EMBERS

A COLLECTION OF DARK FICTION

KENNETH W. CAIN

Let the world know:
#IGotMyCLPBook!

Crystal Lake Publishing
www.CrystalLakePub.com

OTHER TITLES BY KENNETH W. CAIN

Adult fiction:
The Sage of I
These Trespasses
Grave Revelations
Reckoning
United States of the Dead
These Old Tales: A Collection of Dark Fiction
Fresh Cut Tales: A Collection of Dark Fiction
Lifeblood
Jade
The Adventures of Alexin

Non-fiction:
Writers on Writing

Middle Grade fiction:
From The Deep Will Rise (Book 1 in the series)

Early Reader:
How Marbles Roll
Hardy the Allergic Cat & Willy the Wrong Way Woodpecker
RE: Animated: Three Apocalyptic Tales for Kids
When Vampires Eat Fast Food & Cooking with Monsters
3 Fun Tales About Monsters
Math Is For Mummies: Addition & Subtraction
Frankie's Alphabet: an A to Z alphabet picture book
The Big Book of Monsters & Friends activity book

OTHER COLLECTIONS BY CRYSTAL LAKE PUBLISHING:

Visions of the Mutant Rain Forest by Robert Frazier and Bruce Boston

Tales from The Lake Vol.3, edited by Monique Snyman (includes a story by Kenneth W. Cain)

Gutted: Beautiful Horror Stories, edited by Doug Murano and D. Alexander Ward

Tribulations by Richard Thomas

Devourer of Souls by Kevin Lucia

Wind Chill by Patrick Rutigliano

Eidolon Avenue: The First Feast by Jonathan Winn

Flowers in a Dumpster by Mark Allan Gunnells

The Dark at the End of the Tunnel by Taylor Grant

Check out other Crystal Lake Publishing books for Tales from The Darkest Depths.

PRAISE FOR *EMBERS*

"Not a squall, not a blizzard . . . It's a pulp horror AVALANCHE! That's Kenneth W. Cain's new collection, *Embers*."
—Mort Castle, Bram Stoker Award® winner

"Collections such as this are the reason that, even after 45 years, I still enjoy reading horror!"
—Douglas Draa, Editor of *Weirdbook Magazine*

"Kenneth W. Cain's imagination is on full display here. He will take you by the hand, lead you into the darkest places, and you'll be thanking him every harrowing step of the way. A bright new talent in horror."
—Ben Eads, author of *Cracked Sky*

"With prose that is sometimes poignant, sometimes unsettling, but always incredibly dark, Kenneth W. Cain takes readers on a macabre journey with the smouldering burn of 'Embers.' A master of weaving tales around seemingly simple premises and ordinary situations with every day folk, Cain never fails to turn a story on its head and deliver a long-lasting sting. You'll need some genuine embers to warm you after this, for some of these tales will chill you to the core."
—Jim Goforth, author of *Plebs* and *The Sleep*

For Mom, who introduced me to dark fiction and
believed in this collection.

TABLE OF CONTENTS:

THE CHAMBER

ECALLING THE DEATHS having occurred here long ago, Karl wavered with nausea, steadying himself on the wall of the chamber. Then, remembering the blood that had once stained these exact stones, he yanked his hand away in disgust.

That had been a day he'd tried to forget. A quick glance at his scarred hand spoke as to why that satisfaction would never come. He'd committed sins, unforgivable evils he could not quell. So, he'd come here seeking to put those troubles to rest.

But can I make amends?

Back then he'd even spoken a different language. Had worked hard to disguise his accent, and now the German language sounded rather foreign to him. Only on rare occasions did he feel any connection to his roots.

Yet the scars will always remind me.

Life had transformed into a walking nightmare. Their tired faces waited for him around every corner. They stood among every crowd. Their recognition evident, they condemned him for his secret crimes. It didn't matter that he'd been forced to follow orders. The dead never forgave.

Here, though, perhaps he'd find some peace from these ghosts, some mercy.

His wife and two grandchildren waited at the doorway to the dank building as he entered. All the atrocities flooded back in an instant. The orders he'd been given, and the chance blockage of the delivery method.

Tears welled in his eyes, and his queasiness worsened as the memories became clear.

A shrill cry startled Karl. Seconds later something heavy struck the wall inside the chamber. He heard the crunch of bones, then an inhuman growl, followed by silence.

He'd been assigned to Sobibor three months prior to this day, and already things had gone sour. His failure unacceptable despite such immoral orders, he couldn't risk speaking of his concerns. Those in charge frowned at the mere mention of such discussions, always eager to meet these altercations with a swift punishment, and they handed out death as if it were tea. So he kept his feelings bottled up, his unreadable countenance giving nothing away.

A masked man emerged from the doorway, rifle hoisted. Klein dropped his gun and yanked off the gasmask. He tossed the mask aside and fell to his knees, breathing heavy. When he did look up, tears left clean trails on his dirty cheeks.

A few years older than Klein, Karl empathized with his comrade. Panicked eyes searched Karl, perhaps seeking affirmation of his compassion. But

THE CHAMBER

Karl refused to offer any such comfort, hiding his expression behind the handkerchief pressed to his face. Doing so would be taken as weakness. Besides, the red splatter on Klein's sleeve kept him distracted.

Whose blood is that?

Desperate, Klein shifted his attention to the man standing beside Karl, Arnold Richter.

Richter showed no sympathy, his features ever rigid. He didn't seem to mind the smell of corpses, the cries, or even the falling ash. Karl ascertained the man enjoyed every bit of this madness.

A haggard Klein exhaled hard and spoke in a crackled voice. "They're alive, Herr Richter."

"Alive? What do you mean alive?"

Klein gasped, refilling his lungs with air. He coughed and hacked, looking as though he might faint.

Where's Heinemann?

A man of Heinemann's size would never fall to these people whom their Führer despised, such a malnourished race. Not even if they banded together in that effort.

Unless they had weapons . . .

This thought trailed off as Klein rose and staggered away from the door like a frightened child.

"Well?" Richter said. "What is it, Klein?"

Klein seemed unable to answer. Karl prayed his friend would compose himself soon.

Richter wore a stung expression. "Wait, why are you crying soldier?"

Karl couldn't blame Klein. Even he broke down when alone. More than once in fact, an emotion often warranted by these unnecessary deaths. Every last fatality haunted him. He hadn't slept more than an hour or two straight since this war started.

Klein sniffled and finally answered. "I'm sorry, Herr Richter, but Heinemann . . ."

"What is it then?"

"He's . . . dead."

Richter stormed away. When he returned a second later, anger creased his brow. "How could this happen?"

Klein whimpered. "I'm not sure, Herr Richter. We were moving through the corpses, dealing with matters." He gulped in more air, his shoulders dropping. "They were still breathing." He paused, collecting himself. "Maybe a blockage, but for whatever reason the pellets didn't work, but..."

"Well? What was it? Get it out," Richter said.

"A creature, maybe."

Karl remained silent. Sure, this piqued his curiosity, but he thought the stray gases might have made Klein hallucinate.

A faulty mask maybe?

"What are you talking about?" Richter said. "And this better be good."

Klein wiped his forehead, and then his cheek. He stared at the blood on his sleeve. "Something brushed up against me." His tone weakened. "I felt a spray of blood. Next thing I know Heinemann's body is flying across the room, and they're coming for me."

Klein paused for a long moment. Seemed to need time to muster enough strength to divulge the next part. "And then I saw something horrible."

Richter stared down at a trembling, sobbing Klein. He appeared to ponder the details. Then he removed

his glove and swatted Klein across the face. "Stop this incessant sniveling. Now get back in there and finish them. They're rats, mind you. The lowest scourge of this Earth."

The harsh tone of these words stung Karl. He understood that if Klein failed he'd be killed. And Klein's entire family would pay for this letdown. But even more daunting to Karl, he knew what would follow. This task would fall on him.

Klein gazed up at his commanding officer with hopeful eyes. "Please, Herr Richter. Let's refill the chamber."

Richter cocked his head as if considering this idea. No doubt it would do the trick, but Karl suspected it could be seen as a sign of weakness. Richter would never go for it.

Again, Richter lifted the glove to strike Klein a second time.

Klein raised his hands in defense, but the blow never came.

Richter's face tightened like the strings on a violin. "I said, get back in there. Right now!"

Klein collapsed. "Please, sir. Please, Herr Richter. I beg of you . . . "

Again with the crying.

It had become too much for Karl to bear. Now he struggled to suppress his emotions. *If I do nothing I'll join Klein in this suffering.*

This chamber saw less anguish these days. All the same, the memories persevered here. Just like the acute pain behind his right eye, hidden but still felt.

Pawing at his cheek, it relieved him to discover sweat instead of blood. Still, the pain intensified, shooting back over his scalp and piercing his skull.

He raised his hands like guns, struggling to see. Shook his head in an effort to alleviate the mounting headache, but it continued to ring.

He staggered a few steps forward in the darkness and backed against the wall. There he waited for something to move, anything.

A skitter drew his attention to the far left of the chamber. He spun away from the wall, scanning up and across the ceiling. For a split second he spotted something, a grotesque foot maybe. Then it vanished.

A shortened exhale escaped his lungs. Soreness spread through his chest. A voice, pleasant yet worried interrupted his thoughts, his Annabel.

"Karl?" she said. "Are you okay, honey?"

She knew so little of his past life and the ghosts that haunted him. She'd never understand why he'd done these things. He stared into his grandchildren's faces and saw their concern.

Where has the time gone?

Neither of them were children anymore. His granddaughter, Anna Marie, had been in college for a year now. His grandson, Dillon, would head to college this fall.

"We should leave," Anna Marie said. Her eyes filled with tears.

What will they think of me when the truth is revealed?

"No," Karl said, "I'm okay."

"Grandpa?" Dillon said. "What are you pointing at?"

Karl glanced down at his hands. He'd balled both into fists, the forefinger of each pointed out.

He eased his nails from his palms. Fidgeted for a brief instant, and shoved his hands in his jacket pockets.

"Nothing." Karl said. "It's okay."

His wife's arms crossed, her eyes searching him for answers. Over the years, he'd told her what he could, but never the particulars of that war.

She'd think me a monster.

Such happenings drew out the madness in a man, like a thick poison being pumped into the bloodstream.

It made him sick. And as this disease worsened, he drifted back again.

"Schultz?" Richter turned to Karl. "Relieve this man."

Karl hesitated, unsure of what Richter expected of him. But deep down he knew.

Richter tapped an impatient foot. "Well, I'm waiting."

Karl pocketed the hankie and drew his Walther. Pressed it against Klein's temple. Klein's eyes opened wide, and looking into them Karl faltered.

How can I do this?

"What is this insolence? I said to relieve him, soldier. Now do what you're told or I'll relieve you both, myself."

Tears streamed down Klein's cheeks. "Please, Karl."

Karl's heart ached. He struggled to steady his hand.

Tried to look away, enough so Richter couldn't tell. He closed his eyes to slits in case he did notice.

"I'm sorry," Karl whispered.

A bullet tore through Klein's skull. His arms slackened at his sides. His body went limp, and he slumped to the ground.

Keep your shit together.

Karl lifted his eyes to the splatter of blood now covering the wall. The red blemish unraveled him all at once.

Men would hear this story, likely from the lips of Richter. Whenever one of his men dared disagree, they'd remember this bloodstain. But none would know the truth of what happened this day, or how Karl's sanity deteriorated in that instant of time.

Sorrow rose inside of him. But he forced it back down, gawking at the blood on the wall.

"Schultz?"

Startled, Karl did his best to snap his feet together. "Yes, Herr Richter?"

"Get in there and finish this fool's work."

"Right away, Herr Richter."

Karl leaned forward and unsnapped Klein's holster. He retrieved the man's gun and a spare clip that hadn't been fully loaded. He seized the discarded mask, wiped it clean, and tugged it over his face.

Most of the gas would've settled by now, but one could never be too sure. With both guns raised, he breached the threshold and started his search.

Bodies lay entangled on the floor. A thin haze of gas persisted as if lingering to taste its prey. But he saw nothing like Klein described.

He ventured farther into the chamber, hesitant to

let the door close behind him. It slammed shut anyway, loud enough to surprise him.

Among the corpses, he identified Heinemann. The man had been Karl's elder by nine years. A thin line of red had been carved from the left side of his neck to the right, disappearing under his body.

With everything so still, Karl considered matters might have taken care of themselves. This hope waned as they came into view.

Karl's world spun with him being unable to discern his past from the present.

Where are they?

He scanned the floor for the bodies. Searched the ceiling and the walls, but saw nothing. Then the mass of corpses materialized. He stood dumbfounded, staring at them.

One arm hitched. Then a leg from another corpse shot out at an angle.

He took aim and fired. His bullet struck the deceased leg. Something beneath the corpse buzzed a most unnatural noise that sounded like a hive of bees.

Only this is a giant critter.

A man's head bobbled. Several arms waved all at once. Whatever creature came for him amidst this death, it moved without hindrance and remained hidden beneath these corpses, leaving them where they lie as it passed.

He fired twice. Unsatisfied, he shot two more bullets into the bodies.

Still the beast hurried his way.

Backed into a corner, he had nowhere left to retreat. He raised his guns and fired the rest of the bullets into whatever corpses writhed.

When the unseen thing came within a few meters, evidenced by the shifting bodies, he aimed as best he could and fired again. The telling click of an empty clip resulted. He glared at the gun, cursing it under his breath. But at least the creature's advance had stopped.

Must have wounded it.

Bodies dissipated into the air. Her voice once more pulled him out of this vision.

"Honey, you're worrying me," Annabel said.

She wiped her eyes.

Once again he'd balled his hands into fists, each forefinger extended. He released them and returned his hands to his jacket pockets.

This is killing me.

His eyes softened on her. Why couldn't he see the truth? They were all alone in this place, he and his family.

Anna Marie and Dillon flanked his wife, and an unexpected familiarity overwhelmed him. The vision of the three of them standing there resurrected his most heinous remembrance.

The woman had abandoned the supplied shower cap, her shaved head marred and bloody. Her wounds painted a picture of her struggle.

She limped forward, one hand on her hip, and the other clutching a sliver of steel she'd likely pilfered

from the metal shop. The agony of broken bones showed in her effort. She bore her teeth, lips drawn back in a dreadful snarl.

He went to fire but couldn't pull the trigger. He'd been distracted by the two round faces that appeared behind her.

The children trembled to the point of near collapse. Tears streamed down their young faces.

Is this their mother?

The answer didn't matter. He'd observed firsthand how women would care for another's children. It had always been so endearing. Often made him wish the world were a much different place.

She thrust the steel out at him. He'd been too shaken by the children to notice. Anger burned in her eyes. Not the slightest hint of fear showed in her demeanor, as she drew back the blade, ready to strike again.

Panic seized Karl when the woman vanished into thin air. He observed the swell of bodies forming on the floor where he spotted a hint of unnatural claws from somewhere beneath these corpses.

He knelt, neglecting to take the time to reload his guns. Setting one aside, he retrieved his knife and jabbed it into the mass of bodies.

When nothing stirred, he thrust the blade deeper. Again and again, he stabbed into the bodies. With his other gun, he shoved men and women aside. When only ground remained, he stared at the empty floor in disbelief.

Scanning the corpses, he searched for any peculiarity. And he found one, a familiar deceased man with a smile as wide as the slit in his throat. In fact, all of the corpses were grinning, as if Heinemann encouraged them to follow his lead.

He rose and retreated to safety. Brandished his blade and slid along the wall to the exit. A heavy form brushed against his shoulder and despite not wanting to face it, he did.

The creature's shocking yellow eyes stared back at him. Terrified, he felt a scream rising in his throat. Like a spider creeping up his esophagus, he struggled to choke back the shriek.

The shriveled face grinned, its mouth filled with awful pointed teeth. The eyes beamed with revulsion. A single withered hand lashed out at him, carving deep burning lines in his cheek.

He dropped the knife and pawed at his face to relieve the pain.

When he opened his eyes, Annabel's hands were on his cheeks, warm and caring. She caressed his face, wiping away the tears as they sprouted from his eyes.

Behind her, Anna Marie and Dillon watched with quiet uncertainty.

"Karl, honey, what is it?" Annabel said. "What do you see?"

He tried to answer. Wanted to tell her everything. But although his lips moved, he produced no words.

Instead, he fell into her arms. Laid his head on her shoulder and sobbed. His body heaved, and the memory returned.

THE CHAMBER

As the woman's blade came down, he tried to fend off the attack with a raised arm. Her weapon pierced the back of his hand.

His grip faltered, and one of the guns rattled along the floor, lost to him. A hint of fat billowed out of his wound, followed by a flush of red. Without hesitation, he lifted his gun and fired.

Her angered face twisted in a knot of instant pain. She collided against him, the shiv knocked free of her flaccid fingers.

They were forced into an embrace. He stared into her weakened eyes. This dance persisted down to her final breath. When she finally collapsed, her gaze fell on the frightened children standing against the wall.

As the children disappeared into thin air, he hurried to reload his gun. Somewhere in this chamber, he heard a noise that terrified him. It clicked and chattered, insect-like mandibles opening and closing, sounding hungry.

He yanked the empty clip free and attempted to load the spare, but his hands were shaking. The gun slipped away, landing in the corpses. There, it vanished.

Shit! Shit! Shit!

His eyes zeroed in on the other gun.

It's too far away.

He rushed across the floor and dropped to his

knees. With eager hands, he reached for the gun and released the clip. Before he could reload, something knocked the gun loose again.

Bolting for the door, he made it only halfway before a deep pain seized the meat of his right leg. The burn ran from his thigh down to his knee, from his calf down to his ankle. He flung his arms out in an effort to break his fall. Still he plunged face first into—

Oh, dear God, no.

The grinning face beamed, looking pleased by their unexpected reunion. Heinemann's limp arms bounced and embraced Karl.

While Karl tried to free himself, Heinemann's hold constricted around him like a python. Karl attempted to spin away, using his legs in an effort to loosen the grip.

When they finally broke apart, Karl sat up and scurried across the floor on his butt. There, he stared at Heinemann's corpse with disbelief. Cold steel touched his fingertips and upon seeing it, he seized the fallen gun and jammed the half-empty clip in.

A shadow drew his attention to the ceiling. Then to his left, and back to his right.

How many are there?

He counted three. They were closing in fast. Before he could fire, a pair of yellow eyes honed in on him. In them he saw his own death.

The creature's inconceivable physique froze him. Never had he seen such razor-sharp nails, as long as blades. The fanged teeth chattered. Its shriveled black flesh appeared riddled with scars.

Her voice surprised him. "Karl, please," Annabel said. "You're scaring me."

THE CHAMBER

She pawed at his shoulders. Tried to encourage him to stand, but he knew something she didn't. He'd succumbed to these ghosts, whatever fate they desired.

Here in this chamber she became the distant future, her voice barely audible to him. Only the business of the past remained, and his sole duty to complete this horrid task.

He pushed the weight of the woman off and stood. Loosening his shirt, he tore a length away and tied it around his bleeding hand. Then he turned to the children.

In that brief fraction of a second, he knew death would find him. The pain in his chest so distinct, his heart felt as though it were on fire. He nearly collapsed.

He prayed for his own demise, but death had never been so kind in the past. And these children seemed to sense his thoughts.

His right eye throbbed with pain. When he reached for it a rush of red blurred his vision. The woman had pierced the mask and nearly taken his eye. He hadn't even noticed.

Now that he had, he raised the gun.

Pain shot through his chest. Three claws pierced his breastbone and pushed their way between his ribs. The creature's smile broadened as its talons explored the cavity of his chest for the morsel it desired.

When it found his heart, those menacing claws grasped the delicate organ in its blade-like digits.

He glanced down and saw a gun in his hand. Uncertain where it could have come from, he lifted it and fired. A click resulted.

Keeping the gun elevated, he fired again. Another click. He fired as fast as his finger would allow but heard only more empty clicks.

Surprising enough to temporarily shake him out of the pain that had seized him, three distinct crashes followed loud as thunder.

A gruesome smile filled the creature's face and its grip tightened.

Death had never been so close as it became now. Karl's vision cleared as the pain deepened. For a moment he saw those two children from so long ago, their bodies strewn across the floor as he'd left them. Beside the boy and girl lay the woman, sprawled out, their apparent mother whether by birth or otherwise. But those bodies faded and the horror of what he'd done took shape.

His wife and two beautiful grandchildren, all of them lay on the musty floor. A pool of blood spread out from beneath Annabel. He couldn't see Anna Marie's face, but she'd ceased breathing. Still alive, Dillon's eyes strained on Karl. One bloodied hand extended to him as if asking why he would do such a thing.

The misery ended when the creature yanked Karl's heart free of his chest. For a few final beats, he gazed at the organ, appearing as black as night. Decades of lost tears found him all at once.

VALERIE'S WINDOW

A MONSTER STAGGERED down the barren street. Even one posed a significant threat to her survival.

Valerie let the drape fall back into place. Stared out through its thin fabric as night blotted the orange and red hues of day.

The monster's silhouette crossed the front lawn, and she shrank away from the window. Halfway across the yard, the man paused and gazed up at the wavering curtain.

Did he see me?

Her heart leaped, and she retreated behind the couch where she kept very still and tried to steady her nerves.

The monster shuffled around outside the front door. When the doorbell rang, she jumped. So much that her foot slid across the floor, producing a brief but loud squeak.

Please go away.

She raised her eyes above the back of the couch and stared at the door. An unexpected screech of metal forced her back down to her knees. Her heart pounded as several items spilled in through the opening in the

door. Even when the dead man trudged away from the door dissatisfied, she remained where she knelt in case he returned.

"Why do you bother looking out that damned window at all?" Jasper said.

His appearance startled her. *I didn't even see him.*

Or maybe he'd been sitting there all along, dissecting her actions. Despite everything, he looked cool and calm. He wore that familiar sour expression she'd learned to disregard.

She abandoned the area behind the couch and returned to the window. From this vantage point, she made sure the man outside had moved on, watching him stagger from house to house. Only when the man could no longer be seen did she turn back to Jasper.

Jasper's piercing gaze met hers, making her feel vulnerable. *I was wrong to ignore him.*

She chewed a fingernail. "You're right. I shouldn't."

He leaned back in his rocking chair, hands folded across his chest. "Damn right. It's like I always told you, what's out there ain't no good. You don't want no part of it."

A grin spread across his lips that made her skin crawl. This was all true, of course. He'd been telling her this since the day they met.

That day seemed so long ago now. Everything went to hell so fast. She'd been lucky Jasper had been there to protect her. To bring her here where he could take care of her.

So why test him then?

She dismissed the concern and allowed herself forgiveness. "I know. It's just that . . ."

"What?" He raised an eyebrow. "You miss it?"

She did, too, with all her heart. She missed having someone to talk to, maybe a person who could relate to her situation. There'd been others, of course. But all of them had been older, and not one ever returned once they went upstairs.

She hated those stairs. Just the thought of them made her shudder.

"Well, don't," Jasper said. "We got everything we need right here. And mind what I learnt ya or you'll spend a week in your hole of a bedroom." He beamed his awful grin, providing her a perfect view of an empty gap between his yellowed teeth. "Or maybe I'll take you upstairs and remind ya who's in charge round here."

The threat concerned her enough she conceded.

Jasper pushed up from his rocker. Both the wood and his bones cracked. "There are more of them out there now. I think it's time we got some shuteye and let matters settle. What do you think?"

He crossed the hardwood floor to the stairs. She followed. There, they parted ways.

This surprised her, and more so when he ascended. She tried not to watch, but couldn't help but notice how hard it had become for him.

Certain he'd forgotten, she headed for the musty closet beneath the stairs. With some effort, she pulled open the door and slid inside. After a brief pause, she shut the door and waited for the sound of the deadbolt. But it didn't come.

He must've forgot. Or maybe he trusts me enough not to lock it.

The sound of the deadbolt sliding into place indicated otherwise.

Part of her remembered having broken this lock

once. Surely he would have repaired it by now, but for the life of her, she couldn't recall when he'd had the chance.

It couldn't have been that long ago.

Then again, time moved differently these days. Being so weak and hungry made it hard to remember much of anything let alone when the deadbolt had been fixed. Also, Jasper hadn't gone out for food in a long time, so most of her thoughts were consumed with memories of specific tastes.

She considered testing the door and even lifted herself up on her haunches to do so. But as she reached for the handle she heard him climbing the stairs again and stopped herself.

Each footstep came heavier than the last. Jasper got so angry whenever her faith in him wavered.

She wiped her sweaty palm on her torn jeans and slipped into her makeshift bed. This was the only place she felt safe anymore. Although cramped, her worn blanket and shoddy pillow offered some comfort. She pulled the cover over her body and when sleep finally found her, she dreamed of better days. Back when she'd been innocent and the world hadn't yet perished.

She thought him charming, but at twelve her heart tended to flutter at the slightest bit of attention. Still, he'd compelled her to divulge secrets that made her blush. And with no one there to keep her in check, she would've revealed most anything if he asked.

They spoke of topics that made her curious, so it had been natural for her to want to know more. Plus

she liked the way he brushed his long hair back from his collar and cocked an eyebrow whenever he asked her an inappropriate question.

She answered every query, no matter how dirty it made her feel. Some even flushed her cheeks. But she answered them all, rocking back and forth on the park swing.

He listened and shared how the dead had started coming back to life. She didn't believe him, of course. Not at first. But then he pointed one out to her and although she couldn't see the man, panic consumed her.

Before she could get a good look, he'd swept her up from the swing. As frightened as she felt, she let him.

His terror seemed to equal her own, thus heightening her fear. She saw something else, too. The way he kept licking his lips in a creepy and weird way. By the time she knew what was going on, he had her in his car and whisked her away to what he insisted would be a safe place.

She roused from a dream and saw him staring at her in the darkness of her room.

Not again.

She shrank away. Her blanket snagged on the rough floor and hindered her progress, but still, she wriggled away while wrestling the blanket. She squirmed back like a worm until she hit the wall.

Pressing her eyes shut, she opened them to the door, and his face began to dissipate. *What made me think he was in here?*

She squinted. *That knot in the wood maybe?*

There'd once been paint there. Over time it had become faded and worn, replaced by dried bloodstains from her fists. Awareness dawned on her as she spied the trickle of light beneath the door.

Oh God, it must be morning.

He detested when she overslept. If he caught her, he'd be angry. Might even punish her. *Or take me upstairs.*

She tugged her shirt down to cover her belly and reflected on her dream for a brief moment. She'd come here of her own free will without even her mother's knowledge. To think, Jasper's hair had only been a wig. That day when she'd first seen his mottled scalp and receding hairline it had sickened her.

How old was he back then? She remembered thinking him much older than she originally believed. *He must be quite old now.*

She stepped to the door and waited for the deadbolt to slide away. When it didn't, she assumed he'd already unlocked it. Pushing the door open an inch, she leaned forward and stared out through the crack. The early afternoon light revealed an empty room. No sign of Jasper.

Opening the door wider, she stepped out into the living room. When she turned to shut the door, his voice startled her.

"Well, well. Lookie who finally woke up."

Her heart leaped, pounding out several hurried beats before settling. She didn't want to look him in the eye but did so anyway.

"Sorry. I didn't sleep well."

Convinced this would be enough, she stood before her window and waited for a reply.

VALERIE'S WINDOW

When he didn't protest, she took to her familiar spot and gazed out at what remained of the world. There were so many dead outside today. Most stuck to groups of two or three, as if socializing. Others roamed about with no apparent purpose. One dead woman chased after a dog, its leash dragging in the street.

She's gonna eat that dog.

"After all these years, you still refuse to give up on them, don't you?" he said.

She didn't answer.

"They'll kill you if you go out there. You know that's truth?"

She did.

"Bastards will tear the flesh right off your damn bones." He hummed knowingly.

She ignored him. Her focus remained on two of the dead, watching them disappear into houses. Another stumbled out of the house next door. There must have been a dozen dead out there at any given moment, all of them ignorant to her existence. She needed to keep it that way.

But what good is life if I'm stuck here?

Jasper interrupted her thoughts. "Bastards tore my dog's guts right out. All those others in the basement, too." His voice sounded stern and unappreciative of the fact she resented being holed up with him. "You don't want to end up like them, do you?"

No, I don't.

She shook her head and stepped away from the window. She'd return when there weren't so many and when Jasper wasn't around. Although she remained grateful for the brief moments he afforded her at the window each day, this hadn't always been the case.

"Stare out that cursed window if you must. It'll do you no good." He cricked his back and started up the stairs, already laboring. "I've been up since very early and need to lay down a spell. Mind how long you stare out that window daydreaming or I'll have you upstairs."

Sometimes she wondered about the last two girls he'd taken upstairs. She'd heard muffled screams for weeks on end. Their constant weeping still haunted Valerie's dreams now and then.

She gazed up the stairs. *I haven't heard them in so long.*

An hour or two passed before she could return to the window. There wasn't much left to eat. She'd found a few stale crackers and drank water straight out of the faucet.

The crackers didn't sit right in her stomach. They felt like a moldy lump that wanted to come back up. She'd ran to her closet several times afterward to retch into her waste bucket but nothing came out, and her insides continued to squirm.

Why hasn't he gone for food?

Through her window, she spied one of the dead ambling to the end of a driveway. This woman stood beside a mailbox, staring off across the road. Then she opened the mailbox and pawed inside.

Valerie nearly fainted. *The plague, it must be fading?*

Perhaps everyone would be cured in time. Unable to contain herself, she hurried up the stairs. But in her excitement, she'd forgotten his rules, how she wasn't allowed upstairs without his permission.

I should—

Her foot reached the landing, and she froze in place, quivering. She considered withdrawing the foot but couldn't will it to move.

She took a deep breath and pushed herself up, tiptoeing to the first room. A battered bed with torn sheets draped over half the mattress sat in the middle. A woman bound in chains lay on the bed, her naked body deteriorated. A bright-red ball held her mouth ajar in an eternal scream.

Sorrow consumed Valerie. She forced herself to continue down the hall. In the next room a woman lay in a fetal position upon the bed. The white shroud she wore offered Valerie an unnatural view of the woman's bony frame. A look of terror and hopelessness defined the woman's hollowed face.

Tears stung Valerie's eyes. They'd suffered, and she felt guilt for wishing at times they would stop their incessant crying. Even if they had been infected, no one deserved this fate.

She arrived at the last room, the door still closed. This would be Jasper's room. She dried her cheeks with her sleeve. If he saw her crying, he'd punish her.

What will he do to me then?

Would he chain her to one of those beds? She'd never be able to endure such an atrocity in her current state. But she'd come this far, and she only had to turn the knob. Then she could confront him, tell him how she no longer cared whether the dead ate her or not.

She mustered up what little courage she could, opened the door, and entered with her eyes pressed shut. She refused to open them until she stood in the center of the room.

Gradually she eased them open, unnerved by what

she saw through mashed eyelashes. He lay in his bed with his sheets drawn up to his neck. The linens had sunken into his chest and stomach. They outlined his bones, making him look like one of those skeletons from science class. His mouth hung agape. The swollen tongue poked out over cracked blue lips. His teeth were more yellow now. Wide-eyed, he stared up at the ceiling.

Moving bedside, she stared down at his wrinkled face. His eyes had turned into dark pools that filled the whole socket. The corners of each eye angled down.

She leaned in close. "Jasper?"

He jolted upright, and she leaped away. She landed several feet from his bed and raised her hands to defend herself.

Chest heaving, she scanned the bed only to discover he hadn't moved.

What just happened?

Again, she approached him, this time refusing to get so close. She spoke in a quiet tone. "I'm leaving." It felt good. She gathered up what strength she had left and added, "And I'm never coming back."

With much effort, she turned and hurried down the hall. Something plodded along after her. She heard bony heels thumping against the wooden floor. Rotten teeth chattered.

She rushed past each door, trying not to look. Yet, at both doors her eyes betrayed her. She couldn't even slow herself when she reached the stairs.

Before she could brace herself, she slipped and bounced down the staircase on her rear. Ending up on the last stair, she righted herself and spun around fast. To her surprise, he wasn't there.

She waited, listening for the slightest sound, only to hear her own labored breathing.

Beneath her feet a massive pile of unopened letters lay scattered. Her eyes rose from the mail to the door. It should be so simple to open. Yet she knew how difficult it would prove.

Am I really unafraid?

From this vantage point she could see out through the faded drapery of her window. Several of the dead still wandered around outside. Surely, they'd see her.

But I have to go.

"You can't," Jasper said.

His voice scared her. And he spoke as if he'd heard her thoughts.

She didn't respond.

"They'll eat you. I swear it."

She rose from the step. Her bumps and bruises complained. "Let them."

"Don't do it."

She wanted to run when he approached. Instead, she stood her ground.

His voice boomed, "Don't you open that goddamned door."

She turned to him and whispered, "I'll never listen to you again."

With that, Jasper seemed to weaken. His form faded until no longer there.

She stared at the place he'd been. Tears streaked down her cheeks, and for a brief second, she wasn't sure she could find the strength. She seized the doorknob, took a deep breath, and yanked the door open.

Shielding her eyes from the light she stepped out

onto the porch. The instant smell of flowers assaulted her senses, bringing back memories of her mother's garden. She eased down the stairs to the grass.

A dead woman's head turned up. Her mouth opened as if to speak, but no words came out. The woman ran for Valerie.

Valerie saw this and collapsed. The feel of the grass and the aroma of summer pleased her. The sun warmed her. A light breeze drifted across the yard. She heard noises she recognized and others she couldn't place. All of it excited her.

Behind the woman, others noticed Valerie. At least six of them started her way, maybe more. There would be no escape, and that was okay.

She curled up in the grass and waited. *If this is what God will have of me, so be it.*

They were upon her, all around her. The pitter-patter of her heart shifted to the loud thump of a bass drum.

The woman knelt beside her. Her hands pulled at Valerie, who let herself be lifted. She felt the woman's arms embrace her.

Unsure of what to expect, Valerie stiffened. Her eyes widened with panic. She looked at them one by one. Gulped down a deep breath and held it in while she awaited the inevitable.

A WINDOW TO DREAM BY

DESPITE HER TENTACLES and lack of human arms or legs, Seth had an inexplicable attraction to the woman. He observed her hovering amidst a black cloud darkening the sky outside his hotel room window.

All of this should have alarmed him. Alerted him to call the police or fire department, but instead it only piqued his interest. No one could understand her mysterious allure unless they'd also seen her. But he didn't believe this show had been intended for just anyone. She'd come for his sole benefit.

Being a rather compassionate man, the guilt set in right away. Yet he'd avoided calling his wife for fear he might mention the sultry woman. If not for his conscience, he wouldn't have bothered contacting work.

How luscious you are, my dear.

She'd appeared to Seth in a dream that first night of his stay in the historical Gilman House Hotel. After thoughtful reconsideration, the dream seemed rather impractical now.

She'd materialized in a distant fog. Her image aroused him despite knowing she couldn't be real. And although she never gratified him in this dream, he

woke to wet sheets all the same. That such a vision of beauty actually existed hadn't crossed his mind until the following night.

He'd been married for over two decades. As such, the touch of his wife had grown uncommon as the years passed. Because of this, he lived for the subtle indiscretions of everyday life. Especially those in which he'd have little culpability: a passing glance at a beautiful woman, the hint of a smile, a free peek down the front of a woman's blouse or viewing the outline of a woman's panties when she bent to pick something up. After this female reappeared the second night, he could no sooner deny her authenticity than he could the way she made him feel inside.

Prior to his initial dream, he'd suffered some worry over the dark hole forming among the distant clouds. He'd believed he would bear witness to the end of all humanity. God would finally descend upon the Earth, having come to reap the souls of all those who'd sinned, as Christians had long professed. He even considered running and seeking shelter in the basement of this facility to wait things out. Once the torrential storm dispersed, he noticed how the rest of the sky remained untouched by any threat this darkness posed. This provided him some clarity to what he'd seen in the gloomy clouds outside his window. When the storm later faded, a strange emptiness shrouded him. He stared out his window for several hours.

As a precaution that following day, he'd stopped after work to purchase the best telescope his funds would allow. He then returned to his window, eager to scrutinize the hole, should it reappear. To his shock, when it did rematerialize, it was twice as big as the first time.

Then it occurred to him the cloud wasn't larger but closer. And within the terrifying void at its core, he glimpsed something most unexpected. Still distant but ever so obvious in its shape, the figure of a woman filled his eyes, so dissimilar to any female he'd seen prior to this day.

That night he sat beside the plain window, surrounded by bricks whose years stretched back far beyond his own. He gazed down, noticing the vagrants who stood in the dampened streets below. Their pasty faces upturned, they studied him through thinned eyes, perhaps curious of what interested him so.

Do they see her, too?

It seemed more plausible they only saw him, a middle-aged man gawking up at the sky with wide eyes. Perhaps they thought him intrigued by the moon or the stars. He hoped that was all they saw because he didn't want to think about sharing her. She revealed herself exclusively for his eyes, and that excited him.

All night he contemplated the woman who seemed trapped within the dark mass. Considered the likelihood he'd gone mad and accepted it as a distinct possibility. He hoped it wasn't the case because more than anything he longed for her return. He wished she would come closer. Near enough he might touch her and fulfill his most passionate yearnings. He sneered with lust-filled eyes at the empty sky.

When she did arrive that night, he no longer troubled himself with the disquiet of being crazy. Only this growing need to satisfy his most primal desires mattered. For all he cared, they could lock him away in a straightjacket and cast him into a padded room for the rest of eternity. As long as he got his wish to touch this woman. To make love to her before they carted him away.

This dusky night she loomed closer to his window, although still too far away to perceive without the aid of the scope. He focused on her and filled the eyepiece with her physique. She enamored him with her slender torso, her beautiful breasts, the furry mound he longed to experience. And she seemed to sense his excitement, responding to his probing eyes by laying back on some unseen surface. There, she pleasured herself for his enjoyment.

Drooling, he engaged himself. He studied her gyrating hips and seeking tentacles, and tried to match her pace. Caught in the middle of this self-gratifying moment, he wished he'd splurged for a stronger-powered scope. Then again, his wallet had failed him, and he could no sooner afford such a scope than he could a fine meal. Having already spent most of his budget, he'd have to scrape to make ends meet. He squinted, tried to focus on the eroticism unfolding in the sky, but his thoughts wavered.

What will those bums think of me if they look up and see what I'm doing now?

He realized he didn't care. Ignoring them, he felt no humiliation in his actions. His lone concern the woman in his telescope, he wished for her to come closer.

As if sensing his difficulty in seeing her, the woman's actions became more animated. Nearing completion, his thoughts waned once more, this time to work and the fact he'd be leaving come morning.

A WINDOW TO DREAM BY

The sheer frustration of this detail denied him an end to his ecstasy. And the irritation of this interruption persisted long after the woman vanished for the night.

The following morning while he spoke with his wife, he attempted to mask his desperation. It would be the first in a small string of lies.

While Sarah's displeasure had been evident, she'd tolerated his decision to stay, no doubt thinking it necessary. He never thought she would give in so fast. Perhaps in some way she also enjoyed their time apart.

Persuading his boss proved even easier. He conveyed the need to extend his trip and finish up business, mentioning how he'd been too sick to call. Having made a convincing plea accompanied by sniffles and coughing, he took a spell before detailing his dizziness. Through it all he maintained a relentless concern that business with their latest acquisition hadn't been finalized.

His call garnered urgency from his boss, who deemed leaving matters unsettled as more troubling than depleting any excess funds he'd allotted for this trip. The man's sole interest could be defined by monthly sales figures and whether they'd seen significant growth or not. So, as long as the individuals at Global Securities didn't contact his employer, Seth would be in the clear for another few days.

With his thoughts consumed with ogling his evening visitor for an additional three interruption free nights, he hadn't planned on any need to barter with the front desk manager to retain the room. However,

checkout time had passed, and they'd taken the liberty of handling the paperwork for him. Pleading with the man, he pointed out what an inconvenience changing rooms would be for the both of them.

When that didn't work, he resorted to begging. Even felt the urge to cry at one point when he became certain the manager would still deny him this request. In the end, the manager accommodated him once Benjamin Franklin made an unexpected appearance.

This latest expense drained his wallet. If he withdrew more money his wife would become suspicious. He didn't want to deal with her concerns these next few days. She'd be annoyed enough when she learned of his impulsive enthusiasm for space after discovering the bill for the scope. But none of this mattered now. He'd go without eating, so long as it meant he could behold the beauty that existed within the murky depths of that hole in the sky.

Although he didn't have the resources to buy a larger scope, he considered stealing one. Though he wasn't sure he'd need one, because each night she appeared, she'd been closer than the previous evening. Somewhat optimistic his wish to touch her might soon be realized, he tossed his guilt aside, knowing if the opportunity presented itself he would indulge without question.

When night cloaked the small New England town, he waited by his window. He tapped an impatient finger on the sill. Took a moment to gaze down at the sullen faces below.

She blinked into existence, so close his heart leaped in his chest. Any remaining guilt washed away the second one of her tantalizing tentacles breached his

window. The glorious scent of her perfumed feeler teased his nostrils, and he drew in the aroma. A bulge formed in his pants, assuring he would refuse her nothing.

A second tentacle entered the room and began to disrobe him with delicate precision. He breathed heavy and let her do whatever she wanted. She prepared to pleasure both herself and him simultaneously.

He caressed her tentacles. Unsure of himself, he disregarded the foreign texture and let her guide him. He had all but forgotten his wife's tender skin, entranced by these probing appendages. They crept across his naked body. Their peculiar suction cups stuck to his flesh and pulled away with light kissing sounds. The daunting teeth at the ends of each limb nibbled at his body.

His eyes filled with passion. Mouth agape, he couldn't stop staring at her pulsating body. She gleamed with the sweat of love, and he yearned to lap up every last drop. He wanted to taste all of her passion.

The urge to take her, real or imaginary, and quench his desire frustrated him. One cool feeler squeezed and another slithered up to his lips. He kissed and licked the appendage as she let her teeth drag across his tender flesh. Soon they climaxed together.

Then, as if she'd never been there at all, she vanished. Her departure left his soul vacant. He barely slept that night, overanxious for her arrival the following day.

He dared not leave for fear of missing her. Taking a quick shower, he made himself presentable, dressing in his finest suit. He ate a melted candy bar and some crushed crackers, both of which he demanded the front desk deliver to his room. Having misplaced the lone glass, he drank water from the sink like a dog. Each time he hurried back to the window, afraid he'd missed her.

His wife had become the farthest thing from his mind. Both she and work had called several times, but he neglected every call. Both would have only one reason to bother him. No doubt work had contacted Global and discovered his absence. Work had likely informed his wife. None of that mattered anymore.

When she arrived, darkness clouded his window. It thrilled him when she slithered into his room, a coy smile pressed upon her lips. He started undressing, never letting his gaze fall from her.

She climbed into the bed and braced herself by coiling four of her tentacles around the bedposts. In this way, she offered herself to him, free for his taking. The other four feelers coaxed him with some urgency, exploring his naked form. They tugged him to her while he hurried to remove his underwear.

He crawled on top of her with eagerness, and they made love. He'd never tasted sex so sweet. Taken part in such carnal acts of love. And now that he'd experienced this level of satisfaction, he found himself obsessed and wanting more. There could be no one else.

In the morning, he awoke by his lonesome. The sweet smell of her lingered on him and in the bed beside him.

He rolled to his side and breathed in her scent. Afterward he stared at the empty space she'd warmed and thought of her.

When the hotel staff broke in, he resisted. Still, they managed to force him outside. They tossed his possessions into the street after him.

That night he wandered below the window, his ultimate alternative to loiter about the exterior of the hotel, staring up and dreaming of seeing her again. He considered calling work to see if he could make amends and secure the room again. Certainly, that would prove pointless.

Although he felt somewhat guilty for cheating on his wife, he couldn't bring himself to contact Sarah. Nor did he want to. He'd ask her for money, and she'd have no part of him. Besides, his feelings for the mysterious window visitor took all precedence. Yet without any source of income, he wouldn't be able to secure the room to visit her.

For fear he might miss his love, he dared not leave these streets. Then, he became aware of the other men around him. Many of them also stared up at the window. Their faces appeared gaunt, their eyes glazed over and lost.

When the man who'd taken over his room showed up in the window, Seth observed the way he stared off into the stars. That man looked startled at first, but soon his expression eased to curiosity.

Seth envied this man for what he saw. He suspected the woman would seduce the man, as she had Seth. But even in his jealous rage one thought continued to infect him.

I cannot rest until I can be with her again.

EACH NEW DAY UNKNOWN

HE SHOT UP in bed, dismayed by the unfamiliar surroundings. Splotches of reality bled back together, forming shapes he knew. Dim light penetrated his widening eyes while one of those shapes turned into a figure, sitting across from him in a large chair.

The man spoke loud, "No, leave it. If he wants it, he'll get it himself."

He eased to the edge of the bed, distracted by its rigidness. The crumpled white linens and flattened pillow hadn't felt as uncomfortable as it now looked.

It's some sort of gurney.

Rethinking matters, he wasn't so sure he even remembered being asleep. But one detail rang true.

My name is Lucas.

He squinted at the balding man in the deep, leather chair. Watched as the man tugged at his peppery beard, his eyes sparkling.

Then he noticed the long, white coat and put everything together. "Have I been in an accident?"

The doctor smiled but didn't answer. Something about him seemed familiar, but Lucas couldn't put his finger on it.

The room itself appeared rather plain. The white

ceiling, gray walls, and standard tiled floor, all indicative of a hospital room. A row of cabinets lined the far wall with no identifiable objects on their surface. Windowless, an imprisoned feeling overwhelmed him.

He took a deep breath and exhaled slow, trying to alleviate his immediate stress.

"You can have some if you'd like," the doctor said.

Only then did he see her.

She regarded him with a troubled smile. Then nodded to the table beside his gurney.

There he found a glass of water. His eyes searched the doctor. "This?"

The doctor nodded, shifting and straightening the lapels of his white coat, appearing somewhat anxious. "If you wish."

He folded his hands across the clipboard in his lap and extended the fingertips of his left hand. "It's merely a formality, Mr. Bradley."

Bradley? My name is Lucas Bradley. Yet, the name didn't sound as familiar as he'd hoped.

His throat dry as the desert, he picked up the glass. Its unnatural warmth surprised him. Several tiny anomalies floated about in the water, so the liquid no longer held any appeal.

"I'm not that thirsty," he said. He returned the glass to the table. "But thank you."

With an understanding nod the doctor's face grew sullen. "I understand. We have such god-awful water here in this . . . this purgatory." He scoffed. "So much for hospitality's sake."

Lucas didn't know how to respond.

The doctor retrieved his own glass and lifted it. "To good health, sir."

EACH NEW DAY UNKNOWN

In one swig the doctor emptied the glass and returned it to the table. He leaned back to a symphony of complaints from the worn chair and began tapping the end of his pencil on the clipboard, regarding Lucas with interest.

Uneasy with this scrutiny, Lucas looked away. But his eyes defied him, stealing paranoid glimpses of the man. It gladdened him when the doctor's eyes shifted beyond him.

"Thank you, Lilith," he said. "That will be all."

She exited through the lone door with slow deliberate steps. Once she left, the doctor returned his attention to Lucas.

The doctor snickered. "Quite the woman, isn't she?" He breathed an exaggerated sigh and spoke in a whisper. "What a rack on that one."

What sort of doctor speaks like that? His cheeks flushed, but Lucas managed an affable, "Yes . . . I suppose."

To this, the doctor cackled.

A waft of cool air crept up his back like icy fingers, and Lucas pawed at the opening at the back of his attire. He observed the floral pattern on the standard issue hospital gown.

Such clothing has to be the work of the devil. Only that fiend could design an outfit without any consideration for one's backside. And hospitals seemed to have a never-ending supply of drafts, too.

"So, was I in some sort of accident?" Lucas said.

"You could say that."

The doctor flipped the clipboard open. With haste, he thumbed through a dozen or so pages. "Well then, let me see—" He hummed to himself while he turned the pages. "Oh yes, well, that won't work at all."

Lucas strained to see over the top of the clipboard. "What does it say?"

The doctor beamed. "This?"

He flipped all at once back to the first page and read it aloud, looking down and then up after speaking each name. "10:45 with Mrs. Ross. What a wonderful specimen. 11:30 with Mr. Kline. He hasn't had much success, like yourself. Don't you get it, Mr. Bradley? This is nothing more than my schedule."

The doctor placed the clipboard aside. He retrieved a thick book from beneath the coffee table and sat it on his lap. He tapped his fingers on the cover, as if awaiting a reaction.

Concern washed over Lucas.

Satisfied, the doctor wrestled the book open but said nothing at first of its contents. Finally, after a long moment, he cleared his throat and offered this tidbit. "It's quite thick, isn't it?"

"Excuse me?"

"I said that it's thick." He raised and lowered the volume to demonstrate its weight. "I'm referring to the book."

Lucas twiddled his thumbs. His eyes widened with concern. "Yes."

He examined his surroundings more closely. *Is this the sort of room they conducted sleep studies in?*

A large camera fastened at the corner of the ceiling and surrounded by several dull red lights offered some confirmation to this suspicion. But whatever ailed Lucas wasn't a sleep issue, so he couldn't be certain. In truth, he felt quite rested and alert.

From the corner of his eyes Lucas spotted the doctor pawing through the book. "Is that about—"

"It's rather empty, isn't it?" the doctor said.

Now Lucas did gaze at the doctor and swallowed hard. "The book you mean?"

The doctor laughed. "No, the room." He twirled his pencil in a circle, pointing out their surroundings. "So damn empty down here." He tapped his pencil again. "Oh and yes, this is your chart." He glanced at the book and found Lucas with a gummy grin. "Or rather, your book."

His jaw agape, Lucas couldn't withdraw his eyes from the book. *Good Lord, what could require so much paperwork?*

The doctor licked his finger and skimmed through several pages, whistling a charming tune. He scanned each, appearing dissatisfied by what he found, so he turned them more briskly as if he meant to rip them right out.

When the doctor reached the page he'd been searching for joy spread across his face. He jotted something down, of which Lucas had no idea.

Nose still in the book, his pencil dipping and dragging across the page, the doctor addressed Lucas in a more serious tone. "Tell me, Mr. Bradley, what's the last thing you remember?"

Lucas tried to recall. Whenever he made the slightest connection to his past it slipped away like water through his fingertips. He did have some recollection of his mother and father, their house, and a few trivial details of his childhood. He believed himself in his thirties, if not then his early forties. His parents would have grayed over by now. His father might even be sporting a receding hairline.

With that, a thought struck him like a brick to the skull. *I have amnesia.*

This would explain a lot: the fact he hadn't known his name and how the few memories he'd retained were all from his childhood. He knew nothing of the present.

The doctor tapped his pencil on the book, shaking Lucas out of his thoughts. *There is that, though.* He stared at the book and couldn't help but wonder what glorious secrets were hidden within its bindery.

Seeing this inquisitiveness, the doctor crossed his hands over the tome. Wrapped his fingers around its edges and gripped it tight, as if guarding it.

"Don't worry, Lucas." The doctor exhaled a slow breath, exuding patience. "We're going to figure everything out together."

Lucas wasn't so sure.

The doctor's eyes thinned on him. "Now, back to my question. Do you remember anything at all?"

And he did recall a few other particulars. His father's name was Ted, and his mother, Elise. They'd lived in the suburbs of Chicago for eight years in that same old blue house. Those visions flashed into his thoughts with such vividness, as if they'd only just happened. Yet, at the same time, everything seemed wrong, as if it never occurred.

I'm a grown man. He considered this for a long moment. *What if I've been in a coma all this time?*

He choked back some tears.

The doctor made an awful attempt at exhibiting sensitivity. "Please don't worry yourself, Mr. Bradley. I assure you this is all quite normal." The doctor sounded somewhat optimistic, and Lucas clung to the hope. "In time, everything will come back to you. You'll see. In fact, you're making excellent progress."

His eyes dropped. "Am I?"

"Yes, quite. Excellent progress, indeed." A sly grin crept across the doctor's face. "More so than any of the others."

The doctor returned to his paperwork, but Lucas couldn't get those words out of his head. If there were others then he hadn't suffered a coma? This disappointed him. He'd been circling the notion like some cerebral shark, believing it the only possible truth. Now that it didn't seem probable he felt as though he were drowning in that same bloody water.

"How many others are there?"

The doctor scoffed. "There are many, many others." He sounded delighted. "So many others."

Whatever ailment had inflicted Lucas must have been something catastrophic. A plane crash, or maybe a bus, a terrorist attack, or it could have been a bombing. *Think, damn you.*

The doctor yanked his eyes up from the book. "Listen, and you must grasp this: you are far from alone here. Your situation is not the least bit unique from many of the others. They, like you, are here right at this very moment taking part in similar studies. And I'll assure you of one thing. They've made far less progress."

He threw out his best guess. "Was it a plane?" Lucas fidgeted his fingers. "Did my plane wreck?"

Disappointment stretched across the doctor's face. "Is that what you think happened?"

Lucas frowned. "No."

"Good."

He gazed at the doctor for a long time before realizing the doctor stared back at him.

"Can you remember anything?" the doctor said.

Lucas offered a halfhearted shake of his head. With an unsteady voice, he added, "Nothing."

The doctor flipped the book open all at once. There he scribbled away. "Interesting."

"What is it you're writing?"

The doctor didn't respond right away. "It's of no consequence. You're still making excellent progress, however . . . "

Lucas loathed this word.

"I fear you've experienced a slight setback just now. I hadn't expected this from someone as far along as yourself, but we can't always control these things, can we?"

He felt his heart sink. His eyes followed as the doctor rose and sat the book aside.

Is that it? Just like that it's over?

Taking note of his panic the doctor retrieved the empty glass and wobbled it. "Relax. I'm only getting some more of that dreadful water."

Defeated, Lucas placed his head in his hands and wept. When the door clicked shut, he glanced up at the book. Everything he needed to know within an arm's length, all he had to do—

He forced his eyes away. Hadn't he regressed far enough for one day?

Damn me to hell.

He launched himself to his knees, seizing the book and heaving it to the floor. There, he threw the volume open, anxious to devour its knowledge.

The first page displayed nothing more than a childish drawing of a unicorn. The next, a rudimentary depiction of a demon with oversized horns.

EACH NEW DAY UNKNOWN

Lucas flipped through several pages at once, catching glimpses of a vast array of doodles. He stopped on a page depicting a monster standing beside a crooked tombstone. He ran an unsteady finger across the drawing, smearing its rough lines.

Even my doctor no longer cares.

The door opened. When he looked up, the doctor stood over him. His smile had become elastic, reminding Lucas of the thick rubber bands that held a medical skeleton's jaws together.

"Well, well. What do we have here? It looks like the devil's gotten the best of someone, hasn't he?" The doctor sipped his water and winced. "Whatever shall we do about this predicament?"

Lucas jabbed a rigid finger at the doctor and turned the book so they could both see. "What the hell do you call this?"

"Why it's a monster, Mr. Bradley. And a damn good one if I do say so myself. Except that you've gone and ruined it with your greasy fingers."

Fury boiled inside of Lucas. He jumped to his feet and wanted to hit the doctor, to hurt him as much as he'd been wounded. The man deserved it.

"I go through something horrible, a plane crash or maybe a car wreck, and all you can do is sit here and draw pictures? You offer me nothing to help myself? And . . . and—"

He tried to refocus his thoughts. His cheeks burned as the words came to him. Still he couldn't get them out fast enough. "And this is what you think will cure me?"

"Oh, dear. How do I put this, Mr. Bradley?" The doctor paused and sipped the warm water. "My

intention was never to help you. I was just having some fun."

His emotions running rampant, Lucas felt his legs tremble. He rushed the doctor, who met his assault with a grin. An instant of pain followed, and then nothingness. Nothing at all.

His world spun. He sat and steadied himself, trying to remember what happened but had no recollection.

"That's okay, Lilith. He can get it himself."

Eyes still blurry, he acknowledged the balding man across from him. Saw the man's white lab coat, the way he tugged at his peppery beard, and those beaming eyes.

Dear God, what happened to me?

He thought long and hard, trying to recall anything. But he could barely remember his own name.

Lucas.

Hopeful eyes found the doctor. "Have I been in an accident?"

The doctor grinned but didn't answer right away. "You can have some, if you'd like, Mr. Harrison."

GONE

LESS THAN A second and Ryan realized his worst fear. The air in his lungs left him as he glanced back to Jane, but his wife wasn't there. So he turned back to the area his son had been playing.

Where's Noah?

He spun in every direction, searching for any sign of the boy.

Memories flooded his thoughts: the first time he'd held Noah, the day his son choked on a piece of hot dog, when Noah had been knocked unconscious by a baseball. One after another these flashes hit him like a battering ram.

Noah had endured all of those obstacles. Ryan's gut wrenched. *But will he survive this?*

His question went unanswered as he abandoned the blanket for the sand. He found his voice. "Noah?"

No answer.

He hurried to where he last saw Noah. Stared at the bright-green algae that had discolored the surrounding beach and water, noticing its localized coverage. The green water lapped at his feet, but he ignored the cool sensation. His concerns returned to his son, skimming the shoreline like a bee flying from flower to flower. His toes tingled, but he refused to acknowledge it.

He shouted louder, "Noah?"

His voice ended up lost in the crowd, but he continued to call out for his son again and again, ignorant to all else. Each subsequent holler came with more desperation. A kaleidoscope of emotions weighed him down.

Would he run away?

Not at eight. He was still too young for any such rebellion. And he'd always seemed happy enough.

Then the cruelest thought popped into his head. *What if someone took him?*

Were there signs of a struggle? Nothing out of the ordinary, but that meant little when it came to such matters.

The waves crashed with some regularity. Seagulls screeched overhead. Children played. People milled about everywhere he looked.

Someone would've seen something. Or he would've screamed.

His eyes returned to the sand. The tide had already washed Noah's footprints away. He watched a rolling wave curl in, dragging out the sand.

The undertow?

Wasn't it somewhat stronger today? His feet sank into the sand. He refused to move, staring out at the sea.

He's a good swimmer, isn't he?

Visions from camping trips, neighborhood parties, and occasional beach vacations all popped into his mind. Noah knew how to swim, that much was certain. But he was far from exceptional.

This early in the season a chilly bug like Noah didn't even like to venture ankle high into the tide. Plus, the lifeguards would've seen him.

The nearest lifeguard sported a pimply face. His arms folded lazily across his scrawny chest, it did nothing to reassure Ryan.

Is he even awake?

The lifeguard shot forward in his seat as a child lost their footing, answering his question.

All of this transpired so fast, yet it felt like an eternity. He stepped back and the sand loosened from his feet. The greenish water rolled over his toes again.

He wiggled them, noticing a numbing sensation. And the tingling worked its way up around his ankles. It felt as though he'd been stung by a jellyfish?

Backing away from the greenish water, he tried to refocus. A reddish ball of fire rested on the horizon. The sun lingered there as if awaiting his fate.

The numbness reached his knees, spread up his thighs, and around his waist. His chest tightened, already overwrought with concern now he believed he might be experiencing a heart attack.

Oh God . . .

He spun back to Jane's chair, hoping she'd be there. His head twisted in slow motion. Her still barren chair intensified his unease. There were lotions, towels, an umbrella, but no Jane.

She must be looking for Noah, too.

Up the short span of beach he spotted a familiar pink blanket. The indention of the attractive woman's body remained fresh in its folds, but she wasn't there, either.

His eyes darted in the other direction. *Where did they all go?*

The other end of the beach also proved deserted. Even the monolith lifeguard perches were now empty.

A sudden void replaced the common sounds of the beach. He stepped back from the wet sand, noting the tingling had stopped.

He hurried to the dunes. From there he could see the shops on the boardwalk. There should've been hundreds of people crisscrossing paths. Their chatter would have competed with the rolling sounds of the ocean. But only the alien beeps and buzzes of Wonderland Arcade persisted.

His feet touched the wooden planks and felt the heat of the afternoon sun bearing down on them. So, he rushed to a souvenir shop and secured a pair of cheap flip-flops.

When he came to the first side street, he paused and glanced back at the lifeless beach. A large bubble had formed on the water's surface, increasing in size at a snail's pace.

He ducked down the street and put distance between him and the bubble. Still, it felt as though something trailed him. He tried to focus on his immediate surroundings, on finding Noah.

Each empty store he passed drained his spirit all the more. Not only did his legs feel heavier, but also some unseen force tugged at him. Pulled him back as if urging him to return to the beach.

He pushed onward in search of Noah. The sounds of the abandoned boardwalk followed him, not yet willing to relinquish their hold. Soon, they too diminished, replaced by unexpected laughter.

Hurrying to these voices, his heartbeat matched the slap of his flip-flops on the sidewalk. The more ground he gained, the fainter those voices sounded.

Upon reaching the restaurant terrace, he peered

through the screen. He'd hoped an audience of blank stares would be looking back at him. An eerie emptiness ruined this expectation.

Have I died?

An image popped into his thoughts, that of his wife and son standing over his unmoving body. Something about this scene wasn't right. He didn't feel dead.

The shrill cry of a seagull surprised him, sounding much like maniacal laughter. Had his sensibility slipped this far?

After a few moments, the bird cocked its head and flapped away. He stared at the place the bird had been, watching as an odd-shaped storm cloud rolled past. Its purplish form reminded him of an elephant.

It seemed a fitting image given the world had somehow become heavy. His feet dragged, the force required to move each foot to its next destination ever more arduous. Whatever pulled at him worked hard to exhaust his stamina.

Deep down, he thought he knew what had happened. He would forever be one step behind. Each effort-laden stride would carry him to no end. Whatever horrible thing he sensed lurking behind him would eventually catch up. When it did it would devour him.

He glanced back but saw nothing.

Voices interrupted him. This time they sounded only a block or two away.

Despite his growing agony, the voices taunted his curiosity. Before he could convince himself otherwise, he hurried down the sidewalk. A lump grew in his throat, making it difficult to swallow. Still his rubbery legs carried him onward, and he would've fallen if not for his momentum.

Upon reaching one of the most popular restaurants in town, he was certain the experience would be no different. He'd run up the stairs to the rooftop deck only to find himself completely alone. Whatever had been trailing him would utilize this time to make up ground. But, although the voices had dwindled, he still heard them quite well.

He burst into the establishment. Panting, near fainting, he searched for the stairs. His heart pounded. Lungs burned. He drew in air with loud gasps. But the solitude he'd anticipated hadn't been the precise circumstance.

Alone now, he replayed the brief instant in his thoughts. There had been people sitting at these tables. They'd been talking and drinking, eating their food. Not one of them noticed his intrusion, save for one. He didn't think she'd seen him, though. She'd shuddered, caught by a stray draft from the open door, and pulled a sweater over her shoulders. Less than a second later they were all gone.

No, they didn't vanish.

To him it looked as though they'd been created with fresh paint. As if some disgruntled artist had thrown a bucket of water over the canvas in an effort to wash the brushstrokes away.

He observed the empty seats, the half-consumed food and drink. Steam still rose from the freshest meals.

He exited the restaurant and scanned the street behind him to ensure whatever had been following hadn't gained. For whatever reason, he no longer sensed this presence.

What would happen if it caught up to him? Would

he vanish? Or perhaps die? Maybe he'd be thrown back into his proper reality.

The cackle of a seagull mocked him. He squinted at the bird. On the ground he spotted an empty bottle and threw it at the bird. The glass came within inches of the gull but hadn't even warranted a sideways glance. It clanged against a rooftop, rolled down the incline, and shattered on the ground.

Unfazed, the seagull flew away, providing Ryan a clear view of the cloudy sky. He watched, unmoved by the scenery. Then a purple cloud paraded by, swaying its wispy trunk, and everything inside of him stirred.

His eyes darted across the road. Car after car remained immobilized. Somewhere in the distance an occasional engine purred, albeit weak. Faint voices murmured, but they were still far from his position.

His attention returned to the cloud, and it surprised him when he couldn't find it.

Weaving in and out of the stranded cars, he followed the clouds, searching for the elephant-shaped one. He continued until he could no longer stand the burning in his chest.

It forced him to a stop. Bent over, hands on his knees, he gazed up and continued to scan the sky. *Where the hell is it?*

"Dad?"

He shook his head.

"Is that you, Dad?"

He turned to Noah, overcome with joy. "No . . . Noah?"

He fell to his knees, and they collided in an embrace. He kissed Noah's forehead and hugged him. Held him at a distance so he could look into his eyes.

Noah buried his head back into Ryan's chest. When he spoke, his breath warmed Ryan's flesh. "I was so scared, Dad." Noah lifted his head and stared off at the beach. "There's something awful back there."

"Yes, I felt it, too." Tears stung Ryan's cheeks. "Whatever it is, I think it's gone now."

Noah's weeping moistened his shirt. "Where are we?"

He wanted to answer but couldn't. He stared off into the distance, interrupted by a shrieking seagull. When the creature departed, he dared the cloud to reappear.

Soon the purple elephant meandered past.

"I think—"

Ryan paused, scanning the immediate area to confirm his beliefs. He reflected on the abandoned vehicles, how they still moved. The front wheel of a fallen bicycle spun as if set in motion seconds earlier. After several rotations the tire slowed and physics suggested it should come to a complete stop. Before it did, the wheel whirled back into motion.

Noah pawed at his shirt. "What is it?"

Ryan's eyes narrowed, listening to sounds both near and far. He noticed how they'd changed ever so slightly.

Time is being swallowed up.

If that were the case, everything behind him would have ceased to exist by now. All else would be rewound and then slip away.

Like the old reel-to-reel movies.

Sometimes those projectors got stuck. The same frame would play over and over until the projectionist fixed it. If they didn't, though, it would eventually burn.

But it's not slipping. It's skipping. A flicker.

He stared at the bike, deliberating whether he could outrun such an occurrence.

Looking in the direction opposite the beach, he pondered his assumptions a second longer. "Maybe, if we can get out in front of it—"

He rose and took Noah's hand, pulling the boy to the nearby bike. He lifted the cycle, threw a leg over it and steadied the bike. "Get on."

Noah climbed up and cinched his hands around his waist. Ryan's legs pumped to pick up speed. The faster they went the more Noah leaned in against his back.

After they'd travelled about a hundred yards the voices formed complete words. At first, they sounded like an old-time radio show, accompanied by constant static. As reality tuned itself in they no longer broke up so much.

Painted blurs of cars whooshed past. He weaved in and out, the muscles in his legs cramping. Nearby shops and houses offered faint glimpses of ghost-like figures. Pale streaks of color took form as if someone were detailing a paint-by-number.

When Ryan spotted the terrifying creature, he surmised it had been the thing they'd both sensed. Somehow it had gotten out in front of them. Its withered body, a mass of weeds and purplish veins, blocked their path.

Noah's hands tightened around Ryan's stomach but there was nowhere else to go. He sped straight for the creature.

As they closed the gap, its haggard face turned to them. Its enormous eyes were empty pools of muddied water, Ryan felt lost in them for a brief second. The

creature flailed its arms—large fists cutting through the air like boulders, trying to end Ryan and Noah's escape.

One came much closer than Ryan preferred. If he hadn't ducked it might have knocked them right off the bike. The beast roared as he sped past. And he didn't look back, afraid he might see it racing after them.

An unexpected jolt startled him as time caught up all at once. Out in the middle of the road, he no longer needed to dodge a creature. Now he evaded cars, cringing as they peeled off in every direction. He swerved to miss one, saw another and veered toward the sidewalk. When he reached the safety of the walkway, he brought the bike to an abrupt halt and breathed heavy.

The ground beneath him steadied. His legs regained some of their strength. Danger averted, his heart slowed. All of it left him tired and withdrawn.

A single seagull drew his attention upward. It hung there but soon passed. Behind the gull a dark cloud lumbered past. Ryan watched until the cloud dispersed and no longer resembled an elephant.

But he hadn't noticed the missing weight against his back. *Where's Noah?*

Desperate eyes retraced his path. Cars zipped by without worry.

No, it can't be. Please. Please let him be back at the beach.

He rode to the boardwalk where he abandoned the bike. He sprinted over the dunes and down the sandy trail. The bustle of activity shocked him, but he ignored it all and scanned the shoreline for his son. The flip-flops fell away as his weakened feet slipped

in the sand. He leaped, doing whatever he could to reach his wife.

Finally, he collapsed and called out for her. "Jane?"

She turned in her beach chair and regarded him with a puzzled expression.

"Where's Noah?" he said.

Each day before dusk, he visits the shore. He lingers at the water's edge, at this precise location where Noah disappeared fourteen years earlier. There he waits, praying for the strange green water to return.

UNDER A DRIFT OF SNOW LIES ANOTHER WORLD

CLAIRE HAD SPOKEN the words. She'd taken a vow to love me until the end. But I'm still alive, and I feel cheated.

I remember the day Claire died in the hospice with clarity. As I slept in the chair beside her, I wanted to reveal the truth. I'd been planning to leave her for months and if not for her illness, I would've done just that. But the sickness came on like a torrential storm and there'd been no time for confessions. Every hour filled by her needs, it became a rarity that I had time to leave her side. This spoiled my plans.

Because of my obligations, the details of our marriage still haunt me. In hindsight, I believe she may have suspected my infidelity all along. We'd been arguing a great deal over insignificant matters: the color of old cars, when we had our first date, the names of distant acquaintances. These were the sorts of disagreements most couples were capable of overcoming. But Claire and I never could let the dust settle.

We both knew our friends and family had grown uncomfortable with our bickering. Over time, most of

them stopped visiting us altogether. This forced us to endure each other's company without distraction. And I think that above all else corrupted us. We nitpicked every detail, and I felt us spiraling out of control as we sped through the tunnel of time.

My biggest regret, though, wasn't the inability to inform Claire of my betrayal. The growing impatience of the woman I'd planned to leave my wife for took higher precedence. At least she should have. But she hadn't been willing to stomach the constant postponing, nor the demeanor in which a man like myself suffered his betrothed's gradual demise. Mia doubted my intentions. And I had my own doubts, too. But I found it difficult to look into my wife's fading eyes and deny having ever felt love for her.

Before long, Mia moved on. Being young and pretty, she found a new man within a few weeks. How could I despise her for wanting to get on with life with me still stuck in the past? But if not for the length of time it took Claire to die, maybe that would've been me with Mia. I tried to hate my wife for taking so long to die, but the bitterness never stuck long enough.

When Claire finally did leave this Earth, I found myself in appalling seclusion. No one cared or visited. I ended up alone, and only then did I truly understand what I'd lost. I missed my wife.

It wasn't fair how she'd left me. I'd do anything to hold her in my arms again.

At her funeral a few days later, I observed how many lives my wife had touched and found myself envious. People I never met came to offer their condolences. And while it moved me, I found myself loathing my wife for all of these secret relationships.

UNDER A DRIFT OF SNOW

How much time had she spent with any one of them when she could have been with me? I'd been home alone a lot in those years before I met Mia, and now I understood why I'd felt so heartbroken, enough to seek love elsewhere. The acrimony had formed out of that separation, blossoming into something horrible in the years afterward.

Then, there was the matter of what I'd discovered after the funeral. With indifference, I walked through the rooms of our empty house. At first I only stared at the furniture, a chair she'd sat in, or out a window daydreaming of what I'd lost. I missed her most in those first few days.

When I finally mustered up the nerve to revisit her possessions, I dug through paperwork, clothing, and myriad shoes. There, hidden among her lingerie, I discovered a small red silken bag I'd never noticed. Inside the bag, I found letters from a man she'd loved during our many years together. A man she'd shared our bed with and had considered leaving me for on more than one occasion.

Tears streamed down my cheeks at this revelation. Sorrow and anger bit at my soul. Not only had I not been alone in my infidelity, but her relationship with this man had started years before my own. It had been the spark to ignite our growing animosity.

Right then my eyes burned with jealousy. I went over the letters again and again, digesting the words of her lover. With each reading I despised her more. No longer could I hold back my temper.

I strode to our bed, tore at the covers and the sheets. Left them hanging from one corner, spilled onto the floor. I stormed to the head of the bed, seized

the pillows one after another and threw them against the wall with all my strength. The last pillow I balled into my fists and threw at her vanity mirror. Although it didn't produce the effect I'd hoped, I felt relieved nonetheless.

For a long while, I stared at myself in that mirror, wishing it had broken. That way I wouldn't have seen myself so hurt and disheveled. And for what reason? Because Claire had been as hopeless in our marriage as I had?

I wish I'd never learned of her secret. That way I might have remembered Claire the way I wanted to and felt better about her passing. But since I had, those letters consumed my every thought. And now that I'd lost Claire, her adultery became my sole obsession.

Having read the letters, I'd discerned the man my wife had fallen in love with went by Steve. I struggled for more details. After many fruitless searches I happened upon the guest book for my wife's funeral services. Sure enough, there among the many names, I found one Steve Hewing. And now, knowing his last name, my anger burned hotter than ever before.

This man who'd stolen my wife had worked for the same company several years back when she'd been a realtor. Discovering this detail made me wonder how many times Claire had gone out, telling me she had a showing, when in reality, she'd been having sex with this man in an empty house. Worse yet, when I Googled the man's name, I found he still worked for Hathaway-Fox, and their website sported his picture.

I stared at this picture for a long time. Traced his jawline with my eyes, wishing I could somehow punch him right through my monitor. His piercing blues tore

at my soul, begging me to close this website and go about my business. But, how could I? He looked the part, the role of the handsome man an unhappy wife sought out for such favors. Only then did I resolve I could not let this matter lie.

As it turned out, Steve wasn't a cheerful man. He spent much of his time at a local bar, drinking himself near death. How could my wife have ever loved a man who drank without any forethought to what he might be doing to himself?

I caught up to the man one night in a back alley, as he staggered back to his apartment. Having gained his attention, we stood facing each other in the darkness, and I said, "Do you know who I am?"

Steve nodded. Of course, he did. She'd probably shown him pictures. Told him of the many ways in which I disappointed her. Perhaps joked about how I'd let myself go over the years.

Even thinking that stoked my fires, and I found myself yelling at him. "How could you?"

He didn't answer. I couldn't help but notice he'd been crying. Then it dawned on me. Maybe he hadn't always been such a lush. He'd lost someone important to him and had been grieving in his own way. This meant he'd been with my wife to the end. Knowing that, I recalled the hours I'd been away from my wife's bedside dealing with Mia. Could he have taken my place in that time, saying goodbye to her and she to him?

No more words were needed. I rushed forward with my knife as he fell to his knees. I did not hesitate, striking his neck like a viper. I wanted him to die. And in bringing this desire to reality, temporary relief settled over me.

I stood over his body, watching him bleed out. Satisfied, I grabbed the knife and went back to my car. I worried not about blood, as I'd clean up later, when my mind settled. It took some time for the realization of what I'd done to reach me. I'd killed a man for sleeping with my wife. Even then it didn't change a thing.

Liberated by his death, my desire to confront my wife had never been stronger. I wanted to tell her what I knew and how it made me feel, to reveal my own infidelity. Use it to return the feelings like a blade of steel meant to cut Claire's flesh for hurting me. This is how my thoughts first turned to the snowdrift and the secret world beyond, found only by mere happenstance on a night when my own darkness had been too great.

Under these drifts of snow, I've glimpsed a world beyond this one. I've ventured close enough to the edge that I could gaze upon this place. Seen golden valleys stretching out before my eyes, so beautiful, yet I could not pass.

One doesn't merely walk into this world. I've attempted to force my way through on more than one occasion and failed. It's a far superior dimension and the manner in which I could gain admittance eluded me for so long. Yet I've never felt worthy until recently, after years of hard work and dedication.

With all my heart, I longed for the day when we could be together again, walking hand in hand upon sacred ground. This desire filled my dreams, my every waking hour with angst and anticipation.

But all my meditation appeared pointless considering the light winter with little snowfall. Even

when it flurried, it never stuck long enough to form a drift, often trailed by sleet and rain and the occasional rise in temperature.

Now I stare out my window hopeful for another opportunity to escape this dreadful existence. I curse the weatherman daily for his inaccuracies and the bad news he brings. When I sleep it comes with great effort, but at least I have Claire to fill my thoughts.

Sometimes I hear the soft pitter-patter of rain on my rooftop and find myself staring at the ceiling. It's been such a wet winter, but I cannot deny how calming the noise is upon my troubled soul. At least it affords me peace of mind that I might reflect on my life. It's in this space of time my utmost regrets find me.

Somewhere out my window the snow approaches. I can feel it in my bones. When it comes, I'll once more be presented with an opportunity to flee this world. It's my belief she exists in this place. Being able to cross over and look into her eyes, see the guilt in her face, this is what drives me.

Why should I alone feel responsible? Must I be the only one to endure this guilt?

When I wake the next morning, my thoughts are at ease. In that moment, I look out my window and witness the fall of snow. I'm filled with a joy I've not felt in what seems like months. I hurry to the kitchen and make coffee, sip it while I watch the sprinkles of white salt the Earth.

I rehearse my words. Can feel my unrest escalating. I twist my toes within my shoes, but this does nothing

to accelerate Mother Nature. All I want is for this storm to intensify. But it isn't until noon that the powder starts to accumulate. By dinner it's a foot deep. That's not quite enough, but I'm patient and ready.

Around three in the morning it reaches the correct depth. The harsh winds tease at the topmost layers, tossing and turning the crystals and forming the drifts for which I've long awaited. I can almost feel the wind through the edges of my windows. Now is the time.

I slip off my shoes and hurry to disrobe. Shed all material possessions from this world. Naked, I venture into the night. The brisk air slaps against my skin, numbing me within seconds. Although I shiver, I push on until I stand waist high in the snow. It bites at my flesh like rats. The cold is unbearable, yet I refuse to leave.

In the drift I dig and keep excavating, packing the removed snow behind me. A clump of ice fills my bellybutton, and I can no longer feel my testicles, toes, or fingers. Still I burrow, searching for that entrance.

After several minutes insanity finds me, and the opening appears to me in the form of a glowing hue beneath my fingers. Lightheaded and slowing, I push onward. My breath frosts the air. My fingers feel like brittle icicles, as though they will snap at any moment. The snow hardens, making it difficult to claw. Despite the bitter cold and my failing limbs and digits, I break through this last layer of sleet.

Finally, I gaze upon the opening. It's far larger than I remember. I stand in its blue glimmer and see all the golden fields of this realm.

I press against the gate. Take a deep breath and hold it in. I expect to find myself refused once more but to my astonishment, I slide through with ease.

The warmth strikes my cheeks. Fills my soul with joy as I observe the picturesque mountain ranges and unique birds fluttering through the sky. These creatures dive at the ground and then rise, driven by some unknown purpose but all the same delightful.

"David?" she says.

My heart skips a beat upon seeing Claire. Then sinks deep into my belly as I attempt to draw up my anger. All the things I've wanted to say for so long fill my thoughts, but they are lost to me like smoke in the air, wispy and dispersing faster than I can gather them.

How can I be angry here?

For the first time, I notice the man whose hand she holds. It infuriates me. "Steve?"

She smiles and releases his hand. Still, he follows behind her as she nears me. "It doesn't matter." Concern fills her expression. "Why have you come here?"

My thoughts flood with every infidelity, every lie, and I long to speak of these issues. But when I look into her eyes I can think of only one response. "For you."

She takes this man's hand again and hurt fills her eyes. "I'm sorry, David, but I can't."

I feel my loss like a punch in the stomach. "But we're . . . married . . . "

With this, he pulls her from me. She glances back over her shoulder as she's escorted away, and I see a single tear in her eye.

"This is not a tear of sorrow," she says.

And with that she's wounded me.

She speaks with empathy, "That was another

lifetime, my dear. We weren't happy there. Why would you ever think we'd be happy here?"

Despite the truth in her words, I say nothing. Can make no gesture or movement. She's ruined me.

My eyes follow her until she's no longer visible. Once more she's condemned me to sadness. To the loneliness I cannot bear. It consumes my every thought. But there's more to my realization, long hidden like her letters.

I do not belong here. Somehow, I must escape this world and find comfort elsewhere. There must be more, and I will not rest until I find its gate.

BLACKBIRD'S BREATH

ANNE ALWAYS LOVED birds. Not Henry, though. The sheer number of them annoyed him. Their constant racket often pulling him out of his book or TV show, and for that he loathed them.

Whenever they appeared, he'd try to scare them off. But they always returned. His frustration with this often made her giggle.

God, I miss her laugh.

She enjoyed the way the birds hopped around the front lawn pecking for insects. He'd even caught her feeding them now and then. And although he'd known it would encourage more to come, he'd tolerated these secret feasts because he loved her. At least she'd been happy.

Now that she'd died, he'd vowed not to harm a single bird. He endured their commotion, even at an odd hour like this. Three consecutive days of rain meant some of the juiciest worms had been lured to the surface, an easy buffet for the birds. At times, they chirped so loud it roused him from his sleep. But he didn't mind because it reminded him of Anne and that brought him comfort.

After a while, the chirping faded. He slipped into

the methodical creak of his rocking chair. The noise escorted him back to his book. Page after page he grew drowsy, and his chair slowed. Soon, he nodded off.

In his dreams of late he saw himself sitting at his dying wife's bedside. He'd been so unsure of how to keep busy while he waited for the cancer to ravish her body. What could he do? They were both helpless to the disease, left hoping for a miracle they both knew would never come. In truth, the wait only increased his anxiety.

Images of her troubled expression flooded his memories. How she'd struggled to flash a smile in those final days, doing her best to keep his hope alive despite her pain. He'd tried to return her smile, but too often failed at being convincing.

The vision faded in a whirlwind of flapping. His heart made a noise similar to the one coming from his chimney. He sat his book aside and leaned forward in his chair, staring at the fireplace. It sounded like a bird.

He watched, expecting the poor creature to discharge into the firebox. But that moment never came. Instead, he heard an awful scraping noise, and the bird hit bottom in the darkened space behind the fireplace. Seconds later, a single confused chirp indicated its predicament.

With some effort, he lowered himself to his knees and stared into a hole in the side of the fireplace where a rivet had gone missing, the opening slightly larger than a BB. A single black eye stared back at him, wide and alert. Startled, the bird leaped, flapping its wings and hopping about. Moments later it settled, and he believed he could hear it panting.

He spoke in a calm voice, not wanting to add to the bird's unease. "Easy there, pal."

Glancing back at his abandoned book, he thought about how reading had become one of the few activities he enjoyed since Anne passed. It had also become his primary means of dozing off each night.

I'll never get any reading done with this hullabaloo.

A terrible thought occurred to him, like a puncture wound at first. It spread like some horrible infection.

Maybe I should put it out of its misery.

Such a selfish notion, yet it would allow him to return to his reading. Eventually, he'd fall asleep and dream of his wife again. In time maybe he'd even forget about the bird.

His thoughts wandered back to Anne, her love for the birds. He shook his head. *No, I can't.*

The sun cast an eerie orange on his windowsill before expiring. The birds had grown quiet, all except for this lone specimen. A quick glance at the clock confirmed his worries: in a few short hours it would be midnight.

Once he would have balked upon seeing that time. Nowadays he slept whenever he felt like it. Sometimes he didn't shower and wore his robe all day. Such was the life of a retired man, let alone a widower. So, after everything he'd been through with Anne the least he could do was stay up and try to save this bird.

Lowering himself back to the hole, he observed what he could of the bird's labored breathing. After examining the fireplace for an obvious means of liberating the creature, he found none. He opened and closed the damper several times, hoping the noise would alert the bird to the way out and it would somehow free itself. But he had no such luck.

He left the damper agape and tried to startle the bird. A fit of flapping accompanied the bird's struggle to reach the opening. With each attempt, the bird slid back down. Its wings splayed against the metal walls, each breath more panicked than the last.

"Why the hell would they build a space like that behind a fireplace?"

He threw his hands into the air and a thrashing of wings followed. "Sorry, little one."

If only I could get you up to that opening.

An idea popped into his head. He ran to his bedroom and pushed through his closet until he found the necessary item. He returned with the wire hanger. Bent and twisted it, fashioning a slight hook at one end that he fished through the hole and maneuvered it to the bird's chest.

He tried to stay patient, but his arthritis started complaining. "Come on. You can do it."

He wiggled the wire, but the bird only flapped its wings, as if frightened by this invasive object. The more he tried to force the bird onto the wire, the more it thrashed. When he felt close to giving up, the bird leaped and landed on the hanger by chance.

The struggle left the bird tired. So he lifted the wire as far as he could, a mere few inches and waited. After regaining its senses the bird fluttered up toward the damper. Henry held his breath, ever hopeful. But the bird fell back again.

Damn it all to hell.

The bird slumped, as if in agreement and thus surrendering to its circumstance.

He tried the hanger again. "You can make it."

But the bird did nothing.

BLACKBIRD'S BREATH

Discouraged, he thumped the side of the fireplace.

The bird sprang to life, flapping its wings. When it did, he slid the unnatural perch beneath it. Upon feeling the bird's additional weight, he once more lifted the creature. "Go on. Save yourself."

It managed to get close to the damper, even stuck there a moment. Elation rose in Henry's chest, certain the bird would succeed this time.

Once more it slid back down to its dark dungeon. *This isn't working.*

The chime on his clock rang, and it amazed him how fast time had passed. He rubbed his eyes.

I'm too tired to keep this up.

He stood over the fireplace, saddened. "It will have to wait until morning."

Although he hated to do it, he needed sleep. He prayed the creature would be silent in the morning, so he wouldn't have to bother. A selfish thought, he felt guilty for it.

Anne wouldn't be happy.

Knowing this, he shuffled off to bed.

He woke early to a clamor of birds outside. They chirped and pecked at the soggy ground. He hurried to the fireplace and listened.

At first, he surmised the bird had either escaped or died. An inquisitive chirp surprised him.

He called an old colleague, Dale Argent. Dale had always been a handy guy, eager to discuss home improvements while standing around waiting for the coffee to brew.

"Hello?"

"Dale? It's Henry Tanner."

"Well hello, Henry. What a surprise. And so early, too. What can I do you for?"

"Sorry to bother you, but I have a problem I think you might know something about," Henry said.

"Sure. What's up?"

"Well, seems I have a bird stuck in my fireplace."

Sounding stunned, "In your fireplace?"

Henry snickered. "Oh no, scratch that. Not in exactly, but sort of behind it."

Dale remained quiet for a long moment. "Can you kill it?"

Bothered, Henry struggled to contain himself. "I'd rather not."

"I see." And maybe he really did. "You got a wood-burning fireplace over there, Henry?"

"Yep, they put it in when we had the house built."

"Well, if that's the case, I'm afraid there isn't a lot you can do. You can tear out the insert and all. But if it came pre-installed, it's likely secured from inside the structure. So unless you want to buy a whole new insert I think that bird is screwed."

These words struck Henry like a slap in the face.

"I was afraid of that. Sorry to bother you, Dale."

"Anytime, Henry. Hey," Dale said, "sorry to hear about Anne. We should go out for drinks sometime. Maybe when the weather is better."

"I'd like that," Henry said.

"Take care of yourself, Henry, you hear?"

"Will do."

Henry hung up the phone and retreated back to the hole. "Looks like there's no other way, compadre."

I should've invested in a chimney cap. Now it was too late for such precautions.

What if the bird's injured, a broken wing or foot? If nothing else it had surely exhausted itself. Maybe it only needed some time to heal.

In the garage, he secured a bag of seed he hadn't touched in months. He rushed back to the fireplace, regretting having let the door slam shut.

The bird's wings slapped against metal. Its feet clawed for purchase. This alone might have injured the bird.

Once it calmed, Henry knelt and poked a few small seeds through the hole. The bird's eye widened but after seven or so pieces it became obvious the bird wouldn't touch the seed.

Maybe it's not hungry. He paused for a moment. *Or maybe I'm feeding it the wrong food.*

He tugged on his slippers and rushed outside. The birds pecking at his lawn startled. They flew into the trees and returned seconds later despite his presence.

With a piece of kindling from his firewood pile he dug. After several minutes he found what he wanted and headed back to the hole, this time more mindful of the door.

When he fed the skinny worm through the hole, it collapsed upon itself like a wet noodle. With his patience worn thin, the worm's guts began to ooze out around the edges. In the end, it looked like he'd spread some awful jelly around the hole. At least part of the worm had made it through.

No doubt terrified of this man who continued to poke food through the hole, the bird looked nervous. And although the poor creature did regard the worm guts, it still wouldn't eat them.

"How are you gonna live, if you won't eat?"

Those words sounded so much like what he'd said to Anne. This similarity made him shudder.

Why Anne? Why send this bird? To torment me?

His options were limited. He could go back to his book and let the bird die on its own. This was what he'd done for Anne, reading at her bedside while he waited for her to pass. She'd begged him to help her along, but he could never have brought himself to do anything. All the while her whimpers had assaulted his senses, painful for him on so many levels.

I can't go through that again.

Log by log, he built the largest fire his fireplace could withstand. He hoped it wouldn't be too painful. But how could it not?

He lighted the fire and watched as the flames licked at the black metal encasement. As if in disagreement with his choice, the birds outside stirred in protest. A turmoil of flapping ensued, as the fire heated the imprisoned bird.

His ears keen, he heard a small chirp, and then something far worse. It reminded him of Anne. It almost sounded like Anne stuck behind the fireplace, whimpering.

Damn, it's suffering. It's in pain.

After an hour, the flapping eased. The lack of oxygen had likely exterminated the bird long before the fire. That seemed somewhat humane.

With the blaze still burning, he settled back into his chair to read. He wanted nothing more than to forget it all. The rocking found a rhythm with the symphony of crackles that escaped the fire and soon he forgot the bird, turning his focus to the words. His thoughts free

of both Anne and the bird for a while, the fire warmed him and soon he drifted into slumber.

Of all things, a squawk woke him.

How long have I been asleep?

His eyes struggled on the clock. He sighed upon seeing it neared three in the morning. Pushing up from his rocker, he stumbled toward his bedroom.

Maybe it was only a dream.

As if in answer to his grief, a single caw shook him out of his daze. His ear trained on the smoldering fireplace. He gazed upon the dying embers.

No, it can't be.

He retraced his steps back to the hearth and listened. Judging by the intensity of heat finding him even now, the bird should have met its demise.

Bending to see through the hole, the dying fire warming his scalp. A single coal-black eye stared back at him. When it didn't move, he thought the bird dead. Then the eye twitched, and Henry jumped, startling the bird.

He rose to his knees and marveled, "Unbelievable."

With no idea what more he could do, he paced. *How could it survive? What can I do to end its pitiful existence?*

An idea came to him, and he returned to his closet. He dug through a box full of childhood memories. Threw aside trophies, his cap and gown from graduation, several school papers, until he found the gun. In hand, he rushed back to the hole.

He shook the replica handgun, indicating a dozen

or so BB's rattled around inside. This wouldn't have the impact of a pump action pellet gun, but he believed those pellets wouldn't fit through the opening anyway.

After cocking the handgun, he aligned its barrel to the hole. His finger slid into the curve of the trigger and pulled. The BB pinged off one wall and then ricocheted off another.

"Missed."

He cocked the gun and fired again. Each pull of the trigger came with greater ease. One after another, he riddled the space beyond with BB's, tilting the gun at different angles to ensure at least one BB would hit the bird.

Most of the BB's brought only the sound of metal. A few offered a dull thud. Before long the gun clicked empty.

When he bent, he expected the bird to be staring back at him, but he found only darkness.

His heartbeat slowed, certain he'd finished the task. But a pang twisted at his heart when the haunting eye returned. An awful blank glossiness judged him as if to inquire why Henry would do such a horrible thing.

"Why won't you die?"

Despite his drowsy eyes, his stubbornness refused him rest. Not until he completed this dreadful deed. Mercy must be delivered. That alone would bring peace to his Anne.

He ran to the kitchen and rifled through the drawers. Each banged against their stoppers, and he left them open when he didn't find the utensil he wanted.

At last, he grasped the metal skewer and returned to the fireplace. He eased the pointed end of the

skewer through the hole and thrust it in blindly. When an assault came away empty, he adjusted his angle and shoved it back in with fervor.

He extracted the skewer to check on his prey. There he discovered the bird, alert as ever. It stared at him with its coal-black eye.

Anger consumed him, and he stabbed the skewer in with reckless abandon. The creature countered with a bustle of flapping wings. Then all became quiet when he felt the extra weight on the skewer and withdrew it from the hole, careful not to pull too fast. He smiled upon seeing blood.

Near five in the morning another caw woke Henry. He thought it one final desperate plea, this bird's last breath.

But the unpleasant squawking continued throughout the next hour, then throughout the next few days. When he thought he could take no more a full week later, the bird finally surrendered.

Astonished, he studied the hole. He stared into the darkness for hours, certain that eye would pop back into view. When it did he would slip farther from reality. But it didn't return and much like after Anne died, he saw his first real sleep in a long while.

He slept most of the following day, waking to a familiar noise. The ping of metal startled him. Followed by the flapping of wings as it descended down the depths of the chamber behind the fireplace.

He ran to the fireplace, collapsing to his knees and staring into the hole. A single black eye peered back at him.

The bird offered an anxious chirp.

DESOLATE

T**HE BOY REMINDED** Emmie of a vulture. The way he squatted on the ground, feeding among the large boulders that lined the back of their three-acre yard.

The infected often evoked images of such ugly creatures. And like vultures, they too scavenged. Always in search of the berries, their sole desire once they'd been diseased.

These berries had been the catalyst for the massive outbreak that brought ruin to their desolate village. All infected were now lost to the community. And they'd never be coming back.

Her brother had been the first to discover the berries. His actions back then still troubled her even with knowing of his addiction. It had been too horrible to forget. The berries ruined so many lives in this way.

It's what led to the people of her village to work hard at uprooting all of the berry plants, their stringy vines dipping in and out of the ground among the underside of large rocks, the fruit safeguarded beneath the cool wet soil. Later, they burned them, so as to prevent further loss of life.

The *lost* as they were called, didn't linger after the

berries were gone. Where there'd once been dozens, she hadn't seen a single one in over three years.

Now there was the matter of this boy. She cocked a brow and surmised the peculiar berries had returned.

That isn't good.

She remembered the discolored appearance of her younger brother's face after he'd eaten the berries and a hint of a fading winter's mud on his cheeks. His fingers were always blistered and scarred from excavating the berries from the frosted earth. She recalled how he shoved them into his mouth so greedily, one after another without pause. How the juice spilled down his chin long after his belly engorged. The vision of it still sickened her.

From what she could see, this boy looked rather emaciated. Tattered clothes hung from his bony frame. He dipped and then rose. Large rocks obscured much of her view. Matted hair dangled in front of his face, and she could make out his mouth chomping away.

She slid open the glass door, and the slight noise drew the boy's attention. His hair spilled to the sides, and those restless eyes locked on her. Only then did she see his face.

No, it can't be.

She considered retrieving her coat. It was still brisk for March. Instead, she forged ahead without it, worried he would leave if she didn't hurry. She needed to identify this trespasser.

Stepping down to the stone terrace, she left the door open in case she needed to retreat. Right away a rush of cool air raced up the front of her shirt. Shivering, she folded her arms across her chest and braved onward.

Father had been explicit in regards to how she should handle this situation. If any of the infected ever returned she was to hole up inside and wait for him to get home. He'd assured her that he would take care of everything.

She knew what that meant, too. He'd shoot them dead. Even kept his gun loaded for such an occasion. He expected she'd keep her distance yet she couldn't resist seeing if this boy was her brother.

Besides, it wasn't the first time she'd disobeyed Father. She and David had often ignored his orders as children. It always frustrated Father and because of it, she'd been responsible for at least part of David's addiction. She hadn't kept an eye on her brother as Father had instructed.

This still saddened her. Mostly because it also meant she'd played a part in Mother's death. Feeling lightheaded from the memories, she shook her head in an effort to relieve the sensation.

A mix of emotions shrouded her as her boots touched the grass. She traced his jawline, the curvature of his eyes, his blistered lips. It was David all right. He'd only been ten when she last saw him.

He's gotten taller. She felt her forehead wrinkle. *How is he even alive?*

The infected lacked the intelligence required to create shelter or secure an alternate food source. Their entire existence depended on their addiction. Once the berries were gone and the heaviest winter in thirty years followed, death for the *lost* had seemed imminent.

By all rights David should've met this end. *So why didn't he?*

Her mind wrestled with what this might mean. If he'd learned how to feed himself and live through such harsh conditions, maybe he'd gotten better. Had he been holed up somewhere? Found something other than berries to appease his hunger? Could the *lost* overcome their addiction?

If nothing else, it offered a sense of hope. Father would have to consider this before he did anything rash.

He won't, though.

Of this she was certain. He'd clung to his resentment for David. Perhaps they would've been better off still thinking David dead. But that was no longer an option for her.

He didn't mean to kill her. It was the berries.

She stood rigid and defiant. *Besides, he's my brother.*

But was he? She recalled walking into her brother's room on that day, frozen as she watched him tear at Mother's flesh. Emmie had been lucky to escape. She wouldn't have if it hadn't been for Father.

They should've seen it coming. Left alone to the berries, the infected were somewhat peaceful. Similar to the scavenging birds she'd likened them to.

Yet, once the berries were gone, the *lost* reacted as any addict might. They lashed out in an attempt to soothe their endless madness. Nothing helped. Things escalated.

There was no changing the past, and she doubted Father would ever forgive him. She wasn't even sure if she could excuse David.

But I won't abandon him.

A brash wind teased at her dark locks. Sent them

fluttering across her face. She brushed them back and when she did, he leaned away.

He's afraid of me.

After a long pause, he returned to his food. Took small bites, as if to conserve. A second later he glared off into the distance at a fox. David stood and dashed several yards toward the animal. He flailed his arms and made wild noises that worried her.

The fox fled, stopping only when David did. There it paced back and forth, daring to come closer, but mindful of its proximity.

David ignored the creature and returned to his meal. It surprised her that he hadn't killed the fox. He could.

Why isn't he attacking it?

Other critters, unseen by her, seemed to pester him. On occasion, he swatted at the ground, and she heard a scurry of footsteps. Then he'd go back to eating.

A large shadow swooped overhead. She looked up and saw a pair of vultures spiraling down on him as if caught in a funnel of wind. They were also interested in David's meal. Although large and ominous, he didn't even bother with the birds until they ventured too close.

When they did, he leaped into the air and waved his arms.

Frightened, the birds ascended back to a safe altitude. There, they began their calculated approach all over again.

Maybe he'd become more normal than she suspected. Visions raced through her mind, memories of them running through the fields together. How they

would capture bees in glass jars and watch them buzz for hours. She missed the simplicity of those days. The smell rising from the grill as Father cooked dinner. Mother humming a tune while she set the table. Those were wonderful days.

David munched, his gaze fully on her. *Does he recognize me?*

He didn't appear concerned by her advance. Not like he'd been with the other creatures. Would he guard the berries as he once had? If that were the case, Father wouldn't even hesitate to shoot him.

He'll likely kill him anyway.

She glanced back at their house. Scanned for signs of Father. He should've been home by now. She half-expected him to come bursting through the door, gun in hand. Yet an eerie emptiness filled her when he didn't.

For the most part, David ignored her. She took precautions and hid behind whatever obstacles the yard provided. Still, he didn't attack. He didn't even look angered.

She paused shy of the large rocks. At first, only his soiled face remained visible. She squinted, focusing on the thing in his hand when he ate. Unable to confirm what it was, she noticed the crimson trail on his chin. That was all the evidence she required. His fingertips were also red, and the gaps between his discolored teeth. It brought back memories that made her cheeks flush hot.

Damn those berries.

The villagers had taken such care in their removal, having dug up every last root and kept a close eye out for their reappearance. Maybe they'd grown too

confident over those years as for some reason they'd neglected to see them return. She whispered a frustrated curse, or—one she hadn't intended to come out so loud. It surprised even her.

David leaped away. His eyes widened on her, full of mistrust. This could have been the first human sound he'd heard in a long time.

"No, wait." She took a brave step forward. "I'm not going to hurt you."

Even as she spoke, he slanted away. Much like a terrified animal on the verge of fleeing, he kept on his toes. His distress obvious, his mouth opened, lips drawn back in a cautious snarl.

What now, David? Will you hurt me? She didn't think so and closed in.

He tossed the morsel into his mouth and chewed. His jaw moved in slow gyrations, eyes glued to her. They seemed vacant of the boy she'd known so well. But he was in there somewhere.

Life could never return to what it had been. But maybe, if he'd gotten better, they could salvage some part of their lives together.

She turned, thankful Father hadn't arrived home yet. *Even if he's running late, he won't be much longer.*

She glanced over her shoulder, which startled David.

He's so skittish.

That wasn't a bad thing. If Father showed up, maybe she could scare David off. Sooner or later he'd return for the berries. With any luck, he'd come when Father wasn't home. Maybe over time she could reason with them both.

David sat back on his haunches. She stretched up on her tippy toes, hoping for a better view. But still, she couldn't see much.

If I gather the berries, maybe I can use them to get closer to David. Father wouldn't approve of this idea, but she was well aware of the danger it entailed.

She ventured closer with careful steps.

Uneasy of her advance, David puffed out his chest. The tiny hairs on his arms stood like the worn bristles of a weathered brush. His dark sunken eyes explored her.

"Do you remember me?" she said.

He didn't answer. She thought he might have forgotten how to speak. But he also didn't retreat. Even stood his ground when she took two steps to the stone stairs.

"I'm your sister, Emmie."

Taking the first step up, she stayed on her toes so she could maintain eye contact. She thought this helped him relax.

He twitched and leaned away from her. She believed he'd flee at the slightest hint of danger.

She edged her way around a boulder, using it to steady herself. All the while her eyes remained on David. "I'm not going to hurt you. I just want to talk."

His distrust showed. This close, she could see the discoloration well. His face, chest, and hands were covered in red. The shabby remains of his clothing were soaked in the juice.

"Do you remember me?" she said.

She smiled, and to this, he took a cautious step back.

Her voice sounded desperate. "No, don't leave."

Tripping on the rocky undergrowth, she stumbled forward. She tried to support herself on the next boulder and had to take a large step to balance.

At this, he scampered several yards away. His hands dragged along the frosted earth like a primate. Once he'd put safe distance between them, he stopped.

Worried he might leave, she lunged forward all at once. She hoped to make up the distance she'd lost. But with her attention on her brother, she neglected her footing and tripped again.

The cool of spring soil found her cheek. Wintery crystals stung her flesh. The shadow of the large rocks forced her to shiver.

She lifted herself up, worried he'd left. Her search began and ended on the corpse beside her. Its body twisted in an unnatural pose, the man's cheek had been torn away. Both of his eyes had been plucked out of their sockets. The empty puckered holes stared up at the bright-blue sky. She tried to deny his identity behind this horrid death mask, but her Father's nose was impossible to ignore. His mouth agape, he wore a permanent expression of terror that threw her world into a spin.

No, not Dad, too.

When she glanced back to David, it terrified her to find him so close. Blood dripped down his chin. His contorted hands opened and closed. A wicked glare filled his eyes. His gaunt cheeks quivered in anticipation of food. His red-stained teeth chattered.

A guttural growl escaped him. She knew he wouldn't flinch again. Even when she began to scream, he did not leave her side.

LOST IN THE WOODS

ALLIE HAD HEARD stories of this wooded path. How it might be a gateway to another world. Rumor had it one boy used it to bring his deceased mother back from the dead. That tale was as old as Allie's grandmother, the first to tell it to her.

She ignored the chill in her extremities. Despite the icy crystals that buried her boots, she pushed onward through the wind. She crossed her arms at her waist and weathered the gusts, reaching the opening of the path in no time at all.

There, she observed the rather ordinary trail. Celestial or otherwise, why would any being intelligent enough to build such a portal, opt to place it smack dab in the middle of suburbia?

Why not a rural location in the South where people often reported such supernatural events? Or maybe atop some estranged mountain where no one would find it except for those who'd created it? The mere thought of any such gateway being right here in Haleyville seemed improbable. But if this place offered even the slightest chance to bring James back, she'd believe anything, no matter how absurd.

Her brother had been involved in an accident a year earlier. The force had been great enough to

mangle his car. Given the closed casket, she'd always suspected he'd suffered a fate similar to the vehicle.

They went out for dinner on the one-year anniversary of his death a few weeks ago. Her parents thanked God she hadn't been in the car with him. Allie, on the other hand, often wished she had.

Forever engraved in her memories, she could still picture his face. She'd always been so proud to call him her brother. She remembered his dimpled smile. The way he'd playfully slug her shoulder each day before school. He'd been the best brother a girl could have.

How many brothers would escort their little sister around high school on her first day? His friends had teased him, but he'd been strong enough to shrug off their mockery. Later, he told her that his friends' idea of a good time revolved around debating how much Janice Delfro's breasts had grown. Not him, though. He'd always been a class act.

When some of the other girls made snide comments about the way she looked or how she kept her nose buried in her books, he'd been there to defend her. He'd always been so witty with his words, too, often leaving other kids without a comeback.

His had been the voice of reason when their parents quarreled. But where was he when she needed him most? Since his death her family had become strained: Mom listless and detached, Dad unsympathetic to anyone else's needs.

I can't blame Mom.

Maybe Allie was too young to understand everything, but she had a good idea what it might be like to lose a child. After all, she'd lost her brother. Allie often listened to Mom cry herself to sleep, drinking so

much she began to slur her words as she babbled to no one.

On those nights, Allie hid around the corner outside the bedroom, sitting on the wooden floor with her head pressed against the wall. Tears would run down her cheeks while Mom mumbled inaudible words and Dad listened with indifference.

These last couple of months those nights had come to an end. Mom no longer sought the comfort of a bedroom. Now she passed out on the couch, and Dad slept alone. Allie found herself caught in the middle of a declining relationship, and it had deteriorated faster than she could repair.

A few nights back Allie ventured downstairs to watch Mom sleep after Dad had gone to bed. The hurt and pain had been evident as she watched Mom dream. She imagined she dreamed about the night he died, what her parents had seen upon arriving at the wreck.

Yesterday everything exploded: her parent's relationship, high school. It had all become so fractured, like a well-travelled sidewalk. She'd vowed to fix things, and that meant she had no choice but to believe in the legend surrounding this wooded path.

She rubbed her hands together, the coarse fabric of her mittens scratching against her sweaty palms. "Hello?"

There was no response. Not a single creature stirred. The blanket of snow lacked any tracks.

"If you can hear me, James, I miss you."

Her eyes studied the path, glancing from side to side and then upward. Swells of snow rested upon limbs, weighing them down. It looked as though the

trees were wearing sparkling gowns, preparing for a ballroom dance.

From these branches hung hundreds, maybe even thousands of icicles. They shimmered in the afternoon light. Each blinked off and on like stars in a night sky. This captivated her imagination. The backdrop had certainly been set for something magical to happen.

What will happen if I can bring him back?

Would she feel whole again? Maybe. Would he heal their family? He'd always been the better peacekeeper. Of course she thought he could mend matters.

She frowned. *That's if he can get Dad to come home.*

If Mom were having one of her good days, she would have found out she'd cut school by now. That was if she wasn't still sleeping off last night's drinking. Even then the school would have called Dad. He'd be out looking for her, maybe even called the police.

A sense of worry shrouded her like a fresh coating of snow. *Stay strong, and hurry.*

If James were here he wouldn't have wasted so much time thinking. He would have continued on, fearless as ever. In his absence she'd become vulnerable. Her quality of life had dissolved and desperation took over. Enough for her to come here.

What if I can't return? Does anyone even come here anymore?

Most people didn't, either afraid or indifferent to the lore. How long would it be before anyone found her?

Likely days.

Darkness enveloped her as a cloud passed in front of the sun. A dismal shadow covered the path,

eliminating the dreamlike quality. Now the trail looked terrifying.

As if mocking her uncertainty, an owl hooted.

Startled, she scanned the whitened treetops, but could not find the bird. A cool breeze nipped at her cheeks. And the more she searched for the owl, the more she began to loathe the creature for its intrusion. It had made her heart—

A voice whispered behind her. "Allie?"

Who, indeed?

She expected to see her brother, and her heart leaped when she spun around. But all she saw was their town, looking barren for a Wednesday afternoon. Doubt churned in her thoughts.

Am I hearing things? She felt like running. *It's not too late to leave.*

Water splashed across the bridge of her nose, and she screamed. Her shrill cry faded as the cool droplet worked its way around. From there it wet her cheek and touched the corner of her mouth.

Her eyes shot to the icicles, hanging there like precarious daggers. Another drip landed squarely on her forehead. It meandered down her temple to her earlobe.

An awkward laugh escaped her. She wiped her forehead with her mitten and only then realized she'd entered the path by accident. A steady thump pounded inside of her.

She mustered up some nerve. *No turning back now.* But she still couldn't bring herself to take the next step.

As if in response to her fear the cloud cover thickened, and the temperature seemed to drop several degrees all at once.

That same whisper came again. "Allie?"

She turned faster this time, and her eyes lingered on the space she'd occupied seconds earlier. The snow revealed only her footprints.

But somebody had been there. She'd heard them.

Obscured by the bushes dotting the shoulder, her apparent intruder moved. This couldn't be her brother. He would have made his presence known. But still, this impostor plodded along through the fallen snow, rustling the dried leaves hanging from the lowest branches.

With each step she took, her heartbeat struck louder. The trees felt as though they were crowding her. Their joined canopy made the temperature plunge even farther.

When the creature burst out from the shrubbery, her chest hitched. Hands on her heart, she struggled to keep the organ from leaping right out of her chest. Several uncontrolled shrieks escaped her as the rabbit crossed to the other side of the path and vanished into the bushes.

Nervous laughter bubbled from her dried lips. Her red locks danced before her eyes, obstructing her view. But she didn't mind. She needed the distraction.

Hot breath tickled the back of her neck, and her despair returned. Her flesh prickled as she gulped in a deep breath of air and held it.

She wanted to look, to spin and confront this stalker. But she knew they wouldn't be there. Instead, she bounded through the snow with large unbridled leaps. Cool air stung her throat as she inhaled deeply in her effort. Her heart raced her footfalls, pounding out a steady *thud-thump, thud-thump* rhythm. Tears

pinched at the corners of her eyes, making it difficult to see.

At the end of the trail she ducked into the brush to lose her pursuer. She glanced back and several thin branches swatted her. If not for a large limb impeding her path, she might not have fallen.

Cold bit at her exposed flesh. She lifted herself out of the snow, eyes wide and searching. A tingling sensation washed over her, but not due to the snow melting on her face.

"James?"

After a long moment, she thought she might have only imagined hearing him again. She stood and wiped the snow from her clothes, still searching, but saw nothing.

Maybe he's here, but not here.

And if she could convince Mom she'd heard James, she'd help Allie bring him back.

She hurried home, kicking at the foundation to free the snow from her boots. A shadowy figure loomed in the bay window. Mom's silhouette hunched over the stove, cooking like she did before the accident. It smelled delightful.

A frown formed on her lips, as she considered this might not be real. *No, this can't be a dream.*

Mom's shadow crept across the living room wall, and Allie could barely contain herself. Telling Mom might start the healing. But maybe somehow it already had happened. *After all, Mom is cooking again.*

The woman's face floated in the window, her eyes broad and dark. They were deep unnatural pits on a misshapen skull. Her flesh had paled, riddled with purple veins that creased her cheeks and forehead. Her

teeth were uneven and pointed, reminding Allie of the jagged rows of trees that saddled the wooded path. Drool moistened her chin as she saw Allie and smiled.

This creature rushed to the door, already struggling with the knob. And Allie ran, her screams giving away her route. But she couldn't stop herself.

She headed for the path, her only hope of escaping. By the time she reached the wooded trail, she spotted someone familiar in the distance. She recognized his smile, even from this far. Waiting for her at the entrance, she darted for him, and he opened his arms to embrace her.

When she crashed into him, it forced the boy back. They stumbled through the path, her trying to keep them both afoot. She struggled with his weight until they were almost on the other side. Before they reached the end, she fell, and he tumbled to the ground beside her.

Buried in snow again, her eyes darted up for fear he might not be real. He sat looking away from her, staring off at town. A smile found her lips, and she threw her arms around him, hugging his back.

"James!"

He turned and held her tighter than ever. It felt so good.

The sun lit his silhouette, but she couldn't quite make out his face. Imagining his smile, his dimples, she shielded herself with a hand. She wanted to see it for real. To take in everything she'd been missing this last year.

His eyes were so sunken. Uneven fangs poked out of his grin. She hiccupped with surprise as his smile widened. His arms constricted her, a cold embrace

similar to that of a hungry snake. A pinch hurt her shoulder and the warm sensation of pain spread fast down to her stomach.

She listened for the noises of nature. All she heard was the desperation of suckling at her neck. This and the owl, still unseen somewhere up in the trees.

FINAL BREATHS

A MOTHER SHOULDN'T have to suffer her child's death. Above all, she shouldn't be here, alone. Alas, her daughter's father had died back when she was four, so Glenda had no choice.

It felt wrong sitting here, waiting like this for such a dreadful end. She couldn't bear the thought of letting Laura go this soon. Yet she'd come to do just that. She clung to her daughter's weak hand. Felt what little life Laura had left slipping away like seconds on a clock.

A gurgling noise startled her. Glenda rolled Laura to her side and patted her back to loosen the mucus. Through it all, Laura remained asleep. She wheezed in relief and settled back to an absolute still.

Her shallow breathing steady once more, Glenda relaxed some. As much as any mother could, given the gravity of her situation. If for no other reason, she'd remain calm in case Laura woke.

But she won't, will she? Glenda's hope waned. She rolled her eyes to the sky. *How could you take my little girl?*

Only she wasn't so little anymore. Laura had grown into a woman when Glenda hadn't been looking. One who'd only just started her adult life.

A frown creased Glenda's face at the realization

she'd never see Laura marry. Or have children. Knowing this panged her heart too much, and she forced herself to push the thought away.

If I could just switch places with her, I would. I wish I—

The door opened, and she gathered herself. She wiped her eyes with the balled up wad of tissues in her trembling clenched fist.

The night nurse poked her head in, regarding Glenda with a kind smile. "I'm sorry. I need to check her vitals."

On any other day, Glenda would have found the woman's accent charming. She believed it, Russian. Under other circumstances, she might have even inquired about it. Right now, though, the accent bothered her, so she refrained.

It will be this voice that will soon confirm my daughter's death.

"Okay," the nurse said. "She's doing well. Quite peaceful."

The nurse stared at Glenda for a long moment. In that brief interlude the woman resembled Laura. They were about the same age. Both had shoulder-length blonde hair and soft round eyes. Like her daughter, she seemed so full of confidence.

"Can I get you something to eat?" the nurse said.

Glenda repeated the question in her thoughts, trying to make sense of it. Once it registered, she shook her head.

She hadn't eaten since arriving. Before that she'd consumed a few packets of crackers with some water, struggling to keep even that down. How could she eat knowing Laura would soon die?

The nurse wore a disapproving frown.

"She woke," Glenda said. She wanted to refocus the nurse's attention on her daughter.

"What do you mean? Choking?"

Glenda nodded, and it seemed so minor hearing the nurse refer to it in this way. She found herself wishing it had been more.

A confused look creased the nurse's face. She let go of Laura's arm and skirted back around the bed to Glenda's position.

"Just so you're aware, if she does wake, it's quite common in the final stages for the patient to hallucinate." Her frown grew as if realizing how this must've sounded, but she made no attempt to alter what she said. "But I don't think she will." She hummed lightly. "You know, because of the meds."

Glenda sat quiet. Watched the nurse return to Laura's care, pumping more drugs into her daughter's already weakened system.

Why so much?

She waited for the nurse to leave. Once alone with her daughter again, everything felt better. She prayed God would find mercy. But couldn't help to question whether God even existed at a moment like this.

She stared at her daughter's peaceful face, trying to will Laura to wake. In the silence, the only noises were the incessant ticking of the clock on the wall and Laura's light breathing. They blended into one. Became a sort of static background noise. Listening to them, Glenda soon nodded off in the yellow pleather chair.

Laura started choking and Glenda shot awake. When she looked, Laura's eyes went wide, searching Glenda's face. Glenda didn't know what to do. She couldn't do anything if she wanted. Then she realized Laura had said something.

Glenda took Laura's hand and pawed at it. "What did you say, baby girl? Tell Mommy."

Laura's eyes passed from Glenda to the door and back again. Her voice sounded weak. "Who are they?"

Glenda glanced over her shoulder, expecting to see the nurse. She remembered the nurse's warning. "There's no one—"

By the time she'd spun back around, Laura had settled. Once more she rested, her breathing steady, but shallow.

No, she isn't resting. She's gone back to dying.

With this realization, Glenda's heart ached all over again. Still, delusion or not, she felt thankful to hear Laura's voice one last time. To look into her eyes and see her little girl looking back at her.

Only Laura's eyes had lacked that same deep blue hue she remembered so well. They'd taken on a muddied appearance, like a starless night sky.

Tears strained Glenda's eyes. She'd been crying so much it hurt, but the tears flowed despite her pain.

"Mom?" Laura sounded panicked. "Mom, they're coming for me."

Laura stared at the door again. Still, Glenda saw no one.

What can I say to ease her worry?

FINAL BREATHS

Sometimes, when Laura had been young, she'd crawled out of her crib in the middle of the night. She'd slipped into Glenda's bed before she woke. Laura had been so terrified of the dark and the noises that old house made.

What did I do then, when I put her back in bed? She remembered.

"Hush now, baby." She took Laura's hand and patted it. "It's okay. Don't you worry, Mommy's right here. Hush now, child."

She hummed a tune, but couldn't recall its name.

Laura interrupted her. "Please, Mom. They're awful."

"I'm so sorry, honey. I wish I could take the pain away." And she did, very much so.

Laura's face twisted in a knot of worry. "They want me to come with them, Mom. Please don't let them take me."

"No, Mommy won't let that happen. Stay with me, honey. Stay here."

Glenda's heart skipped, thinking the end close. "Don't go," she said. But Laura had already drifted back to sleep.

Her heart rapped as she studied her daughter. Traced every curve of her young face. The round of her closed eyes, and each and every eyelash. She lingered on Laura's lips.

Are they moving?

When Laura struggled for a breath, Glenda struggled with her. And when Laura settled, she couldn't decide whether she was still alive.

Then Laura did breathe. Ever so subtle and slight, her chest rose and fell. With it, so did Glenda's, understanding the conclusion of this state.

No, I refuse to accept it. I can save her. Be there for her. Take it all away. I can—

The door opened, and the pleasant young nurse peered in. "Everything okay, Mrs. Farrell? I heard something . . ."

She waved off the nurse but said nothing.

"Did she wake?"

Glenda nodded, breathing shallow herself now. She started crying again. "She woke. Sat right up, looked at me, and spoke."

"Hmm." The nurse crossed to the bed and checked Laura's pulse. "What did she say? Was she in need of more meds?"

No, not more drugs so soon.

The nurse had told her the drugs would help ease the pain. But Glenda doubted they relieved anything but the conscience of the living. They somehow believed it made everything easier. But this shouldn't be easy.

"No," Glenda said. "She asked who *they* were."

"Who, dear?"

"I . . . I'm not sure."

The nurse studied a machine, checking the ticker-tape readout. "Everything looks normal." She glanced up at the clock. "It's still early, but do you think more medicine would help?"

Glenda knew she'd ask this and had prepared to say no. Yet she found herself nodding and despised herself for doing so.

The nurse administered another syringe into the port. "There we go. She shouldn't wake again for a while. She'll be able to rest." Concern dawned over the nurse. "And I think maybe you should try to get some sleep, too."

Glenda had napped some, although she had no idea how much. Her eyes felt so heavy as of late, like she hadn't slept in months.

She waited for the nurse to leave and returned her attention to her daughter.

Did I imagine Laura speaking?

Given both her lack of food and sleep, she thought it possible. Maybe Glenda had been the one hallucinating.

She blinked her eyes. Her eyelids drooped as if weighed down. A puffy sensation behind them urged her to keep them shut.

A rustle shook her out of this temptation, and she shot upright. It surprised her to see Laura sitting up in bed, her eyes intense on Glenda.

"What would you give them, Mom?" Laura said.

Glenda didn't respond at first, thinking this wasn't real.

Then a new hope found her. Even if this were a dream, what harm would it do to answer?

She heard her own voice, distant. "What do you mean?"

Laura seemed unhinged. "I have to give them something, or they'll take me away." Her hopeful eyes scanned Glenda, awaiting instruction. "What should I give them, Mom?"

She wanted nothing more than to alleviate her daughter's concerns. Exasperated, she said the lone thing that came to mind, remembering Laura as that child who couldn't sleep. "They can't have you, Laura. Tell them you have nothing to give."

Glenda thought hard, her eyes searching her motionless daughter, trying to come up with a

better answer. "Me, Laura. Tell them to take me instead."

Laura settled back against her pillows and quieted fast. She didn't move for a long time, and an angelic aura seemed to form around her.

Laura jerked in swift movements. Arched her neck, gasping for air that would not fill her lungs. Her eyes closed tight as the struggle intensified.

"Nurse?" Glenda stood, leaning over Laura, but not knowing what to do. "Nurse, come fast!"

Glenda held Laura's hand. Laura's frail digits squeezed hard, and Glenda tried to roll her so she could pat her back. But Laura jerked away.

Unable to find her own breath, Glenda watched Laura's color fade. Her skin turned a dreadful gray in a fraction of a second. Laura's entire body trembled one last time and then her baby girl laid still. The insistent buzz suggested Laura's fate.

"Laura?" Glenda said.

As per Laura's wishes, the nurse would not resuscitate her. But regardless, Glenda would fight it.

She pleaded. "Laura, honey? Don't go . . ."

The nurse entered and rounded the bed, taking Laura's pulse. She leaned over her motionless body to listen. Her eyes found Glenda. "I'm so sorry, Mrs. Farrell."

Glenda sobbed, pouring every remaining ounce of sorrow left in her fatigued body out into that room. The nurse left her to grieve. Glenda remained by her daughter's side until they asked her to leave. Even then she resisted.

She drove home in a fog to the house where she'd raised Laura. She went to Laura's room, turned on the

TV, and threw herself onto the bed. Even this comfort did nothing to alleviate her memories of what had happened.

Staring up at the ceiling fan, it spun round and round. Outside the chirp of locusts rose and fell. The TV flickered on the wall, then dimmed as the scene changed.

In this disquiet, Glenda found sleep despite her battle against it. Images of Laura's final moments filled her dreams.

A weight shifted at the end of the bed, beside Glenda's feet. The corner of the bed slanted, irritating her.

She rolled away from it but felt the weight lift. Then something cold gripped her leg.

She shot up, staring down at her legs. *Nothing there.*

Her fuzzy eyes explored the room and saw a figure looming beside the bed. Glenda flung herself across the bed to safety. There, she stared at the girl, realizing only then it was Laura.

Oh dear God, she's lost her way.

But Laura didn't look lost. She trembled like she had when she'd been young. Barely discernable, her daughter's form swayed back and forth. The blank expression Laura wore did little to alleviate Glenda's apprehension. Neither did the lifeless eyes Glenda glimpsed behind the blonde locks of hair that dangled in her daughter's face.

Laura murmured something incomprehensible. Sounding like a mantra, she repeated it over and over.

"Laura? Why are you here?"

Laura lifted her face and her eyes shot open. Empty pools searched Glenda.

A scream rose in Glenda's throat, but she contained it. Still, her voice crackled. "You need to go, honey." She slipped over the edge of the bed to her knees. "Go to the light, Laura. Just please go . . . "

Laura's mouth opened. Her lips looked pale and blue. She spoke, but the words came out disjointed and not in synch with the movement of her lips. "I can't go."

Glenda scampered across the floor, to the farthest corner of the bed. There, she folded her hands as if in prayer. "Please, Laura. You have to go."

But Laura remained, her gaze vacant. "I can't."

"Why?"

Laura's tongue licked her bottom lip. "I need you. You have to come. I'm scared, Mommy."

Her words saddened Glenda and in this sorrow, Glenda found some determination. "Okay, Laura. I'll do anything you want."

Glenda rose to her feet, mustering up her courage. "You hear that, Laura. I promise, I'll do anything you want. I would—"

Laura didn't allow her to finish. Her ghastly form lunged across the surface of the covers and passed right through Glenda's chest.

Unable to control her body, Glenda's arms shot out. The pain came instant, deep in her heart. Each limb went numb, forcing her to collapse. On the floor, her chest tightened and twisted, stomach retching. Vertigo seized her, eyes shuddering in their sockets as she attempted to keep them open.

Laura stood over her, her image flickering, seeming to weaken with Glenda.

"No, not like this," Glenda said.

But Laura expressed no sympathy. Glenda had made a promise. An offer that couldn't be retracted. Her frightened little girl meant to collect.

Glenda beheld her daughter's empty gaze as the darkness encroached. Shadows ebbed across the walls like sponges of paint blotting out all existence. The pain in her chest intensified, and then the darkness consumed everything.

Glenda opened her eyes. *It's only a bad dream.*

But absent was the softness of Laura's bed. Something rigid and unpleasant had taken its place. And this new surface warmed her in a most unnatural way.

She sat up, meeting Laura's gaze. She tried to speak, but Laura hushed her.

"I did it, Mom. I told them what you wanted."

Glenda's eyes darted around. "Told them what?"

Laura stood unmoving, her hair matted and eyes full of hurt. "That you wouldn't let them take me. That they could have you instead."

When Laura stepped aside, Glenda saw them in the distance. Four figures stared back at her, hands clasped together to form an inhuman chain. Their long nails clacked against one another. Their mouths opened and closed, teeth chattering.

What do they want? But she already knew.

Rotted flesh clung to their scrawny frames, but

they had an obvious strength. Although compact, the muscle masses appeared firm, and their legs plenty capable of running her down. Long pointed ears twitched at the sound of her sliding back on her rump. A second later, they came.

Glenda leaped to her feet and seized Laura's unwilling wrist. She pulled her daughter into motion, dragging her behind as she raced up the uneasy cobblestone incline. Now she saw what brought the red glow and caused the warming sensation. On either side of the path, lava surrounded them. Its heat lessened the farther they climbed up the odd hillside path.

Fire sprouted up among furls of black smoke. The flames twisted and turned in the air, close enough to lick at her flesh. She dodged each burst. When she stumbled, she righted herself fast and pulled Laura along. All the while, her relentless pursuers gave chase, one coming close enough to carve a nasty wound in Glenda's forearm. The gash burned but no blood came, and Glenda pushed both herself and Laura to put distance between them.

The pathway narrowed as they rose to some unseen ceiling. The lava far beneath them became a smoldering pit at this height and seeing it made her dizzy. The flames still rose but from here they looked more like surreal balloons bursting. And the farther she and Laura ventured upward, the darker their surroundings grew.

Pressing her arm to her chest, she led Laura to a pair of tall doors. The intricate designs on these doors were hard to discern in the absence of light. She traced the carvings in the mahogany wood with her hand, searching for a doorknob.

These will never open.

Glancing back, she couldn't see the fiends but sensed they hadn't given up. To her surprise, the doors gave, opening away from them. They slid into the darkness beyond, pushing the doors shut. With nothing more than this obscurity, their fate seemed so unsure now despite their solitude.

Her limbs weakened, and she couldn't go on. Not that there appeared any way out of this room. This was it, the end of the line. There would be no escape.

She dragged Laura to the farthest end of the room and huddled to the floor with her. Despite her heavy breathing, she heard a familiar sound, yet it worried her all the same as it did so long ago. The image of her little girl returned to her, as she listened to Laura sob. There, she found courage and turned to her daughter.

"Hush now, baby. I won't let them hurt you." She spoke softly. "You hear me, you bastards? You're not going to hurt my Laura!"

Even as she said these words, she knew they couldn't possibly be true. She'd already failed her daughter by not allowing these *things* to take her instead, as she'd promised.

The door creaked open, the slight gap glowing a warm red. Horrific silhouettes paraded through the opening.

They're here.

She shielded her daughter from the impending threat, refusing to give up. "Stay away!"

A hand fell on her arm, Laura's she thought. Her daughter turned Glenda until she could see a hint of that warm glow from the door on Laura's face. Her eyes had a certain calm look. In that moment the entire

world stood still. There were no fiends chasing them, no worries, just her daughter and her staring at one another. It warmed Glenda's heart, a feeling that brought with it a sense of defiance.

"Mom," Laura whispered. "You should—"

Glenda shook her head. "No. We can fight this."

Laura held her at a distance. "We can't. This is going to happen. And it's okay."

"No, don't leave me. Please, not yet."

Laura took Glenda's hands and held them tightly. She squeezed every so slightly. "You'll be fine without me."

"No. I won't. I swear." Glenda felt panicked. "I need you, Laura. I want you to live."

Laura pulled her in close. "Run!"

Glenda refused. She pressed her eyes shut and hugged her daughter. There, caught in an embrace, they awaited their fate.

Inhuman feet stomped along the ground, finding them in the darkness. Each shriveled arm seized hold of her and Laura. They tried to pull them apart, but no matter how hard they pulled she clung to her daughter.

"Get off!" Glenda swung her shoulders in an attempt to shake them.

They'd almost succeeded in separating them, but Glenda lunged forward, clutching hold of her daughter again.

Glenda shrieked. "No!"

For a brief moment, she looked into her daughter's eyes again. Whether or not she'd conceded to this end, Laura wouldn't be fighting alongside Glenda. Somehow during the scuffle, Laura had passed out.

FINAL BREATHS

Seeing her this way made Glenda's heart wrench with pain, the anger inside building to no end.

"You can't have her." Glenda glared at one of the fiends, its eyes calm as seas of black. "Leave her the fuck alone!"

A twist of pain shot through her back as something pierced her flesh. She pressed her eyes shut to the agony and covered Laura's body with her own.

"Get off, you bastards. Get off!"

The pain came again, deeper this time, forcing her to keep her eyes shut. But she wrapped her arms around Laura and clutched her fingers together. No way she would give up.

"She's staying with me!"

Then more pain found her. It twisted into her back, feeling like bones cracking. The agony was becoming too much to handle.

Glenda held Laura tighter as they pummeled her with their bony fists. Each blow felt heavier than the last. They struck her arms, her back, the back of her head.

Despite her hold on Laura, a new sensation fell over her. Though she fought it, she knew there was no escaping what came next. The blows continued, one after another, and her awareness wavered. Then, with her huddled over her daughter, still holding her as tight as she could, she gave in to the darkness and passed out.

Glenda opened her eyes, shocked to find herself back in the hospice. Her eyelids still felt heavy.

What happened?

Then she heard choking and understood everything. All of this had been a dream.

No, it was more than that.

Laura gasped, struggling for air.

"Wake up, baby girl," Glenda said.

She tried to roll her daughter on her side, readying to clear her airway if she could. Then she spotted something most troubling. And now that she saw it, she stopped everything. She traced a finger along the fresh wound on her left arm and winced.

That's not possible.

Yet, here it was, and it served as a reminder of what may or may not have happened. Sure, maybe some of what transpired in her thoughts and dreams wasn't real, but she couldn't deny this wound, and that should have been enough.

I can't let her go.

But in her head, she heard her daughter's words: *You'll be fine without me.* And then, *It's okay.*

Laura's figure heaved, her body ever so fragile now. The movement roused Glenda out of her thoughts, and she wrapped her arms around her daughter as if once more shielding her from death.

"Don't worry." She rubbed Laura's back. "Mommy has you."

Laura trembled in her arms. A horrid rattle escaped her daughter's throat.

"Mommy's got you, baby girl. And I won't ever let go again."

Laura shook hard, but Glenda held her tight. She made sure she held her through it all. Even when Laura's body grew still, when her eyes remained open,

gazing into the unknown, when the cold worked its way into her body Glenda kept holding on. She'd hold on forever if they let her, and she'd never let go.

"Mommy loves you, honey." Glenda stroked Laura's hair. Hugged her tighter. "Mommy loves you."

CLOSER

HUNTING NEVER APPEALED to Travis. Death, killing, anything connected to the sport, it all sickened him. This repulsion persisted even now as he narrowed his vision down the length of his gun, centering the crosshairs on the target.

There were other reasons for him being here, though. A quick glance back to his father revealed how pleased he was that Travis had tagged along.

The old man lived for the hunt. Always had. Loved it maybe even more than his son.

Travis had to admit, holding this rifle conjured a feeling of power. More so than he'd anticipated. The gun seemed alive in his hands, ready to spring into action with the slightest twitch of his finger.

No mistaking it, this gun wanted to kill. It needed to taste blood. Knowing this, Travis struggled not to misfire.

Better keep your cool. He'll get angry.

It occurred to him he might want to pull the trigger early out of spite alone. Here Travis was, having always been so precise with his hands, yet he'd surrendered some of that control when he entered these woods. But any internal conflict on whether to fire didn't matter.

His father had been specific about listening for his cue. The old man demanded perfection.

He recalled his childhood. Back on his tenth birthday when he'd fired his first BB gun. He'd missed the blue jay by mere inches, doing so on purpose.

His father saw through his ruse, too. Snatched the gun from Travis's trembling hands and struck him over the head with the butt of the weapon. The old man's cruelty hadn't ended there, either. His father spent much of that summer mocking Travis for his kindness.

As Travis aged, the verbal abuse deepened. So like his mother, he eventually distanced himself from his father along with anything the old man enjoyed. But the insults still followed him through college, forever scarring him.

'You ain't no damn good, boy.' Those words, in particular, haunted him to this day.

Travis believed this trip could somehow bring the two of them closer. Hunting had been the catalyst for a couple of his friends and their estranged dads. And he could see how being out in the wild stalking prey could bring a son and his father together. But he never thought it would come without effort as it did now.

This isn't even hunting. Not really. The thought of killing anything made him feel so—

I think I'm gonna puke.

His abdomen writhed. Guts twisted into knots. He snuck a hand down and cinched his belly, but it did nothing to ease the discomfort. His stomach growled in complaint of what he would soon take part in.

As a child, he'd thought his dad the coolest. The old man had been so dark and mysterious. After all these

years he realized he'd never been far off with that thought. These were indeed traits that defined his father. Characteristics that had become far scarier now that Travis was older and better understood what made his dad tick.

A sudden realization triggered. *This goes against everything I believe in.*

Yet here he was, making a poor attempt to emulate the precise thing he loathed the most about his father. He wasn't even doing a decent job at pretending to enjoy it.

Mom would be disappointed.

He'd always favored his mother. Lived with her when she remarried. Enjoyed tending to the gardens with her and even worked toward a degree in botany because of her. That degree seemed so far away at the moment, nearly out of reach.

When he opted to accompany his father out to these woods he'd traded one reality for another. He couldn't believe he'd ever made the choice.

At least we're closer.

He considered this, trying to decide whether they were any closer. He wasn't so sure.

A fly landed on the gun's barrel, pulling him from his thoughts. His eye drifted away from the scope. The gun wavered off its target.

His father growled and swatted him in the back of the head. "Steady, damn you. Don't screw this up. Steady—"

Travis cringed but hurried to correct his aim. He waited, taking a second to observe his dad's demeanor. A certain glimmer showed in the old man's weathered eyes. How many times had this man put him down?

When did the novelty of having a child wear off? Was it when Travis started thinking on his own, without his dad's approval?

Whatever the case, the abuse didn't stop until long after the divorce. Once they no longer saw each other and only spoke over the phone on the rare occasion.

His father's eyes widened. They found Travis and a slight smile spread across his lips.

Now he's proud of me?

Travis resented the admiration.

Of all Travis's accomplishments this pleased him most? Not his straight A's in college. Not making the Dean's list twice. The killing made him proud.

Have things between us always been this fragmented?

He contemplated this, listening to the sounds of the forest as they flooded his senses. A delightful chirp fluttered away from him. The peep encouraged him to leave this place. A nearby stream trickled over a bed of rocks, leading away from these woods. That water called for him to follow before it was too late. The smell of pine trees and aromatic patches of wildflowers wafted past, demanding he leave.

But he needed to stay here with his father. He wanted to form some sort of bond with the man.

A branch crashed through the tree. It struck the earth in protest of his resolve. Seeing the shattered limb reminded him a lot of himself. This was how he'd felt for much of his life, broken. Things had never really clicked.

For years now, he'd thought his father's affection was the key. That seeing his love returned would somehow mend him. It had been a long time coming.

CLOSER

The hiss of his father's breath teased at the back of his neck. The sensation moved over him like a snake, reminiscent of death itself.

Travis forced his eye to the scope. *Steady. Don't be a moron.*

But this sounded like his father talking. *Stop it. Things are different now. He respects me.*

This was true. Travis had all the love he wanted and more, as long as he was out here and willing to kill.

This is everything you wanted.

His stomach churned. Beads of sweat formed on his brow. The sickness grew. Numbness spread to his legs and down to his feet. He stretched his toes for fear of falling.

"Easy," his father said.

Travis flinched, needing to adjust his footing.

"Don't fall, dumbass."

His father drew close to Travis, the old man's hand slithering along his backbone. Slow and calculating in his approach, his father steadied him. With Travis anxious to strike, he marveled how patient his father could be despite his labored breathing. The snake was hungry but so relaxed and . . .

"Steady," his father said.

It made Travis feel dirty.

"Almost time," his dad said.

Travis pictured his mother in her favorite Sunday outfit: a white-fringed checkerboard dress, pumps on her feet, and a thick black belt. She'd always looked as though she'd been drawn right out of the past. Yet she'd been so perfect within her surroundings.

He'd admired his mother's ability to ignore his father's degrading remarks. Travis had never been so

resilient. Worries rolled right down his mother's back like water off a duck's ass. And the woman fought hard to the end.

Cancer had eaten away at her from the inside. So calculated in how it dealt out the pain. Took its time to invade every nook and cranny of her body before claiming victory.

With plenty of time to say goodbye, he had been witness to his mother's gradual decay. It had left a longstanding memory he hadn't been able to shake. One he never would.

His mother's weakened voice was alive in his memories, warning him of this exact future. "Your father will want you to visit, maybe even stay with him for a while," she'd said.

He remembered nodding but hadn't given it much thought. His hand tightened around hers. His focus on the pain she endured rather than her words.

"He is a complex man," she'd said.

Again Travis had nodded, already knowing this.

"Travis?"

He raised his eyebrows to indicate his attention. Still holding her hand, he'd seized each remaining fraction of time.

She continued. "He might—"

Her words broke off as her struggle intensified. Travis recalled hushing her. Tried to let her know she didn't have to say anything at all. He'd already gleaned what she'd been trying to convey anyway.

But she'd still continued. As if in her weakness she'd found strength for this alone. "If he tries to get you to—"

She shook her head, attempting to rid herself of the

pain long enough to share the rest. But a fit of coughing overcame her.

Ever patient, he'd waited for this bout to ease.

When she did, she tried again. "To hunt!"

Her breath wheezed. Her eyes turned up under her eyelids. Then for one brief second, she refocused on Travis. "Do . . . don't—"

All that effort she'd put into those words. Her dying wish and yet here he was, hunting with good old dad.

Why, Travis? Does this somehow complete you?

He ignored his conscience. Still, it argued from the darkest recesses of his mind.

Is this some means of pacifying emotions left over from years of neglect?

He shook his mother's frowning manifestation from his thoughts. Once more he refocused his scope. Adjusted his aim back to the target.

"That's it, shithead," his father said. He sounded elated by the fact his son would soon join him in this ritual. "Shoot now!"

Travis felt his finger squirm. For some reason, he couldn't bring himself to pull the trigger. His mother's stern voice invaded his thoughts. Her last request echoed in his mind.

"Now, moron," his father said.

When he still didn't fire, his father elbowed him aside. The old man leaned forward in the tree on a thick branch. He took up his own gun and hurried to adjust his aim.

Travis eased back, the uncomfortable dirty feelings overpowering him. He considered the act he'd come so close to committing.

He'll never accept me for who I am. He doesn't even care. His only concern is killing.

He lifted his gun to his father's temple, rested it there.

The old man glared at him. A twisted grin spread across his wrinkled face.

Before he could change his mind, Travis pulled the trigger. A loud bang reverberated across the hillside. The noise rattled all that was wholesome to him. The recoil shook him so hard it almost knocked him out of the tree.

His father's body went limp and slumped forward. The thud of his body striking the earth lasted only a fraction of a second, yet the echo of the gunshot seemed to live on forever.

Wide childish eyes far below his position turned up and found Travis amidst a clutter of leaves. Even from here he could see how curious but unknowing those eyes appeared. The girl called for help, and a woman screamed. An older man yelled for someone to call the police. People scrambled.

Travis stared at his father's fallen body. Then his eyes went to the broken branch. The two had so much in common. These were the feelings his mother had tried to spare him. But something had awakened inside. Even now, it begged for more.

He corrected his position in the tree, took aim, and fired off a single round. Down below, in the street, his stepfather collapsed.

FLOCKING BIRDS

A CHORUS OF CHIRPS drew Chad's attention away from the breakfast table. He welcomed the intrusion to this tense quiet.

He stole a glance at his wife. Watched Jane chew, constant dissatisfaction smeared across her face. Her eyes never left their daughter Angie.

Jane sighed. "What's with those girls you chum around with anyway?"

Angie continued poking her fork into her egg yolk. "Huh?"

Jane had an extensive laundry list of complaints regarding Angie that she kept detailing as of late. Of them, the most popular were Angie's taste in clothes, her subpar attitude, and her trampy friends. But Chad believed some of this came more because of how Angie's choices made Jane look to other moms.

To him, Angie always looked fine, so he wasn't sure why his wife cared. She herself looked great despite never exercising. And with him sporting a belly these days he was lucky she felt any attraction to him at all.

In Chad's experience, matters between a mother and daughter had a way of working themselves out. Still, he'd just endured a long workweek and now this? Truthfully, it annoyed him.

"You heard me," Jane said. "Those floozies don't befit you. They certainly don't exemplify what I'd call nice girls."

"Really, mom?" Angie's face puckered, an expression he'd seen a lot since she became a teen. "How would you know anything about my friends? You never even talk to them."

Angie glanced at him, searching for help. He felt small under her young gaze but knew better than to interfere. He rifled through the items on the kitchen counter, looking for the paper: a few cups, Jane's reading glasses, a bowl of apples, the checkbook, and a tiny brown bottle.

What is that? He squinted. *Ipecac? What the hell is that doing down here?*

It bothered him that he didn't find the paper. He hurried to finish his toast while Jane continued.

"Look at you, dressing like some sort of low-grade hooker. Those black tights offer every hint of what's underneath." Jane eyed Angie up and down. "No wonder those old men took advantage of you."

And there it was, like a dagger to his heart. He recalled Jane's snooping and what it revealed. He often wondered if they would've been better off never seeing the picture Angie posted of herself to some social website. He'd tried to shake the image of his daughter stripped down to her underwear out of his thoughts, but even now it haunted him.

I wish she hadn't done that.

Angie's eyes welled with tears. A similar sting found his own but for a different reason. She looked so skinny these days.

Angie's eyes were like lasers on Jane. "That's what you think of me?"

FLOCKING BIRDS

When Jane didn't respond, unwilling to offer even a sideways glance, Angie shoved her chair back and hurried for the stairs.

"At least have the decency to take your breakfast with you," Jane called after her.

Angie stormed back to the table and seized the plate with rigid fingers.

Jane didn't falter one bit. It made him feel sick.

Heavy thumps tracked Angie's retreat, followed by slamming her bedroom door.

He drew his gaze from his wife just in time. But he could still see Jane's eyes searching him.

"And what about you?" she said.

"Me?" He considered some of the things he wanted to say but didn't want to get into it right now. "I need some fresh air."

Jane sounded much like their daughter now, "Really?"

Grabbing his coffee, he made a hasty escape for the front door. "The birds, dear." He thumbed at the door. "I'm going to see what's up with those birds."

He could sense Jane's eyes dissecting his departure. Before he exited, he glanced back to confirm this, but she'd already started cleaning up.

Thank God.

The morning air filled his nostrils as he bent for the paper. He breathed it in, surprised by the pungent odor.

What the hell is that?

Leaving the paper, he rose, and sipped his coffee while he scanned the horizon for a possible source. *Maybe some local farmer just fertilized his crops.*

He stepped out into the yard and stood there for a

long time, watching as the birds bobbed up and down, playing musical chairs along the gutter. Seeing this made him laugh, which proved a good release.

Angie's bedroom window slid down fast. Had she been watching him?

He considered how detached she'd grown since the problems started. His grip tightened on his coffee cup as he recalled the comments to his daughter's post, titled "Am I pretty?"

Of course, she is. He seethed. *Not to those bastards, though. Heartless grown men.* Most of them had been older than he cared to consider. Shock, dismay, worry consumed him as the longstanding wound reopened. But the birds fluttered, stealing away his fury.

Telltale clomps foretold of Angie trouncing down the stairs. He pushed those intense feelings down and adorned his best fake smile for her.

She burst through the door, letting it slam shut behind her. This had likely been meant to provoke Jane. Their eyes met briefly, and then Angie's went up to the birds. She came to an abrupt stop, her shoulders seeming too bony to hold up the tank top straps. Seeing this, his gut wrenched and his facade faltered.

She looked worried. "What's with all the birds?"

For a brief second, he couldn't answer, consumed by her appearance. *She's too pale.*

She sniffed. "Is that . . . ? Is it the birds?"

He sipped his coffee and looked up at the birds. "I'm not sure."

Only then did he realize the birds weren't as interested with sitting on the gutter as they were with something in it.

FLOCKING BIRDS

Might be a bug infestation. Maybe I can—

A steady thump approached. The black car sidled up to the curb, but he couldn't make out the driver or the passenger. He loathed their awful music and how they played it so loud.

Her squeaky voice disrupted his thoughts, as she pushed past him. "Gotta go. Ride's here."

"Be careful," he said. But he didn't think she'd heard him.

She hurried around the front of the car and slid in fast. It worried him when he couldn't make out the other two silhouettes due to the dark-tinted windows.

Damn it. The car sped away. *I should be relaxing on a Saturday instead of . . .* He watched the car vanish around the corner. *Worrying about birds.*

He leaned inside the front door and listened for his wife. Could hear her fumbling about the kitchen, cleaning with some intensity, evidence Angie had accomplished what she'd planned by slamming the door.

He put on his sweetest voice. "Honey?"

She sounded bothered. "Yes?"

"Mind coming to get me when the ballgame starts?"

She paused, likely cursing him under her breath. "What ballgame?"

"The baseball game, dear."

She left the dishes and appeared in the foyer hallway, hands on her hips. "How would I know that?"

He mustered patience. "Can you check the guide for me?"

She approached, her anger seeming to subside as she neared him. Her nose wrinkled. "What the hell is that smell?"

The birds stirred.

"I'm not sure."

Her eyes turned upward as if she could see through the overhang. "Are those—" She tried again. "Is it coming from those birds?"

"Maybe."

"Good Lord. I'm going to toss my cookies."

He tried to keep the conversation lighthearted. "Thanks for the visual."

She scanned the front yard, her eyes condemning the emptiness. "Was that Angie I heard?"

"Yes."

"Did you see whom she left with?"

He shook his head but answered as best he could. "Hillary, I think."

Staring off to where the car had gone, he hesitated to respond. In truth, Hillary had been the lone friend of Angie's he'd met and only recently. So it was a guess at best.

"Nothing but skin and bones on that kid these days." He rubbed the back of his neck. "Hey, maybe you should take it easy on her."

Jane's already weak smile wavered. "You better get busy on that stink. Can't have the mailman unwilling to stop. That would ruin my dating life."

She left the door open, turned and wriggled her butt suggestively as she headed back to her work.

Her joke wouldn't have bothered him so much if the mailman hadn't arrived seconds later.

"Morning, Chad."

He nodded. "How you doing, Glen?"

"Just fine." He leaned to one side and glanced into the house. "How's the missus?"

None of your fucking business. His eyes narrowed on the man. "She's good."

Glen pawed through his sack and retrieved a few odd-sized mailings. Handed them over to Chad.

He took the mail. "Thanks."

Glen sniffed. "You . . . cooking something?"

Chad eyed the birds. "Not that I know of."

"Holy Jesus!" Glen's eyes widened. "There must be fifty of them up there."

No shit, Captain Obvious.

"Might be what's causing the—" He grunted. "Sorry, Chad, I—"

"No worries. I smell it, too." Chad thumbed through the mail: coupons, a political ad, a lawn service flyer, donations needed, all of it crap. "Well, I'd better get to it."

"Have a good one," Glen said. He hurried off.

Chad sat his coffee cup and the mail on the foyer table. When he returned outside, he took note of a thick patch of grass near the drainpipe.

Now, what's that?

He crossed to the end of the porch and stared at the lush grass. It ran all the way down to the backyard. There, it expanded into a large circle of thick grass.

Must be something up there causing this.

He fetched his stepladder and found a level spot on the thawing ground. The higher he climbed, the more his weight forced the ladder's feet into the softened earth. As the legs sank, it became difficult to steady himself. He didn't see any bugs anyway. So when the ladder swayed, allowing him a split second to swipe inside the gutter before he lost his balance, he did so without hesitation.

Landing on his butt, a large wet spot formed on the seat of his jeans, cold against his flesh. He took a moment and sniffed his fingers. It smelled awful. He wiped them off in the grass.

Whatever would possess me to do such a thing?

He went inside and managed to avoid his wife. If she saw the mess he'd made of his clothes he'd never hear the end of it. At least he could delay that grief.

Upstairs, he washed himself and changed into a pair of old sweats. He'd need to attack this problem from a different angle. Angie's room sat right above the gutter.

The sign hanging on her door written in overlapping pink and yellow highlighter warned him to "Keep out!" This had been meant more for Jane, but he didn't believe himself any more welcome.

He considered asking Jane to help but thought that might complicate matters. Without much more consideration, he turned the knob and entered, immersing himself in a colorful world of pinks, purples, and black. Angie had long rebelled against her childhood bedroom theme by adding beards to all the cartoon princesses. The flowers looked diseased and the butterflies like alien pterodactyls.

I think it's time I offer to change her décor. Maybe that would ease some of the strain.

He saw the plate sitting on her dresser, her breakfast half-eaten at most.

Crossing to the bedroom window, he noticed her computer was still on and approached like a child sneaking downstairs on Christmas morning. He considered turning it off but stopped, his finger lingering over the power button. His conscience begged for him to make sure she hadn't been up to any mischief.

FLOCKING BIRDS

No, that wouldn't be right.

After a second longer, he bumped the desk with his hip. This roused the computer from its sleep, and it awakened to a bright neon-green desktop. A picture of a punk rock singer stared back at him, eyes glaring and mouth agape mid-scream. Dazed by his intrusion, it made him happy that he hadn't discovered anything too bad.

As he lifted the windowpane, he noted how the screen had gone missing. *I should've seen that sooner.*

Speculation infected his thoughts. *How many times has she snuck out in the middle of the night without us knowing?*

In his mind, he pictured any one of a dozen middle-aged perverts picking her up in their cars. His worry transformed into rage.

An irate Chad threw open the window. Chirps, flutters, and a spasm of birds sent him sprawling back a step. Some flew a short distance before returning. Others stood their ground, cocking their heads and staring at him with uncertainty.

He returned to the window and observed those closest to him. Then his gaze fell to the strange sludge trailing down the roof to the gutter. There, beneath his daughter's windowsill, resting on one of the shingles he saw some unidentifiable partially digested food remnant.

He heard Jane whistling in the hallway.

Can't let her find me here. If he did, she'd have an accomplice. He couldn't stand being part of what had been going on for some time.

He hid in the closet, staring out through the slats of wood, able to see her as she entered the room. Only then did it occur to him she might have come to put away laundry. When she walked in with a basket his heart sank.

What do I do? Where can I go?
He prepared for the inevitable.

She sat the basket near Angie's dresser. After opening the top drawer, she rifled through the contents. She removed something and put it in the basket. He hadn't been able to see the object, but he saw the one she replaced with just fine.

With his daughter's bottle of Ipecac renewed, she'd continue doing whatever Jane had taught her to control her weight. That above all else terrified him. His heart crushed, he knew then he had no choice but to put an end to this somehow.

When he stepped out of the closet, Jane regarded him with surprise. "Chad? What are you—"

"Never mind that." He stormed to the dresser and dug inside. Came up with the Ipecac. "Is this what you've taught our daughter to do?"

Jane didn't respond.

"You'd have her slowly killing herself like this?"

She scoffed. "That won't happen. She's—"

Anger filled him to a point he could no longer bear. He'd never been the tough sort but now his rage took over. He raised his hand, prepared to bring it down, and then the phone rang.

A worried Jane picked up the receiver. "Hello?"

Chad breathed heavy, his anger not even close to dissipating.

Then Jane collapsed to her knees. Her eyes trembled. The phone fell from her ear to the ground. And Jane followed.

Still upset, "What is it?" Chad said.

"It's . . . " She gasped. "She's dead.

PIROUETTE

MADDIE HEARS THE screaming, but what can she do? She's only a ballerina. Nothing more.

The yelling intensifies, and she spins. Twirls upon her small platform and watches herself in the mirror. She tries to focus on her effort, but it's hard.

Spin, and spin. Keep spinning. Don't look.

Still she hears the yelling. It comes more often now that Father has been drinking again. And he starts earlier each day.

Father shouts at Mommy. She catches glimpses of them in the mirror with each rotation. She spins so fast their faces become a blur. Her world dizzies, and that is good.

First position, second position, third, then fourth, fifth. Back to first.

Their argument escalates. Actions become more animated with each exchange.

He paces from one end of the dining room table and back. His hands ball into fists, nails digging deep into his palms. Even while spinning she can see this much.

Mommy looks uneasy. She moves from where she stands and leans away from Father as he approaches.

These actions are minor, something others might not even detect. But they're significant enough the ballerina sees it all.

Mommy's afraid. The ballerina knows this fear.

Maddie's energy mounts along with the tension. Spinning as fast as her little figure will allow, she twirls. She forces her attention to the dance, on being a ballerina.

Allegro. Spin, and kick.

She places her toe to her knee and observes herself in the mirror.

But beyond her dance, she still sees them. It saddens her. Makes her feel helpless. All she can do is spin faster. And for the briefest moment, her dance rivals the fighting.

Spin, toe lift, pirouette, then spin.

Try as she might the voices prevail. His voice always triumphs. It's so maddening. Forces her to push to the extreme.

Her heart races as the fright deepens in Mother's eyes. Maddie is too young to know this expression, yet she does.

The yelling stops as if cut by a knife. When it does, so does Maddie. Holds her breath and listens for the slightest disagreement. She waits, patient as one can be in her situation.

Mommy composes herself, as they discuss the issue in calmer tones.

Father picks at the mess on the table. Examining each shard of pottery, he tosses each back on the table with disgust. He acts as though these fragments are precious pieces of his life, yet he's done nothing but despise the vase for years.

PIROUETTE

Sadness permeates the room. Fills it to the point she imagines each window will soon crack under the pressure.

Everything remains still and quiet. Sorrow fills her as she anticipates matters will soon degrade. Their arguments always deteriorate fast. So much it reminds her of sand slipping through fingertips. There's never enough time to resolve anything.

Knowing this, she holds at first position. Breathing shallow, her pink tutu wavers.

Father asks a single question, nothing more. Once again his query goes unanswered.

It's such a simple question, too. One either of them could answer.

A wrinkle of doubt creases Mommy's forehead, and her cheeks flush. Her lips tighten and form two thin lines that match her determination. Now he'll do more than just insult her.

Despondent and hurt, Mommy ignores the question.

His voice grows brasher. He flings words at her. Such belittling insults come easy to him these days.

He tells Mommy she's worthless. Calls her dumb and an idiot. He remarks that she's a bitch, a whore. Expletives accompany each slander, a few the ballerina hasn't heard before.

I must not dwell on such hate.

Visualizing herself in the mirror, she readies despite the hurt she feels for Mommy. Regret and worry fall to the wayside as she strives for perfection.

She hurries through the positions, this time much too fast for her tiny legs. Spinning and kicking, she places her toe against her knee. The process starts

over, going through the positions time and time again. Her dizziness increases, but she cannot stop. Because if she does—

She freezes mid-pirouette when she hears her name.

"Maddie," Mommy says again, "go to your room, honey."

Maddie starts to rise.

"Why?" Father says. "Shouldn't she know what her mother has become?"

His voice is loud. Much louder than ever before. This scares the ballerina. She returns to first position and waits.

"What I've become?" Mother says. "Me? Really, Charles?"

He doesn't back down. After a deep breath, he jabs a quivering finger at the remains of the damaged vase on the table. "You know this vase has been in my family for decades. It's been handed down from one generation to the next. I wanted to give it to Maddie."

He pauses, sucking air. "Now I can't, can I? Yet you refuse to tell me the truth." He growls, sounding like a tiger. "Sarah, if I didn't know better I'd say you took it. Now, where'd you hide it?"

Mommy is hiding something, of course. But he has no idea.

"What if I did?" This will escalate everything. "Are you going to do something about it?"

With that, it comes. Maddie closes her eyes and covers her ears. Still she hears a loud slap. It's followed by the sound of Mommy collapsing to the floor, crying harder now.

Maddie forces her eyes open and stares at Mommy

in the mirror. One cheek is redder than the other. She knows why. This isn't the first time. Nor has Mommy always been the recipient.

A dreadful silence follows. It feels like an eternity. Hours, minutes, seconds have no place at times like this.

Mommy buries her face in her hands, but her tears escape her fingers and fall to the floor.

Release. Then back to first position.

The ballerina rushes through her moves, hitting every position to near perfection. She lifts, kicks, and pirouettes.

She wishes she could dismiss all that has happened here this night. And the many other nights since Father lost his job. He'd been working the late shift at the docks and that led to him drinking again.

Once, she prayed for his drinking to go away and when it did, life had been better. They'd moved on. But now that it had returned, she knew in her heart what he'd done could never be forgotten again. Even if Mommy did forgive him.

Spin, and kick, and knee, and spin. Back to first position and working her way through again.

A dark form blots out the sunlight. In the mirror, she sees him and a cold washes over her. His shadow creeps across the platform, secludes her in darkness. She stops dancing and holds her breath, praying that he'll leave her alone.

"Stop!" Mommy says.

He turns back to her. "Why? What are you hiding? Where did you put it?"

The ballerina knows.

"I'm not telling you anything, Charles." Mommy

takes a deep breath and lets it out with perfect calmness. "I've told you over and over again, this isn't my fault. Now will you take a minute and look at yourself?"

He growls again, sounding more and more like a monster. "I ought to—"

But he doesn't finish, and the ballerina starts to spin again. It's difficult with him standing so near. She struggles to wind the key because her fingers keep slipping. Instead, she resorts to holding the key, freezing the ballerina mid-kick.

Mommy looks nervous. "Please, Charles, I told you the truth." Her eyes are wet, cheeks streaked with tears. "I was cleaning the house, using the vacuum to get in that corner over there when I knocked over the vase by accident. And I found your scotch and dumped it in the toilet. That's all. I'm sorry, okay? I'm sorry."

Doubt shows on his face. The ballerina knows he doesn't believe her. Besides, he'd gotten home before Mommy, and he likely didn't remember hearing any vacuum. But he also doesn't seem capable of fully trusting his own memory, either.

Mommy takes the blame. Always does, but hasn't always been successful at doing so.

The ballerina closes her eyes for a moment. *Please, God. Make him go.*

As he backs away, the ballerina eases to first position and watches. In the mirror she sees him standing over Mommy. His hands become fists, loosen, and ball up again.

Nerves tingle throughout the ballerina's entire body. Every last hair is on end. She holds her breath again and waits.

He grumbles, and his fists loosen,. "You better not do it again."

His words drown out as he heads to the piano. He lifts the lid and retrieves a bottle of tequila he's hidden inside. He unscrews the cap and takes a long drink.

"I won't, Charles," she says. "I promise."

He continues to stare at her for several seconds. The entire time the ballerina refuses to move. He turns and heads off to watch television. A sigh escapes this room when he leaves, a breath of relief that has been held in far too long.

When the television clicks on, the ballerina stares at Mommy through the tiny mirror. Between them, the small plastic doll stands in first position, incapable of movement now. Maddie cannot decide what to do next.

Their eyes remain on each other and when it becomes too much, Maddie leaves her jewelry box and runs to Mommy.

"I'm sorry, Mommy. I thought if I took it he'd stop being so angry."

"Hush," Mommy says. "This isn't your fault. You did the right thing."

They embrace, and that makes everything right for now. But the ballerina knows something more must be done. They can't live this way. And if Mommy isn't strong enough to do it for them, she must be more than just a ballerina.

TO SAVE ONE LIFE

THE KNIFE FELL to the hardwood floor. Blood splattered the foyer wall. Another victim claimed. One more life lost to this cruel world.

She'd been the fourth such casualty. *And what did you do, Boris? Not a goddamned thing.*

It was such a helpless feeling. *But what could I do, being so young?*

His physical limitations alone would've led to his failure against such a formidable foe.

And this somehow lets me off the hook?

He considered this question *No. It doesn't.*

The woman's blank face stared back at him. Her eyes drooped. Perhaps she thought him insensitive. Wondered how he could let her die without even an effort?

I'm so sorry.

One corner of her mouth turned up as if she'd heard this thought and found it amusing. A single tear welled in her eye, forming a bead and trickling down her cheek. Her eyes remained on Boris.

What have I done?

There was no way to relay his reasons to her. Not that she would've cared. What good would alleviating her doubts do now?

Her eyes widened on some unseen place beyond Boris.

Fascinated, Boris also looked. *What is it you see?*

She, of course, wouldn't answer. Even if she could, he hadn't bothered asking the question aloud. But this didn't prevent him from speculating.

Is there an existence beyond this one?

A gasp burst from her mouth, and the woman's chest hitched. Her lips trembled as if trying to speak. But she produced no words.

At this, her killer giggled. It wasn't light-hearted laughter but maniacal, fitting of such a twisted mind.

It sickened Boris to so easily discern her killer's depraved thoughts. The murderer took a deep breath, nostrils flaring as if inhaling her departure. He breathed it in like a feast, hungry and eager all at once.

The woman slid down the wall, a thin trail of blood marking her descent. The hem of her skirt caught on something and tore. She ended in an uncomfortable half-sitting position on the floor, her clothes ruffled.

How many have to die? And each time I've done nothing but watch.

He'd been foolish to believe a heartless man like this could ever love anyone. Yes, the man always kissed with passion. But his desire for murder ran far deeper than any need to make love.

Curse me for being a coward.

Her tongue wagged out of her mouth. Then her eyes glazed over. Giving up on Boris, her gaze shifted left and her body followed.

She slumped to an improbable position. Here she attempted some final words but only a mumble

escaped her lips. Nothing more. Seconds later, she surrendered to her fate.

"Interesting," the killer said.

A sick sensation churned inside of Boris. He himself had killed before, many times in fact. But never had he known anyone so cruel, so indifferent as this man.

What purpose does he have in slaying these women? Could there be any other reason than the pure satisfaction of carnage?

He considered the things the man might have gleaned from each murder. *Is he looking for something?*

Watching intently. *Maybe.* He paused to reflect. *But what?*

The killer stood over his victim, hips swaying back and forth.

What the hell? Is he . . . dancing, again?

There was obvious enjoyment.

Boris stared into the killer's eyes. *Why?*

The killer's gaze lingered on the woman's dead eyes. *Does he see something there beyond this world?*

If he dared get in the way, he might meet his own end. But he couldn't just stand by anymore. If he could stop one of these deaths, it would all be worthwhile.

Next time. I'll stop him then.

Still, he had his doubts.

Weeks later a loud bang startled him awake. His eyes widened on his surroundings, searching for what had made the noise. A long scream alerted him to her position.

I'm too late.

He cursed himself, rushing for the foyer. There, he found the killer already standing over another victim.

Trembling, she held a gun in her hands. She tried to steady the weapon, but it kept wavering. A thin trail of smoke rose from its barrel, the smell strong.

She's done it.

He moved in, cautious despite his elation for her bravery. Then he saw the wound in the killer's knee and stopped. *No, it can't be.*

The murderer wasn't dying.

Why didn't she shoot him in his heart?

Anger creased across the killer's scrunched face. He approached without fear.

Shoot him. His vision amplified in anticipation of gunfire. But the woman did nothing. Her arms shivered so much the gun fell free, landing in her lap.

To his amazement, she didn't retrieve the gun, either. Instead, she covered her face with her hands, staring out through fleshy prison bars. Tears leaked around the edges of her fingers. Then another smell assaulted the air, that of fresh urine.

She's as good as dead.

"Please," she said. "I won't tell anyone."

The killer drew closer, and Boris followed.

Of course, she'd tell someone? Why wouldn't she? But the murderer didn't appear interested in making deals anyway.

"Please," she said again.

Concern overwhelmed Boris. *Grab the gun and finish him. Before it's too late.*

But she didn't seem capable. *She's too scared.*

He crossed to her position without further thought.

The glimmer of the killer's blade flashed in the dull light of the foyer chandelier. For a moment, Boris lost himself in that glow.

Do something.

Roused from his daze, he rushed the killer and lunged for him. This surprised both the murderer and his victim. Enough so he dropped the knife. The weapon slid across the floor, coming to a stop somewhere near the front door.

The man didn't hesitate. He slapped at Boris. The attack missed, but his hand caught on the silk thread supporting Boris. A rush of air forced Boris to a submissive position, being yanked helplessly through the foyer.

Before Boris could regain his senses, the killer backhanded him. This time it connected, swatting Boris to the floor.

Pain erupted at every joint. He scampered to his feet, taking a fraction of the time to acknowledge a lost limb. If he'd hesitated any longer the killer's foot might have squashed him for good.

A determined Boris maneuvered up the cuff of the killer's pants. His world spun as the murderer tried to shake him out. When he reached the killer's thigh, he plunged his mandibles deep into the man's flesh.

The predator slapped at him, missing Boris the first time. On the second try, he connected. If not for the padding of the killer's clothes, Boris might have died. Stunned and unsure of where he was or what he should do, he saw no option but to flee.

Before he could find the cuff of the pants, the man cinched it shut. Trapped in total darkness, Boris considered biting the man again. Instead, he

remained calm and waited for an opportunity to present itself.

A loud crash filled the room and again his world spun. When a small opening formed at the cuff, Boris rushed to it and exited.

Free of the killer, he scampered up a nearby wall. Although he longed for the safety of his web, he took a moment to glance back.

The frightened woman held the gun, its barrel lifted to where the man had been standing. Her would-be killer lay sprawled out on the floor, no longer a threat to anyone.

Boris felt euphoric after such a battle. It delighted him that he'd made a difference.

A vibration roused him, and he listened, studying each strand until he could pinpoint the precise location. He ventured across his web with purpose, anxious to come eye to eye with his victim.

There, he discovered a fly and looked deeply into its eyes. Watched the creature struggle. The fly's wings twitched, and this incited laughter from Boris. No doubt the maniacal sort.

As he closed in on his victim, Boris danced.

OF BOTH WORLDS

WHEN CHRIS ESCAPES into the parallel world, my heart leaps. I long to pursue him, but worry about the creatures of this land. If they find this passage, they'll discover my home world. I can't stand to lose it, so I withdraw into these caves I've called home for so many years and reflect.

The faces staring up at me from the ground look sad. Emptiness fills me but another emotion brews deep within my being. One that is unfamiliar. Anger maybe.

A droplet in a nearby pool echoes. It's a peaceful noise I've learned to appreciate.

I wade through the water, captivated by this man who has intruded upon my calm. He remains ignorant to my presence, ever curious of his surroundings.

Long have I been here, trapped between these two worlds. In a way, I belong to both, one more so than the other.

I've come to accept this existence. Found satisfaction in it until today, when one of those worlds overstepped their bounds. Now all is threatened.

He carries with him a most extraordinary torch. The yellow illumination cast from its end is so unusual. Especially when compared to the blue glimmers I've grown accustomed to seeing when the afternoon sun trickles down through what few cracks it finds in the rocky ceiling.

It's rare for me to leave my labyrinth. The few times I've braved the human world have been in the twilight hours before sunlight. My skin has become too sensitive to the sun's rays. That's why his torch concerns me.

It's been so long since my eyes have gazed upon man. Those I've seen live in the nearest village, a place I once called home.

That seems like another lifetime now. The world has moved on without me, transformed into something I no longer recognize. Human dwellings reach high into the sky, and there are so many of them. I prefer to stay here, away from all the commotion. Where silence is my friend.

Mankind fascinates me, though. They have thick hair atop their round heads. Their colored eyes look so small. Some of them have such pasty flesh it's a wonder they've survived this long. Especially when I consider their apparent inquisitive nature.

I often wonder if there are other settlements. Are there breeds of men different than those I've seen? Their world has become full of objects whose purpose I cannot comprehend. I have little memory of a few of these items and even then they are distant. I'm better off here in my simplistic existence.

Thankfully several smaller organisms also seek shelter in these caves. Their names elude me, but I've

grown quite fond of a few. I savor the little brown ones with their snickering whiskers. How they skitter along the ground. A similar breed flies close to the ceilings with a flutter of wings and squeaky noises. They're all such tasty morsels.

I found this lair long ago when fleeing for my life. It might have been my end if I hadn't discovered the opening, thus losing my pursuers. But desperation makes for keener vision, and my misfortune led me to safety.

Even if the entrance were happened upon by accident, gaining access would prove a daunting task for a human. Perhaps this is what bothers me most. An ordinary man now moves about my lair seemingly unafraid. This leaves me to wonder if I'm still safe in these caves.

Another glow catches my eye. Three more humans breach my lair. They also carry tube-shaped torches, each casting off a similar yellow beam.

I'm surprised when one of their torches shines my way. Not only do they not see me—I blend in well with my surroundings—but this sunlight doesn't burn my flesh as I feared. Surprised by this, for a moment my intruders are forgotten.

A darker skinned male looks bothered as he searches for his friend. "Chris?"

Chris exudes confidence and waves his torch at the others. "Over here."

The three new humans rush to his side. Their torches illuminate him all at once. Seeing the four of them together sends my thoughts reeling. Their numbers worry me, so I keep still.

One of the females brushes back her red locks. "How did you find this place?"

Chris gazes at her fondly. She smiles, but the gesture doesn't appear genuine. I can smell her fear from here.

She moves in beside Chris and allows him to take her in his arms.

"Isn't this awesome, Kristen?" he says.

"Where are we?" the darker man asks.

"No idea, Zack. I've been coming to these parts my entire life and never noticed that opening before."

Zack stretches. An audible *pop* escapes his body. "I nearly broke my back helping the girls in."

Chris laughs. "For sure. That incline was a bitch."

The blonde female darts her head from side to side, leery of her surroundings. She should be, as awful creatures reside close by. This female hesitates, then adds, "This doesn't feel right. We should go."

Of this, I'm optimistic.

The raven-haired Chris bursts into boisterous laughter. "Why would we leave?" He illuminates random sections of the walls around them. He speaks in a booming voice. "There's nothing to fear, Diane. We'll protect you. Isn't that right, Zack?"

Zack nods.

Neither woman appears convinced. Kristen clutches Chris. Her nervous olive-colored fingers wrap around the meat of his arm and squeeze.

He pulls free of her grasp and ambles deeper into the caves, leaving the others behind. All of them hesitate, reluctant to follow.

"I want to leave," Diane says.

Chris thins his eyes on her, then the others, as if daring them. "Not yet, okay?"

They remain frozen in his gaze for several seconds.

Disappointment fills me when Diane agrees with a cautious nod. The stench of her anxiety fills the cavern.

"Chris is right," Zack says.

He also reeks of unease. Diane squeezes his hand, looking perplexed.

Zack turns to Diane. "We're fine."

With an overzealous Chris leading the way, the group explores my caves. I meander behind them, staying out of sight. Every so often one of their torches shines my way. Yet, they remain more conscious of their immediate surroundings and don't notice me.

Chris passes the stunning pool of water where I sleep. The rest of the group stops to regard its beauty. Chris wanders onward. When he discovers he's alone, he hurries back to them and watches.

Kristen leans forward and reaches deep into the pool. Her hands trace the smooth rocks as she withdraws them from the water. "It feels like ice cream."

I barely remember ice cream.

Diane cups some water in her palms and lets it dribble through her digits. Her green eyes widen with amazement. I'm envious. "It's amazing," she says.

"Aren't you glad we stayed?" Chris says.

His query goes unanswered.

Waves of light reflect off the water. They dance upon their faces. I view my own reflection and am in awe of the differences. There are so many.

When they continue, a bold Chris leads the way. He knows nothing of the horrors they approach. My own pace is more deliberate.

Chris stops. "I wonder—" His amusement becomes obvious in the lines of his face. "There's this legend of

a malformed freak that was born in our town. His parents named him Rylak." A wicked grin spreads across his face. "Long ago Rylak killed a woman and despite the pleading of his parents, the townsfolk chased the boy out of town and into these mountains. Maybe this is where Rylak came."

The tale reminds me of my own struggles. Yet I'm unable to recall my given name. Am I this Rylak?

"That's just folklore," Kristen says. Still her voice wavers.

Chris continues. "If Rylak catches you, he'll take you to another world where hideous creatures live. They have fangs as long as daggers that can tear the flesh from your body."

Though his smile widens, it's met with unrest. The others exude a telling aroma, one easier to read than any expression. Easier to see even than the hairs that spring to life along their arms or the tiny bumps that swell across their flesh.

Kristen moves close to Chris again, indicating some mating ritual. Perhaps this is the sole reason they've come here. I'd prefer that to any further exploration.

Should they happen upon this other world they'd find truth in their friend's words. Not all of the creatures there have fangs, but many do. Although they'd liken me to one of these monsters, I'd no sooner lead them to that world than I would go myself. Despite being tied to it in some way that place still frightens me.

Both women scan the void behind them. They appear unsure of what they cannot see. They're apprehensive yet maintain their silence. The men

guide them ever closer. I worry for their safety and for mine. Should they breach this other world, the creatures there may learn of the passage to my home world.

Kristen lifts a doubtful finger to the radiance in the distance. "What's that?"

"I . . . I don't know." Chris stumbles forward. "Another way out, maybe." He wanders ahead and stares into a dimly lit world. "My God." He catches his breath. "You aren't going to believe this."

I had preferred not to alert these people. Now I have no choice.

Slithering up behind them, Kristen sees me first and shines her torch in my eyes. Although the pain is not intense it still hurts, and through it, I can see her terror. I scramble to find the words, but when they come they only intensify her horror. It's obvious they cannot comprehend my dialect.

Screams erupt from her so shrill they bring a steady ache to my ears. I ignore the discomfort. My sole concern is to keep these people safe and the inhabitants of this other world where they belong.

I encircle Kristen's throat with a tentacle to hush her. In my worry, I squeeze too hard. The resulting sound reminds me of tiny rocks being crushed together. When I loosen my grip she falls lifeless to the ground.

Now Diane screams, and I'm forced to seize her, as well. This time I'm more careful. Even as she assaults my flesh with the butt end of her torch my focus is to not hurt her.

Because of this, I fail to notice Zack. Interesting enough, the once brave Chris remains of little concern,

looking as though he might faint. Zack glares at me with condemning brown eyes and withdraws a familiar weapon from his belt. With this knife he attacks.

I shield myself, Diane still in tow. As a result, she slips from my hold and falls to the cave floor gasping for air. Zack glances to her but refuses to give up the fight.

We are caught in a dance, him thrusting his blade and me fending off each attack. I'm infuriated when the sting of his weapon twice finds the underside of my limb. As I'm weakened, it affords him an opportunity. He seizes it and drives his knife hard into the muscle of my arm.

I clutch the man around his chest. Blood drains from my weakened limb. I growl, trying to tighten my grip on Zack but failing. Nevertheless, I find myself unable to stop. I seek revenge for his misdoings and squeeze with all my might.

Squeaks escape his throat. He starts to spasm. His eyes bulge, and his lips turn a bluish hue. Zack's eyes glaze over, and the determination has left them. They are distant and glossy, worried. When he becomes limp I cannot stop myself. I see in his eyes the reflection of my fury, and even then I refuse to let him live.

It saddens me that it has come to this. They're too frightened by my appearance and unwilling to understand what I must convey.

Diane cannot detect my regret. Her color flushes and when she escapes, Chris follows. They flee into this forbidden world and my heart sinks.

I lunge forward in one final effort. My tentacle manages to trip up Diane. I cringe when she crashes

face first into a large rock. Her blood spreads into the alien soil. Once more I've failed them and myself in the process.

Seeing this, Chris races into the obscure world. I'm dismayed by his freedom and retreat into my lair. Two upturned human faces welcome me back. Their lifeless terror-struck expressions lit by their fallen torches. The aroma of their death doesn't repulse me near as much as I expected.

Never has my connection to mankind felt as thin as it does now. Soon, when these creatures discover Chris, it's probable he'll flee to the only place he knows. When he does, he'll lead them right to my lair.

This will force me to make choices I've long avoided. I'll ascertain forgotten truths. My instincts shall prevail. I, Rylak, will have no choice but to become the monster they feared. The monster I myself have feared.

BREATHING CAVE

THE CAVE SEEMED to breathe Kelly in as if smelling her. She didn't want to go anywhere near the cave let alone in. But they expected her to enter despite the sensation, which caused her to drift away from the opening.

In her retreat, she noticed Mike's brow cocked. *Is he mocking me?* No man in his right mind would do that to her so early in a relationship.

Her back banged against a stocky form. Brian's grin clued her in on his opinion of her lack of bravery. "What's up there, buttercup?"

She shook him off and observed Jen's boyfriend's reaction. She thought Jim's judgment an easy read, as well. It said, *what a girlie girl.* She'd heard plenty such comments growing up. Hadn't cared for them then and certainly didn't now. At least Jim had the common sense to keep his mouth shut.

"Just ignore them," Jen said. "Really, it's nothing to worry about."

Jen had been the one to set them up, Kelly having become a sort of project for her friend these last few years. And Jen had an awful track record, so Kelly had gone in with low expectations, sporting a frumpy oversized football jersey and a pair of worn sweats with

frazzled hair. He'd bought her a drink, but when their eyes met for the first time she forgot about the beverage, instead drinking in the deep blue ocean of his eyes.

Kelly forced an uncomfortable smile for her friend's sake. She didn't want to embarrass herself any more than she already had, but it wasn't easy.

If Jen can brave these caves then so can I.

She took a bold step forward. Once more confronted by the peculiar entrance, which looked like a gargantuan mouth, she imagined the opening widened.

It wants you.

This thought forced her back again, staggering. If not for being so close to the rocky wall, she might have fallen. Instead, she played it off as purposeful, bending to tie her shoelaces while she reeled in her emotions.

Come on. He's watching.

When her mother used to refer to Kelly as a tomboy, it had mostly been in comparison to the other two Owens girls. Anyone would look like a tomboy next to her sisters.

Kelly had a passion for the color pink. She preferred movies that made you cry,and enjoyed the comfort of an enticing love story. The dank cool of a cave was a far cry from her comfort zone. But she'd faked it before, and would do so again.

Something chilled her arm, startling her. Jim held the flashlight pressed against her flesh. She seized it with eagerness, flicked it on, and shined the beam into the depths of the cave.

She ducked inside, and the musty odor assaulted her nostrils. A steady beat pounded away in her chest

as the darkness swallowed her. She took a deep breath and held it.

Jim, lanky and tall, edged past her. "There we go. Not so hard, is it?"

What does he know?

He could never understand the torment she now suffered. Jen trailed Jim, offering an encouraging smile as she passed.

Kelly shined the light on her surroundings. This cavity seemed larger from the inside. She wielded her flashlight like a sword, trying to cut through the gloom and ease her panic. It wasn't working.

A bemused Brian sucked in his gut and slid past. Their eyes met long enough for her to notice they were the same height. "I never grow sick of this place," he said.

The three of them led the way. A guarded Kelly trailed. Mike brought up the rear. With him behind her, she felt obligated to venture onward into the ever-constricting darkness despite all her worries.

The farther they traveled, the less light emitted from the flashlights. As their path narrowed, so did Kelly's trachea. She wheezed. Panic swelled up inside of her like a hot kettle of water about to blow its steam.

Brian's voice boomed in the dark. "What do you—"

His words cut off, replaced by a choking sound. Brian screamed, and his beam flickered along the left wall and down the other side. The flashlight tumbled to the ground some fifteen yards away and faded fast. But Kelly had seen more, perhaps Brian being lifted into the air.

But by what?

Shocked, she searched the others with her light.

When her beam lit Jim, his pale face echoed her concern.

"What is it?" she said.

Jim's expression eased. "Nothing."

Kelly wanted to turn around, but Mike blocked the way. Her light illuminated his patient face. Her eyes strained, wondering how he could be so strong at a time like this.

He eased down her flashlight with his hand, then used his to brighten the passageway.

"Brian?" he said. "Brian, you okay, man?"

"What happened?" She knew she sounded hysterical, but she couldn't help it. "Mike, what happened to Brian?"

He sighed and continued staring off into the darkness. "I'm not sure. Let me think a second."

Her light revealed Jim again. His face had regained most of its color.

"He's probably just trying to scare us," Jim said.

A quick wave of her flashlight showed both Jen and Mike agreed. Still, she clung to Mike. Pawed at his chest until she could work up enough strength to mutter a weak protest. "If he is, it isn't funny."

But she wasn't convinced it had been a joke. What she thought she'd seen haunted her, and she couldn't believe she'd been the only one to see it. This alone made her doubt herself, what she thought she'd witnessed.

Nothing could have boosted a man of Brian's size so easily. *Nothing*, she marveled and trembled.

Even if he had been teasing them, she surmised it would be the sort of trick that couldn't be managed without a great deal of preparation. He would need a

strong wire and supports at the very least. Maybe even some help.

But when she shined her light on the surrounding walls, she saw nothing of the sort. *Only rock, dirt, and darkness.*

"Listen, he must be here somewhere." Mike stiffened. "Let's split up and look for him."

She prayed they would go to the entrance.

"I'll take Kelly," he said. "You two check back the way we came."

A scream of objection rose in her throat. She fought to hold it back, unsure why she should bother.

Moments after Jim and Jen left, she heard a panicked cry. Nothing more. No warning. No running. Nothing. She could only speculate on her friend's fate.

Relieved now they hadn't taken the path back, she realized whatever did attack the others could also be waiting for them up ahead. Her heart felt like it might burst right out of her chest. Then Mike would see for himself her level of terror when the loosened organ rolled across this dirt ground.

His gaze lingered in the direction of the entrance. "Come on, let's keep going."

She would have preferred to stay. At least until they were certain the others weren't coming back. But when Mike staggered forward, she followed.

"Wait up," Kelly said.

Mike scoffed. "Goddamned Brian. I'll bet the others are in on this, too. Bastards! You hear me, Brian? You're a real son of a bitch."

She held her breath, uneasy of her boyfriend's boisterous tone. Glancing back every few steps, she became doubtful of what she expected to find. Maybe

she hoped to spot a flashlight, or anticipated seeing something far worse. But she saw nothing and doing so only made it more difficult to keep up with Mike. It surprised her when she crashed face first into him. Kelly's flashlight fell to the ground and cast a dim glow around them.

His eyes strained on her for a brief moment. Then abrupt rushes of air batted her eyes shut. Although she resisted, her eyes surrendered, and she kept them shut until the wind subsided.

Blinded, she clawed for his arms. When she found him, she tried to hold onto him.

He grabbed her back. His fingers seized her wrists and tightened. It began to hurt, and then he pulled at her. He slipped from her grasp, and she tried again. But no matter how many times she reached out for him, her hold faltered until she no longer felt him at all.

The gust diminished, and her eyes sprang open wide. Retrieving her flashlight, she shined it about without care. Her worst fears had been realized. She was alone.

"Mike?" Her voice wavered. "Jim?"

Neither responded. Her lone beam drifted across rocky surfaces. Even worse, the light seemed dimmer. Either that or the darkness had thickened. She couldn't tell which, and a swollen sensation rose in her throat, making it difficult to breathe. Each exhale came with a whistle of air.

She spun in what she thought a complete circle. Somehow she'd lost her way. She agonized over heading off in any direction, and it occurred to her that she should conserve batteries. But the thought of being alone in complete darkness unnerved her.

BREATHING CAVE

Someone will come for me and help me find Mike.

Seconds after this declaration, her light shrank to a minimal glow.

No, no, no. Please don't. The flashlight defied her wishes, turning her world an awful pitch black.

A burst of screams escaped her, unable to contain her terror. With her hands out in front, she shuffled through the unknown, panicked and desperate.

As her cries intensified, it became difficult to swallow. What little saliva she could produce refused to wet her throat, so each gasp felt like a lump. Her esophagus closed and with it, hopelessness intensified.

Heart thrumming, she found herself in unending chaos. She might have lost herself in this madness if not for her whimpers finding some sort of reverberation.

I'm in some cavernous pocket.

Her breathing eased. From this, she discerned the way out and stared off in that direction searching for a speck of light.

A cool breeze whispered by, disorientating her. She tried to ignore the sensation and failed, instead envisioning what might have caused such a wind. Her mind painted optimistic pictures, but the reality of this black canvas denied her any such pleasantries.

Her senses heightened, a steady drip harmonized with her pulse. Bugs skittered across the cave floor, sounding like paper being crumpled and torn. Each new noise added to this chilling symphony. Beyond this horrible music, she smelled a stench reminiscent of her grandmother's house after the woman died, and it had sat on the market for more than a year. For some

reason the linens hadn't been washed, and to Kelly, they had smelled of aging human flesh.

Something's here with me.

It sounded larger than any sort of bug.

It's a rat. Or maybe a bat.

But she knew it wouldn't be either of those creatures. Her conscience assured her whatever lurked about in this darkness would dwarf any known rodent.

Maybe they're all in on this.

She grasped for the optimism of this notion. "This isn't funny, guys."

A rush of wind shot past her. With it came more doubt.

But if I can't see, how can they?

Contemplating this, another thought occurred to her.

Jim bought night vision goggles from that military supply store a few weeks ago.

She stiffened. "I said it's not funny. Now stop!"

Silence followed.

And sensing the hesitancy of her words, a strange confidence overcame her, and with it, her desire to leave intensified.

"Come on, Jim, Jen . . . Brian. Mike. Turn on a light, okay?"

No response. No light.

"Turn on a goddamned flashlight!"

A sour stink assaulted her nose.

It smells like rotten chicken.

A misplaced draft of air touched her neck. While she remained at ease within this warmth, her hair stood on end when this air drew away in a breath. The unseen terror now stood within arm's reach.

She collapsed to the ground. Sought refuge from the darkness in the lone place she thought real. The strange air followed her as if studying her. Her fear whittled away at her soul until only a defeated remnant remained.

Her eyes trained on a single light bounding her way.

What is it? A bug? Perhaps a firefly.

She'd take anything as long as it provided light. Her eyes fixated on it, mesmerized by its movement and desperate for its illumination.

The dim light grew and with it, her heartbeat. It pounded away inside of her like a disgruntled carpenter, hammering at the frame of a house. Before she could avoid it, the light was on her. She shielded her eyes and wanted to scream, but could bring only a weak whelp.

"Kelly?" the voice said.

Jim's breathing wasn't as labored as she would've thought. He bent beside her, holding up his cellphone. Now, they could leave and with the safety of light—

"So glad to see you," she said, gasping. "Did you see Mike?"

"No." He hummed. "And no bars this far in, either." He looked at her. "I wish I'd charged it, too, because it's running low."

With that his phone went black, shrouding her once more in complete and utter darkness. She threw herself into his arms, which caused him to lose hold of the phone. Once more her throat swelled, and the dizziness returned.

A rush of wind disrupted her anxiety. His hold on her tightened, and he pulled at her. She resisted,

pounding on his chest. But as sudden as Jim appeared, he vanished, melting into the darkness. And her fists struck only empty air.

She collapsed into a fetal position and rolled over something on the ground. Heard a crunch.

Jim's phone.

Its weak glow filled her face, which made she smile. Her heart fluttered as she rose. But she wouldn't be able to make any calls unless she backtracked. At least she'd learned what direction she'd need to go.

But how far before I get even one bar?

She searched for the flashlight app and found it. When she clicked it on it didn't work right. She'd broken the screen and now the phone generated a weird flickering effect. But at least she could still see.

The phone illuminated the ceiling. Glancing up, she nearly passed out. The phone dropped from her grip as a flurry of wings erupted around her.

The first to attack looked like Mike, only he'd transformed into something horrifying. Between the flashes of light, she saw tufts of matted hair on his mottled scalp. A membrane spanned the distance between his arms and emaciated chest.

Another flash came. His legs were bent in a most unnatural way. His toes curled into menacing claws.

He spiraled down on her, landing on the phone with a crunch. She caught a brief glimpse of his face before the light failed for good. And those piercing yellow eyes filled her thoughts as his fangs plunged deep into her throat. A numbing sensation seized her, sending her body into convulsions. The disabling effect spread fast, and soon her feet gave way.

He became her support, holding her up so they could all have a taste.

Before her life ended, she drank of Mike's blood. In this way, she became his betrothed.

She drank at first out of need. Then out of pleasure. Soon the light returned, albeit dim, but she no longer feared such things. It burned bright enough to lead her out of the dark for good.

Monique staggered forward and stared into the cave. She didn't like the looks of it despite the fact she considered herself somewhat adventurous.

But it wasn't only the cave that bothered her. Having Kelly along offered some sense of security, but she wasn't sure Brian was the right guy for her.

Jen smiled, her hand in Jim's. Kelly moved beside Monique and placed a reassuring hand on her shoulder. She looked so different now that she'd started dating Mike. Still, both Mike and Jim seemed like nice enough guys.

"It's okay. We've both done this before." Kelly smiled. "Trust me, it's fun."

Monique forced an uneasy smile and entered the cave. She shivered as a cool breeze rolled over the flesh of her arms.

SOUL TAPPED

THEY'D FOLLOWED HENRY again. This time they cornered him behind what had once been McCool's Five & Dime. Now that they had Henry where they wanted him, they'd bring the pain. His body wasn't near what it had been, either. All of his muscles ached without end. His bones were brittle. He'd learned to hate days like this where he felt every bit of his eighty-one years.

He looked each boy in the eyes, but they didn't waver. Henry had never been a fast talker, so he'd have to rely on other means if he meant to escape unscathed.

I wonder if this was how my kid acted.

Perhaps that was what bothered him most. He'd never met his son so he couldn't possibly know. But these boys were the bastards of this town. Teenagers like them went around looking for trouble. His son would be more than twice as old as these youngsters, the product of a late-in-life fling. He often wondered if his son would track Henry down to administer vigilante justice for running out on his mom. If he did, he wouldn't be interested in giving Henry the chance to explain.

Who you kidding? You didn't have any good reason for leaving that woman.

The redhead looked smarter than the rest. More Henry's size, the blond in cutoff jeans acted like a dimwit. He supposed the brunette had a glass jaw. It wasn't facial structure that informed Henry of this fact but something in the boy's eyes. If his instincts were right that boy would go down faster than a sack of potatoes.

Quick as ever, Henry brought his cane around and broke it in half on the boy's chin. The teenager's face crumpled and seconds later so did his body. Afterward, he lay on the asphalt of this back alley, clasping his face and crying out loud. This left the other two boys stupefied.

That'll hurt him much worse come tomorrow.

He lifted his cane and thrust the jagged end at the other boys. Concern for their friend waned and was replaced by distress. When they ran, Henry didn't bother chasing them down. Once the third boy mustered up some strength he followed the others, leaving Henry alone in the alley.

Sighing, he ambled around the corner of the store. This wasn't the first cane he'd broken, and he doubted it would be the last. Once those boys got it in their head to get revenge, they'd be back. Next time he might not be so lucky.

It took him longer than usual to get back to the home. Being such a large plot of land, he felt winded by the time he arrived. There, a man greeted him with a smile.

Damn, what the hell's his name?

The grinning man laughed. "Broke another cane, did ya?"

Henry wasn't in the laughing mood, so he only

nodded. Then something awful happened, and he found his voice after all. "Move!"

Any other day Henry wouldn't have thought twice about seeing a man like this go down. He'd seen a lot of old folks suffer heart attacks. At his age death had become commonplace among the ancient folk living at Divine Acres Retirement Home. The signs were there, too, of course. This man who'd lost his grin was as old, if not older, than Henry. He was far too overweight and likely had thickened arterial walls, maybe worse. So it made sense it would be so-and-so's time. But the man's ticker didn't trouble Henry. He only wished that were his concern.

Despite his arthritis, he'd walked around the entire garden, stopping only at the fountain to stare into that God awful reflective ball, and he'd even endured the scuffle with those young'uns in town. Now Henry hobbled over to the man with lightning speed and raised his broken cane. He wasn't sure he had it in him, but he'd try because what he saw took his breath away.

The man looked shocked by his approach, seeing Henry's panic and the raised cane. No doubt he thought Henry meant to beat the living crap out of him or perhaps stab him in the chest with the now severed end. What he didn't see concerned Henry most—the *thing* looming over the man's shoulder.

Near invisible, Henry almost hadn't seen it. He might not have if it hadn't been for the way it stared back at Henry as if it weren't there for this man but for him. Then the apparition took hold of the man's shoulder and clung to it like a kitten would a tree branch.

Henry reached the man and brought his cane down on the spirit. When it didn't falter, he whacked it again, harder. He kept hitting that ghost with his cane until he'd used up what little energy he had left. But each strike passed right through the specter, weakening the apparition's victim more than the ghost.

The man pleaded for Henry to stop, seemingly unaware of the thing at his back. Henry saw it well, how it gazed into his eyes with spite. The creature grinned and shoved its arm deep into the man's side. The man's hands went to his chest, and all the while Henry kept beating the ghost long after he was spent. Although the blows had weakened, he couldn't stop himself.

It's a ghost, damn it.

The apparition regarded Henry with disgust. That alone caused Henry to strike harder, not knowing the damage he'd dealt to the man in the process. Henry might not have stopped if it hadn't been for an unsuspecting little boy.

"Ma," the boy said. For now, the woman remained unseen. "There's some old guy beating up a fat man."

Ah, the innocence of youth. But all the same, Henry grew aware of what it looked like he'd done, as he didn't think the boy had seen the creature.

The click-clack of high-heeled shoes hurried along the sidewalk. With their approach, Henry lowered his cane and shrank against the door of the home. His breathing labored, his cane broken and the walk difficult, he considered he might have a stroke himself.

Feeling it, he leaned against the building hard. Saw the woman round the corner, but thankfully she hadn't looked his way.

So-and-so teetered in his unsteady kneeling position and finally collapsed. The ghost-like creature writhed about the man's body, in and out, ruining the man. The fact it kept staring right at him bothered Henry most.

The woman ran to assist the man. Henry sucked in a deep breath and yanked the door open, scanned the hallway fast and after seeing no one around, slipped inside. He fled to the safety of his room.

Nimble footsteps pitter-pattered down the hall and stopped outside his door. His eyes trained on the entrance, but still the light knock startled him.

"Come in," he said.

The door swung open, and Miss Nancy stepped in. As far as Henry was concerned, this night nurse was the bee's knees. Not only was she a looker, but she had more smarts than the others. Plus, she was single. If he ever did meet his son, this would be the sort of gal he'd want him to marry.

Maybe if I were a few dozen years younger . . .

"How you doing tonight, Mr. Miller?"

She shut the door behind her. Pulled a chair over to his bedside where she sat.

He loved her accent. Couldn't quite place it, but it sounded European. "Please. Call me Henry."

Her smile beamed in a way that melted his heart. "Yes. Sorry. Formalities and all." She rolled up Henry's sleeve. "Now, let's check your pulse and blood pressure, shall we Henry?"

He thanked God his retirement had afforded him

a place like this, as being a lawyer had provided little else. This home had the best-looking nurses. Most of them, Nancy included, tolerated his mundane stories. Some even asked questions now and then. She might not know it, but she'd been the closest thing he had to a friend these days.

"I'm run down like an old Chevy, you know?"

"Well, seems you are." She shook her head. "Why are your vitals so high? What happened today, Henry?"

A sheepish expression spread across his face. "Well, I had a bit of a scuffle . . . "

She raised an eyebrow. "What? With whom?"

"It wasn't my fault," he said. He worried he'd given away more than he'd meant to.

One of the downsides of being old was this awful tendency to paint himself into a corner. When he'd been younger, he would've snapped off a good lie, maybe even flirted with her. Now, he struggled to hold his tongue.

"Come on, now." She folded her arms across her breasts and offered a playful smile. "Out with it."

He grimaced. "You'll think I'm bat shit crazy."

Her stern gaze ate away at him. Without her saying another word, he caved.

"Okay, okay for Christ's sake." He rolled his eyes. "But you won't believe a damned word of it. I guaran-damn-tee it."

She eased back in her chair. "I understand. Now tell me."

Anxious, he grumbled. "I saw something odd today."

"What was it?"

He'd been convinced then his wife and son were better off on their own. Now regret consumed him because of that choice.

Long ago, Henry had been certain the kid would track him down, curious about his biological father. But his son never bothered, either not desiring a relationship with Henry or unable to locate him. Not that Henry had ever been so impressive.

Around the corner of the garden, that blasted mirrored ball came into view. He hesitated before taking a seat on the nearby bench.

Damn that thing is ugly.

There, staring at his distorted reflection, his thoughts switched to Nancy. She'd make any man happy. He couldn't fathom how she'd managed to stay single all this time.

If only I could introduce Nancy and my son before I die. He tucked the thought away.

From the corner of his eye, he spied someone else rounding the corner of the garden. The teenager regarded Henry with a sneer, obviously still upset with their last meeting. Thankfully it was only one of them and not the whole group.

Damn if these boys won't leave me be.

He pushed up from the bench and stumbled over to the mirrored ball where he steadied himself. This teenager didn't look so afraid of the limb. Not until Henry hoisted it back like a weapon, and then the teenager stood his ground.

When he was still a good twenty yards away, he shouted, "You're pretty tough when you got a weapon, aren't you?"

A wry smile creased Henry's lips. "And you're

damn tough wanting to fight an old man who can barely walk."

The teen growled, unconvincing at best. Secretly, Henry prayed this teenager hadn't come from his loins because more than anything the boy didn't have any sensibility.

Henry considered running to escape the boy. It was too late for that now. He'd plant his feet and maybe give this teen a good whack upside his head. He pushed off the mirrored ball, and his knee cricked. Seconds later the boy lunged for Henry.

To his surprise, the boy never made it. Around five yards away, the teenager simply froze. Staring at Henry with haunting wide eyes, his lips trembling with fear. The teenager pressed his hand to his heart and spun around. Only then did Henry see what had stopped him.

It's that damn ghost again.

Henry pressed his eyes shut, not wanting to watch. Still, they opened, defying him. He considered attacking the ghost again but knew what little damage if any he'd done last time.

The ghost wrestled the teen to the ground. His young fingers clawed at the earth, pulling the grass and ripping it away in tufts. All the while the ghost eyed Henry with hate-filled eyes.

Damn ghost goes after anyone it sees me with.

Finished with the teenager, it left the body motionless on the ground and turned its attention to Henry.

He leaned away, tripping and catching himself on the mirrored ball. There, he ignored the pain and readied to push off as the ghost attacked.

Henry closed his eyes and swung the limb blindly. Nothing. He dared to open them in time to see the ghost fretting over Henry's reflection in the mirrored ball. On this he refused to ruminate any longer, choosing to run for the back door to the retirement home.

When he came within twenty yards of the door the ghost turned and pursued him. Henry glanced over his shoulder, noting how the ghost had gained on him. And because of that, he crashed into Nancy, who was leaving work. The two of them ended up entangled on the ground, a proposition that on any other day might have aroused him.

She pawed at him. "Are you okay?"

Henry got to his knees, feeling his hip twinge in more pain than ever. His attention remained elsewhere. The ghost had somehow missed him due to this collision.

Where'd you go, you bastard?

The ghost spun in a wide semicircle some forty yards away. It headed for them. Only then did she see it, as evidenced by her scream.

Henry lifted her up and dragged her to the door. She followed, although not without some effort. He threw himself hard against the brick wall and opened the door. Without hesitation he grabbed her and lunged inside, turning fast to close the door.

The ghost crashed against the glass, unable to penetrate the surface. When it realized this the apparition glared in at him. Its haunted orbs passed from Henry to Nancy, and back again.

It wants her, too.

For a moment, they remained at the door,

watching the ghost stew over its failure. Afterward, they fled to Henry's room.

Due to the running, his chest felt like red-hot embers burning. The pain rose and for a second he thought for sure death had found him.

Then Nancy was at his back, pounding to loosen the phlegm. He steadied himself and sat on the edge of the bed, breathing heavy.

"Henry, what the hell was that?" she said.

He gasped. "That . . . was . . . the goddamned . . . thing I told you . . . about . . . "

"Can it get in?"

He waited for his breathing to ease. "Don't know for sure. Maybe. But it didn't look like it."

When he shared the story about the teenager, she listened, as always. He noticed how she trembled when he spoke of the boy's demise, which worried him. "You okay?"

She didn't look up and spoke in a whisper, "Didn't you see the way that thing looked at me? I mean . . . "

It struck him, the immensity of her situation. Pain shot down his left arm, the one he comforted her with, and he jerked it away. He stood, woozy, but did his best to keep this from her. She looked too wrought with concern to notice anyway.

"Well," he thought aloud, "that mirrored ball in the garden confused it some. Maybe we can . . . "

Her steely eyes probed him. "You mean we can trick it?"

"I suppose, if we need to."

But he didn't reveal that the mirrored ball had only delayed its pursuit. If the ghost could think, it would have learned from its mistake. Sooner or later it would come for one of them despite any mirror.

She shot out his door and headed down the hall. He slid out after her, watching her disappear into a nearby room. She returned with a full-length mirror in tow.

Yes, of course. They kept one in the lounge so the nurses could preen themselves before their shifts. God only knew why anyone would care to spruce up for old farts like him.

He checked the hall. With no one else around, he shut the door.

She sat the mirror in the chair. "We can use this if we have to."

He stared at his haggard reflection. His eyes were tiny and dark. With his hair nearly nonexistent, the mottled scalp beneath was riddled with liver spots and moles. Maybe he even saw a wart or two. His skin had become so wrinkled, as though he'd been soaking in a bathtub for his entire life.

Good Christ! I look like hell.

"So this thing, it steals souls, right? And now it's after mine?"

He nodded, but she didn't really need an answer.

"I wonder if this mirror will be enough?" she said.

He knew little of ghosts. Perhaps, all he'd learned of ghosts had come within the last twenty-four hours. The extent of his collective knowledge had been derived from watching television, knowing the basics of binding legal documents, and a few common quotes from what many referred to as the good book.

He'd grown fonder of that book in his old age, primarily because each room came equipped with a copy and the elderly gravitated toward hope. In it, he'd read about souls. He could only speculate on their value in the afterlife.

But I won't give up my goddamned soul.

His hardened claim sounded flimsy in light of everything he'd seen. If this thing wanted his soul, he couldn't outrun it forever, especially at his age.

Tears welled in Nancy's eyes. He wished the ghost had never seen her. She was young, had a whole life to look forward to. Such a shame she'd been caught up in this mess. If he could, he would have—

Then it occurred to him. Maybe there was a way to help Nancy. *I have to try, for her sake.*

"Quick, I need a pen and piece of paper," he said. "I think I know how to beat the bastard."

Nancy spent the night, and that suited him fine. They stayed up late, working out the details of their plan. When one of the nurses came around Nancy answered and told them she had matters under control. These nurses worked overtime quite often, so Henry supposed it would go unchallenged. Still, he worried they might interfere, and that would get more people killed.

The nurse nodded, an odd expression pasted to her face when Nancy closed the door.

He'd offered her the bed, which she took after much debate. That orange pleather chair hadn't been so uncomfortable. He woke early and headed off for his usual stroll around the gardens.

After securing another limb, he walked along the tall trees at the back end of the property. The smell of pine freshened the air. A field of brown needles lay scattered across the path and the occasional fallen

twigs snapped beneath his sneakers. He pushed through a few branches at the east end of the pond. There, he found what he'd been seeking.

Appearing somewhat confused by his willingness, the ghost latched onto Henry. He felt its pull deep inside of him. Pain rose in his chest and shot down his left arm. Numbness consumed him, as everything went cold. His vision blurred, and he struggled to stay afoot.

Nancy came running up behind him, the worry apparent on her face. She'd yet to see the ghost, so she stood there holding the paper he'd spent much of the night writing, a simple legal document that she'd also signed. To protect her, this agreement authorized away her soul to the only other person on Earth he could trust, and even then it was a shot in the dark. He'd never gotten to know his kid.

The ghost forced him down to the hardened earth. Its weight shrugged off of him, and Henry did his best to locate the ghost.

That was when Nancy saw it, and she would have screamed if not for it lunging right for her. She held up the document like a cross to a vampire, and the ghost froze six inches away from her.

Henry laughed. "She doesn't own her soul no more, you bastard."

Then something terrifying happened. The apparition glanced back at Henry and grinned. He thought it inconceivable to notice a familiarity in that smile.

Seconds later the ghost assaulted her. Nancy shrieked, her outburst turning to a gargling sound mid-scream. Her hands went to her chest and her knees buckled.

"No!" Henry yelled.

But it was too late. Nancy's eyes looked beyond Henry. She looked older, tired and worn. The ghost reached inside of her, finding what it wanted. It yanked it free, and only then did it return to Henry.

He rolled to look into the eyes of his assailant. A glimmer of joy showed in those hollow eyes. The ghost just kept staring at Henry, observing these final moments as his heart gave.

"Why?" Henry said. No answer came.

The ghost smiled, and now Henry saw it well. This was his face, back when he'd been younger. This was the face of his lost son come back to make sure the loneliness would be repeated. With this knowledge, Henry wanted to die. Unfortunately, he felt better than he had in ages.

THE WATER PEOPLE

THE NOISE IN the living room was slight, barely discernable among the light pitter-patter of rain against his rooftop.

Only the wind I suppose.

Chandler gazed into the fish bowl on his desk. The solitary goldfish swam up close to the glass. Its round eyes stared back at him, tail waving in anticipation of being fed.

How could she leave me, Goldie?

The fish didn't answer. Not that he could blame the little guy. He hadn't come up with any good reasons, either.

His conscience thought otherwise.

That isn't true, and you know it.

He knew all too well why she'd left. She believed his research absurd. But that didn't mean he had to accept her ignorance or give it legs.

Pushing his books aside, he lowered his head to his desk. His eyes were met by what he alleged was the only true illustration of the water people. Only this photocopy of the original, drawn by a person claiming to have seen a water breather firsthand, stayed true to everything he'd seen himself or heard in interviews.

He held the rendering at a distance, studying the

rough lines. It depicted long, slender legs and lanky arms. There were tentacles where there should be hands, looking like slimy fingers. The enormous head seemed too heavy for such a thin neck to bear.

This looks so alien.

It's this hypothesis he'd long believed. That these creatures were visitors from some distant planet, come to live in peace alongside mankind.

This theory did nothing but feed his doubt now that she'd left. Grumbling, he crumpled the paper angrily.

"She's right, damn it. It's stupid to think . . . "

He lifted the paper ball, preparing to throw it in the trash. Then something caught his eye on the other side of the lone window. Scanning the rocky embankment, he searched for anything peculiar. Only the gray horizon and damp black rocks could be seen, along with the occasional flash of lightning illuminating the landscape.

He stared at the balled up paper in his hand. With care he returned the picture to its original form, laying it flat on his desk. His eyes remained glued to the page.

Do they exist? Or was I only dreaming back then?

This paper had no answers for him.

The water people were relatively new to the Chesapeake Bay. He'd been only five years old when he saw one himself. That experience had filled him with enough curiosity to shape a passion for tracking them down.

After a few glasses of wine Lizzie would often laugh while he detailed his research. More than once she'd dismissed his chatter with a mere wave of her hand. She couldn't understand why anyone would fund such

foolishness. But she hadn't seen the things he had over the last seven years. If she did, she might not be so quick to reject his work.

Before she exited the house earlier this day, she'd quipped off one more insult. "You haven't really seen anything."

In truth, he hadn't, not as an adult. Still, he believed them real. There were well-documented cases where those with little faith soon altered their beliefs. Plenty of times ignorance had led to grief. He'd not suffer a similar fate.

Maybe that's what will become of Lizzie.

He shook his head, dismayed he should have such a terrible thought. Why should he expect so much from her? She'd never supported his undertakings from the start.

It sounded rather outlandish now, replaying the accounts of this night. His beliefs were a difficult pill to swallow.

Is this what I've become, a mockery to her?

His eyes scanned the empty doorway of his study. The hall beyond, dark and foreboding, seemed as empty now as it had when she'd been standing there mocking him. He'd felt equally defenseless then. All of it reducing Chandler to a shadow of the man he'd once been.

He'd poured himself into his work. Tried to keep busy enough he didn't worry about her comments or the fact she'd left. Now as he dwelled over the papers and notebooks strewn across his desk it all seemed so overwhelming without her to keep him balanced.

Standing, he observed the stark landscape once more. The view took his breath away. Even at such a

late hour and so soon after a storm, the bay could be so tranquil. Storm clouds drifted by, refusing to complain. A distant rumble rolled across the skies.

Have I wasted my time?

Lightning struck the darkened clouds, and rain poured from the sky again. Droplets formed large circles on the water's surface. Showers once more tapped against his windowpane, distorting the objects beyond the glass. The landscape disintegrated, coalescing to ruin the view.

The gloom intensified. The night grew murky. More so than he'd ever seen in his forty years here. It created the perfect setting for—

The water people . . .

Even thinking about them now sounded so ridiculous. No wonder she believed him silly. She'd been forced to tag along on his fool's quest and had every right to her opinion until he could prove otherwise.

Maybe I can make things right.

With this hope, he abandoned his study. But upon turning into the hall, he stepped in a puddle of water and froze. The house grew colder in that instant.

The liquid proved hard to see in this darkness. Struggling to detect footprints, he fumbled for the light switch. It clicked but no light came.

Power's out.

At best it seemed like a bad trick. Maybe Lizzie had come back, forgiven him and returned to her playful self. It would be just like her.

A grin spread across his face. But before he could call out to her, a single droplet of cold water touched his forehead.

Above him, he identified a darkened stain on the ceiling.

Not Lizzie after all.

This gag came at the hands of Mother Nature, a far crueler joke than he'd expected. Under his breath, he cursed the storm. Now he would need to mend his roof come morning.

While lingering on the water stain, he swore something moved behind him. He spun but found himself staring down the empty corridor. Yet the floorboards beyond creaked.

Sounds like someone's walking around the corner.

He mustered up some nerve. "Who's there?"

No response came except for a few more creaks. A dreadful silence followed.

I'd better be ready.

He reached back into his study and pawed at his bookshelves. There, in a wooden cup, he found one of his letter openers. He seized it, clutching it against his pounding chest. Whatever awaited him in the darkness shifted from side to side.

When he reached the end of the hallway, he rested his back against the wall.

Do I rush out and thrust my blade blindly? His fist clenched the letter opener. *Or should I wait?*

He leaped out from around the corner, letter opener raised. Prepared to rush the intruder but discovered no one there. He studied the next corner, only a few yards away. His anxiety heightened as he approached.

Again, he hid against the wall, once more unsure of himself. Now he heard something breathing, heavy and worried. The breath could even be seen from his

vantage point. Tendrils of cool air caught the moonlight, forming fleeting wispy clouds.

His world slanted, as he felt like passing out. This proved so maddening, and he felt reality slipping away. With difficulty, he contained his terror and once more jumped out from around the corner. He lunged forward with his blade without identifying his attacker. In his angst, he hadn't noticed the puddle of water in which he stood. All he saw were her eyes.

Hurt-filled and fresh with tears, she appeared frightened. Lizzie collapsed to the floor, and he went with her. She looked at him, eyes glazing over and her breathing labored.

"Lizzie?" He dropped the weapon and took her in his arms. "Lizzie, are you okay?"

She tried to speak, but there was too much blood. It discolored his hands while he struggled to keep her alive. Now she stared off beyond him.

Worry engulfed him. "I'll get help."

He rose, but she pulled him back. "You . . . you were—"

"I'll hurry back. I promise."

As he tried to get to his feet, he heard her expel one last word in a hiss of air. A word he'd never thought her capable of.

"—right . . . "

He went for the phone, hoping it still worked. But found himself confronted by something implausible.

The creature gazed back at him with oblong eyes. Translucent skin provided a view of its inner-workings, veins and organs similar to that of a jellyfish. Pink, blue and green hues illuminated inside of the creature, as enchanting as fireworks. He barely

noticed the tentacles until they took hold of his arm and pulled.

The sting immediate, it burned at his wrist and numbed him. He tried to free himself of the creature, but the thin-framed being stumbled along with him. In this way, they were both set off-balance, toppling to the floor beside the abandoned letter opener.

He seized the weapon in his weakened hand and didn't hesitate. Lashing out at the creature, he struck it deep enough to warrant a gurgling roar. Still, he could not stand, so he slid across the floor, crawling as fast as he could toward the phone.

Wet footprints surrounded him. *How many are there?*

He glanced back but saw nothing of the creature. Nor did he see Lizzie.

Sadness overwhelmed him. *They took her.*

He pulled over the phone. Heard a dial tone and tried to push the right numbers. Before he could, the sting overpowered him and he succumbed to the darkness.

Each night he sat at his desk and took in the view. It had been four months since the accident. He never made it to the hospital and as such, the police never questioned him. So he cleaned up after Lizzie's accident and never spoke of what happened that night. No one ever asked, either, assuming she'd finally left him for good this time due to the absurdity of his research. She'd often spoken of starting a new life without him while out in public.

The fact they didn't ask comforted him some, as it was all too painful to recall the true details of what transpired that night. Besides, there was still hope for them.

One day she'll return.

Of this, he felt certain. His hand had ended her life. Somehow they must've resurrected her. She'd seek out revenge soon enough. And on a stormy night like this, he liked to walk through the darkness of his home and wish for her to come.

Tonight, as he left his study and water breached the sole of his foot, he looked up. The water stains were there, but they were old and faint. He smiled.

Come for me, my dear. This time I won't fight.

WATER SNAKE

IT LOOKED LIKE hellfire raining down from the afternoon sky. Amid the reflections of clouds on the pond's surface, crimson streaks appeared by the dozens. Dozens of water snakes hurried across the murky water, heading straight for Sawyer.

Terrified, he jumped back. He landed on his butt, thus yanking his fishing line right out of the water.

Abandoning the rod, he scooted away in case these snakes took land. Thankfully they remained in the water.

What he'd seen weren't garden-variety snakes, either. Not at all your everyday garter snake, these were creatures he feared might lurk deep in the gloomy water. Especially when he went swimming in a lake or a pond like this. The snakes hadn't been around when the boys arrived and started fishing. Yet here they were, chasing him away.

Yuck. I hate snakes.

Both Richie and John reacted to his plight with laughter. But Sawyer accepted that because he saw the same concern in their expressions, too. They'd been just as afraid and were only lucky they hadn't been closer to the water.

The snakes departed, fearless lines squiggling

across the water. They'd turned their interest to the bait bucket, which floated half-submersed at the water's edge.

"Quick," Richie said. "Grab it."

When John reached for the bucket, several of the creatures hissed. He leaped away, and now Sawyer had to admit it looked rather hilarious.

But there's nothing funny about them snakes.

Many snakes twisted into the bucket, weaving in and out through the opening. Their greedy mouths snapped up the minnows. Within seconds they'd emptied the container.

"Those are some vicious snakes," Richie said.

Sawyer nodded, still watching them twist and squirm inside the bucket, looking for more minnows. He hadn't even noticed that his hook had lodged in his forearm when he'd yanked on his line so hard.

Sawyer picked at the hook, carefully removing it. Meanwhile, John retrieved his pole. His line tightened, and he reeled fast. A snake had swallowed his minnow whole and now swam around the center of the pond with fervor. His pole jerked forward with a snap. The line loosened, floating on the surface a second. Then his bobber went down for good.

One branch of the Y-shaped limb keeping Richie's rod tip angled up broke away. His rod skidded across the patchy grass as the guilty snake fled.

Sawyer spotted the hook protruding from the crook of its mouth. He dove for the tackle box and retrieved a filet knife. Turning to cut Richie's line, his effort came too late.

The rod tilted over the edge and vanished into the murky water.

"Dang it all to hell," Richie said.

The serpent turned as if acknowledging their failed efforts. Its crimson tail swirled, and then it too disappeared into the dark water. Seconds later, the others followed, and soon the pond returned to a glass-like state.

"What are they?" John said.

"Water snakes," Richie said. "I've seen them before at Abington Lake. They're greedy little bastards."

"Not just greedy," Sawyer said. "They're the nastiest snakes I've ever seen."

"Their bark is worse than their bite." Richie stared into the water. "One of them got my rod."

Sawyer spat in the water. A single bluegill darted to the surface and gobbled up the saliva. Behind it, a fat snake whirled and snapped its jaws around the belly of the fish. It dragged its prey down into the darkness.

"I tell you what, those are some hungry snakes," Sawyer said.

"Maybe." Richie's gaze scanned the pond and then looked at Sawyer. "But I'm going to try to get my rod back. Gimme yours."

He didn't want to hand over his rod. If nothing else he could use it to fend off the snakes if they returned. That was what he'd done this morning when he'd discovered the rod in the back room of the garage where his dad stored most of the tools.

A garter snake had been resting beneath the clutter, causing him to jump. Chains rattled behind him as he swiped the rod at the snake like a sword. Not even his mother's voice had broken his concentration, as she scolded his Dad about the homemade engine hoist.

His father had endured the lecture, hurrying to gather a bag of charcoal, bottle of lighter fluid, and some matches. All of this he'd placed under the dome of the grill, offering Sawyer a bothered glare before toting the whole thing around back. Sawyer had been lucky, too, as his elbow rested against the release lever. If the safety button hadn't been engaged and he'd knocked that lever hard enough, the engine of the semi-restored candy apple red '69 Mustang Fastback would've dropped fast and likely crushed him.

Richie's voice disrupted the memory. "Dude, your rod?"

"Huh?" Sawyer said.

Richie's face twisted. "Gimme your dang rod, man."

With reluctance, Sawyer handed it over.

Richie dug through the tackle box and produced an enormous treble hook. He threaded the line through the eyelet and attached a small weight near the hook. Then he raced all the way around the pond where they saw a canoe moored to a tree, some thirty yards away. He untied the weathered rope and climbed inside, pushing off into the water.

Concern overwhelmed Sawyer as Richie paddled out. "Be . . . be careful."

Richie laughed. "What are you, my girlfriend now?"

John snickered at that.

Sawyer's face flushed hot. "Shut up!"

Richie didn't stop laughing. "Ease up, Sawyer. I'm only busting your gonads."

"I'm just saying." Sawyer pointed at the pond. "Those snakes are mean."

"Yeah, yeah. I know." But he didn't look so concerned. Upon reaching the center, Richie fished the treble hook up and down where he'd last seen the rod, trying to somehow snag it. "If I can just . . ."

Sawyer inched forward, curious but mindful of the snakes. A hollow thump drew his attention back to the canoe. Richie had gotten to his feet, standing on trembling legs. The canoe rocked and with it so did Richie. All of this made Sawyer's heart skip.

This is it. He's going to fall in. The snakes will get him.

But Richie didn't fall. Although the boat swayed back and forth tempting fate, Richie remained dry for the time being.

"I think . . . is that?"

"What?" Sawyer said. "Did you find it?"

Richie's round face looked at Sawyer, whose eyes darted to the water where he saw what Richie had seen.

A belly far larger than the canoe swelled against the surface. Richie's face went white as a metal *thunk* pinged the canoe. Richie tried to steady himself, bending and grabbing the edges of the canoe. Seconds later he went sprawling face first into the pond. Arms flailing, Richie treaded water instead of swimming for the shore.

While John stood mouth agape, Sawyer ran to a nearby tree and wrestled with a lengthy broken limb, trying to free it. By the time he returned with the branch, the snakes had resurfaced. They were already assaulting Richie, coming in waves. Each time Richie tried to climb back into the canoe, a serpent would bite him, and he'd lose his grip.

Sawyer tried to scare the snakes off. He brought the heavy limb down in the water, creating large splashes. Nothing thwarted the snakes with him being so far away, not at first.

When they turned on Sawyer, he dropped the limb and ran. The branch floated across the surface.

"Swim for that limb, Richie," Sawyer said.

Richie didn't appear to hear Sawyer. Besides, he was in the middle of the pond, far out of reach of the limb. The malevolent creatures swam up behind Richie, found the tender areas of his arms and neck. They bit down hard and whipped their tails to aid in tearing away small pieces of Richie's flesh. Each time Richie yelped, the snakes writhed and flailed as if driven by his pain. Again and again, they attacked, drawing blood with each renewed bite.

Richie lifted himself over the edge of the canoe. While Richie rested and caught his breath, the snakes continued to nip at his calves and ankles. Richie glanced at Sawyer, his back and arms bloodied, and grinned. A smear of red covered his left cheek.

The canoe rocked, and that smile waned. One end of the canoe rose high above the water. Seconds later the entire craft jerked down like an oversized bobber. Richie held tight.

"Richie—"

Sawyer didn't have time to finish. The canoe had taken on too much water and sank fast. Richie struggled to stay afloat, choosing only now to try for the shore. But his effort came too late, and he gasped in an attempt to refill his lungs.

Horror stretched across Richie's face as the creature pulled him down into the water.

"Oh Jesus," John said. "What the hell, Sawyer? What the hell do we do?"

John started crying, his head in his trembling palms. He collapsed to the ground. Unable to control his emotions, they came out in a loud whine.

Sawyer's thoughts reeled. He tried to withdraw from the edge of insanity he'd now stepped up to, but what he'd just witnessed terrified him. He stood motionless, barely feeling the hot sting of tears pinching at his cheeks.

No one would save Richie. He bit down hard on his cheek, causing his teeth to clang together. Despite the pain, all the hurt, he knew what they had to do. "We need to call the police."

"No, Sawyer." John edged up to the water. "We have to help him."

Sawyer wanted to with all his heart, but he'd seen the thing lurking in that pond. "No!" This time Sawyer demanded. "He's gone."

He yanked his cellphone out of his back pocket and dialed 9-1-1.

It was dusk by the time he finished the police. They'd been stuck at the farm all day. No one could leave until they finished dragging the pond.

They found a snapping turtle, a few odd fish, and some algae-encrusted limbs, but no sign of the canoe. No one found Richie, either.

As he lay in bed that night, Sawyer considered one officer's expression. The man had appeared doubtful of their outrageous story. All the while, his father's

hand kept tightening and loosening on Sawyer's collarbone. His father's other hand had been squeezing his mother's shoulder in a similar fashion.

She wept for Richie. But she also cried for Sawyer and John, a balled up wad of tissues pressed to her face.

In the background, flashes burst from cameras. It seemed as though every local reporter had converged on the farm, all of them anxious to capture as many photos of the distressed boys as they could. Soon they'd slander his name by concocting tales of debauchery.

Is any of this real? It doesn't feel like it. Nothing does anymore.

Some of them thought Richie hadn't died. They believed Sawyer might be covering for his runaway friend. Others supposed he and John had killed Richie. They thought maybe that was the reason John remained so out of it? John had difficulty remembering all that had happened, which also drew suspicion. But Sawyer, he knew the truth.

Around two in the morning, sleep found Sawyer. Even then it was a broken slumber, accompanied by images of his friend's haunting grin. Of the blood trickling down Richie's arms and back. Snakes biting at him and something so large it could drag a canoe underwater. Yet he managed to stay asleep until the sound of shattered glass woke him an hour and a half later.

He rolled over and stared out into the darkness of the hallway. A loud creak in the kitchen alerted him as

if weight were being displaced upon the wooden floorboards.

What is that?

His eyes remained in that half-awake state. All he wanted was to slee—

"Sawyer?" his dad said.

Relief rushed over him upon hearing Dad's voice. "Yeah, Dad?"

A brief pause and then, "You okay, son?"

He nodded but realized this could neither be seen nor heard. "Just scared is all."

His father's footsteps grew closer, then backed away. Sawyer could hear his weight shifting from one foot to the other and then heading to the stairs.

"Okay, well, try—"

A rapping sound followed by an awful gurgling noise. Mother shrieked and Sawyer shot up in bed. He wanted to see what had occurred but somehow thought he already knew.

Heavy weight flopped against the floor. What sounded like feet kicked at the wall, then the ceiling. A loud cracking noise followed.

He wanted to help his screaming mother but feared what he would discover. Had the creature from the pond come and eaten his father? He hated that he knew that answer. Was it waiting for him in the dark?

Yes, of course, it is.

It would coil around him, too, and there'd be nowhere to run. Nothing he could do. Its tongue would lash out with a hiss and taste him. Then the creature would eat him whole like it had his friend, like it did his father. Death itself would be slow and painful. He stepped away from the door.

Had the snakes been holed up while the police dredged the pond? That would explain why they hadn't found anything. Sawyer's friend would've been wasting away in its engorged abdomen somewhere far beneath the earth.

He tugged on his sneakers and threw open his window. Mother's screams transformed to an inhuman sound. They came with stifled grunts as she suffered the same fate as his father. Seconds later, her screams were silenced.

It sounded like part of the stairwell railing broke loose and thumped down the stairs, crashing against the foyer floor. Whatever was out there bounded off the walls, slithering toward Sawyer's room.

He crept onto the window ledge and stared out into the night. Below, he spotted their above ground swimming pool. He considered the height. Tried to calculate the odds of surviving. If he broke a leg, he'd stand no chance of escaping. Before he could ponder matters any further, the snake burst through his door and he jumped out into the night.

He almost did make it. Struck water, but his back scraped against the aluminum decking. It tore a large gash in his shoulder. He'd live, but it hurt like hell. He screamed and a gush of water flooded his mouth. He gagged and coughed, sucked in more water. His world spun.

Oh God, I'm drowning.

Finally, his feet struck bottom, and he pushed himself up. Pulled at the water until he breached the surface. Reaching for the decking, once he had it, he cleared his eyes with a swipe of his hands.

A crash drew his eyes upward. The siding of the

house expanded. The snake withdrew its head and pushed again. This time a torrent of house debris rained upon Sawyer. He saw the creature's glistening red skin. The triangular shaped head pressing against the precipice, trying to escape the house. A forked tongue momentarily savored freedom as it pushed out from between terse jaws. It must have been as big as a small airplane.

Rolling onto the decking, he hurried down the stairs. He ran for the grill and threw off the lid. Knocking the small bag of charcoal aside, he snatched up the lighter fluid and the matches. Back at the pool, he doused the decking with lighter fluid. Poured it down the outside of the pool and across the lawn until he emptied the can.

Again, a crash came from above. This time he saw the snake's full size. It looked even larger as it fell.

He lit a match and held it to the fluid soaked grass. A streak of fire raced a short distance across the grass. The flames engulfed one side of the pool, but he didn't hesitate. He ran for what little safety the garage would provide.

When he got there, he glanced back once and beheld the creature's weight collapse the pool. Water splashed up and around, dousing most of the flames. The fire managed to scorch the reptile enough to warrant a painful cry. Then those flames were also extinguished as the beast squirmed out of the debris.

Sawyer shut the door behind him. Heart rapping, he climbed into the back seat of the Mustang and peered out the rear window.

A loud *bang* startled him. The entire garage door bulged inward. Another bang followed by a heavy

whipping sound against the aluminum. The door stretched inward. At the edges, moonlight peeked in. The garage door pulled away from its tracks.

Please hold.

As if to defy his wishes, another bang came and then the sound of metal scraping on the concrete floor, which had the effect of nails on a chalkboard. The huge snake pushed through the fallen door.

Three telling lumps of his parents and Ritchie swelled in its sleek belly. Its muscles cricked. The forked tongue darted in and out, found the Mustang, tasting the windows and doors. It slurped at the air, no doubt sensing a presence. The snake would soon hone in on him if he did nothing.

Trembling, it took everything in him to lurch away. In doing so his foot caught on the seatbelt, causing it to rattle against the vinyl.

The snake's snout burst through the Mustang's window. It pushed hard but couldn't reach Sawyer.

Now Sawyer wriggled along the length of the backseat to the other side. The more the snake pushed, the more Sawyer felt like passing out. The body of the Mustang began to fold in around him.

He scanned the walls of the garage, searching for a better place to hide, perhaps an escape. His eyes moved over the useless objects scattered there. A camping lantern, a sack full of plastic bags, a box of packing peanuts, a baseball glove, another fishing pole he'd missed, a flashlight, all of it useless.

I should've hid in the back room.

In that moment his thoughts turned to his mother and father. He remembered the morning when—

His eyes locked on the lift. He couldn't recall how

much an engine weighed, but it was a lot. He'd seen his father lower the chains plenty of times. Listened as Dad explained the functions of the lift. Once he had the safety off, he need only throw the lever. The engine would come crashing down.

But how do I get it under that engine?

He inventoried his supplies. Tried to think of a way to distract the snake.

What if it catches me?

He wasn't sure he had much of a choice. Either it would get him out there or it would crush him in here.

Just close your eyes and jump out.

That way he wouldn't have to see it. But he wouldn't be able to see what he was doing, either. Yet he'd feel its warm breath all the same.

He fled the safety of the car, his heart wrenching in his chest. He worried he would trip, that he would get stuck outside the safety of the car and the snake would get him. His resolve wavered, and he felt dizzy.

Stop it. Stay focused.

With desperation, he tried to reel himself in. Already he could hear the snake moving to intercept his position. Without much thought, he grabbed several items from the wall and seeing the snake slither around the edge of the car, he dove back inside the car.

There, he dropped everything and clutched his chest, taking deep breaths and trying to calm himself. He fully expected the snake to throw itself against the car. When it didn't, that only made the anticipation worse.

The snake froze and then made its way back to the other side. Meanwhile, he examined what items he'd

managed to secure the packing peanuts, a baseball glove, and the fishing pole.

Not much.

With the small box of packing peanuts in hand, he climbed to the driver side window. He tossed the box high into the air. Watched it rain white packing peanuts.

This hardly distracted the snake, but it was all he needed. He took the fishing rod, yanked off one half, and poked at the metal safety button, hoping to free the release lever.

The snake surveyed his actions. It tried to seize Sawyer's hand and pull him free of the car. Pressed itself against the door so the metal bent inward. This forced the rod against the side of the car.

When the snake drifted away, Sawyer reached for the button again. He could feel the snake's tongue taste his wrist and did his best to ignore the sensation. The rod centered on the button, and he pushed hard but didn't quite succeed.

The snake coiled back to strike. As it launched itself forward, Sawyer leaned and tried again. The button clicked.

Less than a second later the snake banged against the door, pushing the car closer to the wall and busting the rod in half.

Sawyer grabbed the baseball mitt, holding it tight against his chest as he crawled into the front seat. He exited through the driver's side door, keeping low.

The snake saw him and sped to intercept. Slithered through the metal legs of the engine hoist and almost knocked it over. The hefty engine swayed back and forth over the snake's head.

Sawyer aimed and threw the glove before he could think about it any longer. The leather mitt struck the lever, and it hammered back hard. A rattle of chains showered the snake. The engine landed squarely on its head, not killing the snake, but it did stun the creature.

The engine rolled to the concrete with a loud *thunk*, throwing up a cloud of dust.

Sawyer moved fast. He had no idea what to get, only that he needed to find something. He searched the back room where his father kept the tools and found several screwdrivers, a few wrenches, and a handsaw.

All too flimsy.

Then he saw what he wanted. He seized the axe and ran back to the snake. Hoisting it over his shoulder, he stared into the snake's eyes, seeing those black pools close up now.

Do you know what I'm about to do? Can you sense it?

For the first time in his life, he didn't fear snakes. He felt empowered when he brought the axe down and split the flesh around the snake's neck. Hefting the axe again, he brought it down over and over. He continued doing so until the snake no longer breathed.

He sat in the hospital that morning, still shivering from his encounter. Police surrounded him, but that did nothing to ease his emotional pain. They'd managed to free his parents and both were in critical condition. Their outlook grim, he grasped on to the idea of hope because it was all he had left. It saddened

him Richie hadn't been afforded the same chance to live.

Something else perplexed him, though. He stared at the television in the next room. There he saw images of John's house, left in total disarray. But that wasn't what bothered him most.

John and his parents were missing. Neighbors reported seeing a large snake flee the scene. The mate to the one he'd killed.

EVOLVED

WITH ALL ABOUT me forgotten, I flee the men I once considered equals. A spear grazes my flesh, and I'm unable to hold back my screams. Confused and afraid, I rush to put distance between us.

As they intend to kill me, I'm left with no option to discuss matters. We find ourselves at odds, separated by differences I cannot explain. Besides, they wouldn't comprehend my words even if I tried. Would never give me the chance to explain.

Spring's hardened earth cools my flesh. I cast an upward glance and discover a hint of daybreak far beyond the dense field, in the unceasing sky. The heavens are without clouds, and not a single star is left to wink out of existence. I'm reminded of my own emptiness.

I've become an outcast among my people. While darkness has aided me thus far, I will soon be vulnerable should I remain in the open. The moon pales fast. A deep orange illuminates the silhouette of mountains.

Wanting to stray from predictability, I'm drawn to the canopy of trees. Making my way through the forest does not come without effort. Exposed tree trunks, a

drapery of vines, thick brush, and fallen limbs impede me. These obstacles won't prove as difficult to my pursuers. Despite knowing of the stream in the distance, I'm filled with regret for having chosen this route.

Grunts erupt behind me. They communicate with one another in this rudimentary way, their leader barking out orders. One breaks off to my left. Another heads right. Both men gain on me and soon pass.

In anticipation of conflict, my pulse quickens. My chest tightens.

Their knuckles dragging along the forest floor, they close in on my position. My eyes are drawn left and then right. Spears in tow, they use their arms like additional legs. Maneuver themselves over the rough terrain with ease, more like animals than men, as they haven't yet learned how to run upright. Notwithstanding their crude nature, I remain mindful of how skilled they are at the hunt.

Branches thrash against my body. Each lashing creates a unique sting that delays my escape. Trying to avoid all of these deterrents proves futile. While I'm able to sidestep a few limbs, I remain unsuccessful at navigating the surface. Cracked wood and sharp rocks are but a few of the impediments that have punctured my flesh. The pain slows me down, and I consider surrendering.

These men whom I once broke bread with move about these obstructions with minor inconvenience. Here in these woods, I'm not their equal. I'm like a bird with clipped wings, likewise hindered as I am forced through this passage.

An audible whistle alerts me to an object in the sky.

EVOLVED

The spear strikes the earth an arm's length from my position. If I were but a stride faster the weapon would have impaled me.

Up ahead something glimmers, and my heart eases. I'm desperate for this water and hurry to this haven.

As I near the river's edge, one of the men intersects my path. His expression twists into a hateful grimace. He shouts and raises his spear to strike me down. Hurling himself at me, we are thrown back from one another. He steadies with his free hand while I renew my escape.

Now he is close enough I can smell him. He jabs his spear out at me, and each time I must shift my weight to avoid its pointed tip. Still, the weapon slices through the initial layer of my belly flesh. I'm weakened by the cut.

I reel back, coming to an abrupt halt. Blood gushes from the wound. Streaks of wet heat find my lower extremities. Cringing, I find the will to defend myself before the man can ready his weapon again.

Fear shows in his eyes when I turn on him. Although I recognize this man as my wife's brother, I'm too overcome with hatred to care. We clash, the distinctions between us forcing me to fight with desperation.

He looks surprised when I clutch his neck with the flicker of a limb. I squeeze and he attempts to scream. All that escapes his lips is a gurgle. Even in this dimness, I'm able to discern how blue his face has turned.

This man whom I once called brother has hunted me down and endeavored to kill me. He deserves death

for his callous behavior. My sole intent is to crush his throat.

Something inside of me remembers that which binds us. There is a woman who we both love. Through his widened eyes I'm offered a glimpse into another world. In those loathsome pools, I recall the greeting of my arrival to camp earlier this same day.

How can he not see I am the one betrothed to his sister?

The others sound closer now. Thinking fast, I make my choice and know even then I will soon regret it. I throw the man aside, and he tumbles to the forest floor gasping. When the others arrive they ignore me in favor of aiding him.

I enter the river without hesitation, and the water soothes my injuries. Cool spreads over me, stabilizing the anxious beat of my heart. Lungs no longer aching, the calm ushers a flood of memories over me as I move with the river.

In these reveries I see myself scaling the rocky embankment, diving into the water, my spear ready to pierce the swollen belly of a fish. For many years I've trained my lungs to withstand the pressure for lengthy intervals. And this time I notice something unusual among the varied structures of the underwater landscape. I hold my breath and as I near this object, it emits an illumination that blinds me. Even then I sensed the change, though unaware of the severity.

A grunt to my right pulls me out of the brief vision. A man advances in the trees that dot the riverside. On land he is swift, but the water provides me a slight advantage. I glide over the slime covered rocks effortlessly. He does not share in my luck and stumbles and falls.

EVOLVED

The others are not far behind. My wife's brother is with them. I also glimpse the man who has led me for a lifetime. The anger on his face reveals a hatred I've never known in this man. I'm saddened by his resentment, and my only hope is to flee until they no longer follow. This is my penance for being different.

Ambling down the widening streambed, the forest gives birth to the morning light. A ray of sunshine finds me, but this time I do not fear its light. My vision adjusts, and I note how the stream empties into a pool far below.

I know this place well. Women come here to bathe and collect water. A few of them grace this water now.

Part of me despises that I must jump. I'm certain if given an instant longer, they will not hesitate to attack. They would draw more blood from my already anguished body. With no other recourse, I leap.

I'm fearless in these depths. A multitude of tiny bubbles escort me back to the surface where I'm met by shrieks. Two women abandon the crude receptacles they use to gather water and run. A third leaves her skins behind and takes to the brush nude rather than risking to share this water with the likes of me.

Distracted by this last woman's screaming, I too take to land. This is when another attack comes. I lift my eyes to meet the skyward flight of a spear. Its shaft quivers in the ground short of where I stand.

This is meant as a warning. The face of the clan leader is as stony as the rock walls. His form is rigid and bold at the lip of the waterfall. He's an intimidating man.

The rest of the men scale the earthen walls. Their pursuit has not ended, and this angers me. I will run no farther. If these men wish to fight me, then I will face them.

I grab the clan leader's spear and snap it in two. I toss the severed ends aside. I do not require such unsophisticated tools. I glare up at their leader with defiance, daring him to fight me. He only stands watching his men as they near their target.

Having scaled down the walls of the canyon, they reach the sandy beach and come for me. At first, they taunt with their spears, thrusting with quick but short lunges. They spread out to encircle me, a tactic I've witnessed them use on many occasions prior to this day. I stand my ground.

Seizing the first of these men, I coil a tentacle around his neck. He drops his spear as I squeeze the life out of him. His face turns from red to a bluish hue, and I find pleasure in his suffering. I draw this man in closer, so I can watch as I press tighter. His life fades, and I fling his limp body to the shore.

I'm gratified when the clansmen go to his assistance. This is their greatest weakness.

I encircle one man's chest and lift him high into the air. He tries to stab me with his spear but misses, and the weapon falls from his grasp.

When I clutch my wife's brother's leg, he manages to keep a tight hold on his spear. To my surprise, he neglects to use the weapon. I clamp down on his shin with the mandibles at the end of my limb. The teeth there tear into his flesh and when they dig deep enough, he drops his spear. He screams, feeding my indulgence of his agony. I strip away muscle and cinch down hard. The bone cracks and I'm filled with gratification.

EVOLVED

Their eyes wide, the last two men do not challenge me. Although their leader barks out orders, they ignore him and turn to run. Now I'm the hunter.

Lashing out, I trip them up. I pin one to the ground and slide my weight over him. He struggles to breathe, but I don't care. The other, I fend off with one of my lower appendages.

I must admit taking pleasure in the moment. Although it brings me satisfaction, surely there are tastier creatures. But if given no other choice, mankind will suffice. I might even grow accustomed to such flavors. Should I escape and they continue to track me, I will consider this. For now, I pray for an end.

With all my might I heave the man with the mutilated shin at the canyon wall. He strikes the rock with great force. His skull caves in against the rigid stone, and a thin trail of blood marks his descent. He slides to a watery grave, and this end suits my wife's brother well for having opposed me a second time.

Content, I glance up at their leader, and he back at me. My resentment for this man brings me renewed vigor. I hear the ribs of the other man I've taken hold of give. The snap indicates a fracture but before I can see this, I feel the hot sting of a blade. He readies to thrust the makeshift knife back into my limb.

I tighten upon his chest, but my muscles fail. His first assault has already weakened me. I'm forced to switch tentacles, and my teeth claw away at the man's face. He tries to scream, but it comes out as muffled gurgles because of all the blood. Still I collapse his ribs. When I release the man he falls to the ground faceless and near death.

The man beneath me does not struggle. He

succumbs to my mass, perhaps hoping I've forgotten him. I have not.

The last man, having toiled with my tentacle this entire time, runs away. I thrust out both limbs and find his legs. Again he is tripped up and falls forward, gutting himself on his spear.

My attention turns back to their leader. I relieve the sole survivor of the burden of my weight. I take this man into my clutches, his hands in one tentacle and feet in another. He does not struggle, not even as I lift him above me.

Their leader surveys me. At first I tease. Then I sever the man in half. Blood and entrails shower me. I'm overwhelmed with confidence.

There are many things I want to say, messages I wish to convey. It's far too late for any attempt at resolve.

Their leader turns and runs. I consider pursuing him, as I know he might someday come for me again. Perhaps he'll bring others. I don't know why I let him live, but I realize with clarity I might want him to return.

Until that day I will construct an underwater lair at the entrance to the sea. There I will wait for them to interrupt my slumber. Perhaps they'll provide me another opportunity to taste humanity. I will forevermore be the hunter, a fisher of men. Ever patient, I await man's hopeless intrusion.

BURIED BENEATH THE OLD CHICAGO SWAMPS

IN DISBELIEF, TERRELL crouched down with the others and examined the strange structure from a distance. Ari had been right, although despite its size he didn't think it a home of any sort.

What was this? And all the way out here in the middle of the Old Chicago swamps?

Ari beamed, his thick brows jiggling as he laughed.

An image of what it might be popped into Terrell's head, but he couldn't remember the name of the thing in his vision. "Is that what I think it is?"

Ari stood and clapped his hands on his knees. "You're damned right it is. Told you!"

Her discomfort obvious, Rachel held up a hand. "Quiet!"

This reduced both boys to a whisper.

"No, I mean . . .is that a dome?"

Ari's smile widened, revealing his lack of dental care. "No." He folded his arms across his chest. "Like I tell you, it's a witch's house."

Most of the children, Terrell included, had never seen the Earth's surface until last year. As a result, a

lot of his memories revolved around man-made catacombs and the musty smell of earthen tunnels. The ground had sometimes trembled back during the wars. A few of the passageways had even collapsed due to the tremors. Those who'd survived conserved what energy they could by spending long periods of time in total darkness.

When Terrell's family finally did resurface, they did so with caution. His parents, remembering the world prior to taking refuge underground, were astonished by the differences. No one knew the victor, if anyone had won at all, or whether they were safe. They kept the true stories to themselves, but such tales blossomed among the children as steadfast as a field of dandelions. This was the case with the story Ari had shared with them.

Terrell inspected the dome, letting his eyes trace its slick contour. "Doesn't look like no house. More like a boulder if you ask me." But this hadn't been the object that came to mind. He'd seen pictures and knew what it looked like but still couldn't recall the name. "It don't even have a door."

"Witches do not need doors," Ari said.

Terrell's family had spent fourteen long years underground. If there ever had been such a thing as a witch, it could never have survived the bombs. Nothing topside could've endured that devastation. Yet, he noted how some of the animals and plants still flourished, as well as most of the insects.

Rachel's terror made her round cheeks flush with color. Her thick legs trembled, and she pressed up against Terrell. "Quiet, please."

All remained silent for a moment. So much he

could hear her teeth chattering. Evidently, she believed every bit of what Ari said.

Terrell found renewed confidence. "So where are the legs? You said this thing had legs?"

"They are buried."

Terrell approached the dome with bold steps. Rachel tried to pull him back, but he pulled free and continued forward. The name of this object was on the tip of his tongue, bouncing there yet refusing to spring free.

Her voice sounded weak and desperate. "Come back, Terrell."

He disregarded her and ran his hand across the dome's surface. His fingers came away with a thin layer of cool mucous-like mud oozing between them. With the sun so high in the sky, any mud should have baked dry. Yet, the dome wasn't even warm. It felt as though—

"It's perspiring?" he said.

Rachel's eyes searched him. "What do you mean?"

Still trying to recall the object he'd pictured in his mind, he ignored her. Then it came to him. "I think it's a big wrecking ball."

He didn't realize how loud he'd been, but Rachel reminded him. "Shush!"

Terrell frowned an apology.

Ari whispered, "It is not a wrecking ball."

"You're too young to have ever seen one for real, so how would you know? Rachel, tell him this thing is a wrecking ball, will you?"

She didn't move at first, her skepticism apparent. She crept forward and leaned to the dome. When she realized she wasn't quite close enough, she got to her

tippy-toes and reached out for the dome with just her fingertips. She yanked them away seconds later. "Gross, it's wet."

Ari examined her. "Wet?"

"Not all the way. Just a little. Like—" Her eyes sparkled. "Like Terrell said, perspiring . . . "

Ari ran his hand over the dome. Rubbed his forefinger and thumb together, gazing off across the swamp.

Rachel started away. "Okay, we saw it. Now let's go before we get in trouble. We aren't even supposed to be out this far."

Her eyes pleaded with Terrell, and then her face twisted with concern.

"What?" Terrell said.

"You didn't hear that?"

"No, what?"

Ari ran his clean hand through his thick hair. "I heard something, too. Like a grumble."

Terrell laughed. "That's just my stomach."

Perturbed, Rachel pointed to the dome. "It came from—"

Now he heard it, too. Felt it even. This was no growl. It sounded more like a generator warming up, a noise he'd grown accustomed to from living underground.

The land shuddered as if they were standing on some fault line, caught in the middle of an earthquake. He steadied himself on the dome, using it to keep from sinking into the softening mud.

Ari was the first to notice. "It's moving."

Terrell understood what he meant. The ground wasn't moving. It had been the dome that shifted a

good foot or two, maybe more. Now it rose up, unearthing itself.

Rachel unraveled fast, running away and saying nothing. Terrell staggered back on unsteady legs, watching her until she'd gone out of sight.

His eyes returned to the dome, seeing three reptilian forest-green legs lift the structure. He identified thousands of pink suction cups along the underbelly of each leg, as they twisted and slithered about pulling themselves free of the mire. Upon reaching the surface of the swampy landscape, the appendages writhed about as if attempting to cure years of atrophy.

Beneath the dome, Terrell spied something horrible. Blistered lips unsealed, revealing rows of pointed teeth. The mouth opened and closed, the dome itself seemingly a living, breathing organism.

Crowding next to Terrell, Ari cackled. "Like I said, it's a house with legs."

Ari danced with delight, ignorant to the horror lurking above them. Times like this Terrell wanted to slap him.

The dome altered to something more translucent, and a haggard face peered down at them through the glass. Terrell pulled at Ari's arm, but he didn't come. Then Ari tugged back. When Terrell looked, one of the feelers had coiled around Ari's neck and torso. The limb squeezed and Ari's body succumbed with a *crack*.

The appendage lifted Ari and fed his flaccid body into the mouth of the dome. Seconds later, the limb returned empty and anxious for Terrell.

Shaken by his friend's demise, he ran without knowing he'd started. The monstrosity gave chase, the

appendages slithering across the terrain and crashing upon the surface when they flailed out.

Terrell caught up to Rachel and slowed to match her pace. "That thing got Ari."

She ignored him, her terror seemingly having overwhelmed her. She was also running out of steam. And with the dome gaining on them, he worried it would soon catch Rachel if he did nothing.

Scanning the ground for a weapon, he found a sizeable stick. As the feelers came closer he beat them with the branch, trying to fend off the assault. He swung as hard as he could, but an appendage collided with him, spinning Terrell around and knocking the stick free.

He scrambled to regain the branch, but that split second of neglect was all it took. Smothered shrieks alerted him that Rachel was in trouble. He spun to her, saw the feeler wrapped around her face and working its way under her arms. He leaped to help her, but the appendage boosted her high into the air. Seconds later it fed her into the mouth of the dome.

She's still alive.

He'd seen her breathing. Yet his heart sank at the realization he could do nothing for her. A most awful, howling cackle erupted from the being inside the dome, delighted by not one but two children. He also knew there'd be plenty of room for one more.

Lose her in the trenches.

Without hesitation, he fled the swamplands for the rubble of the wasted suburbs, where he hoped to find somewhere to hide. Having gained some ground under the cover of the withered trees, he ducked into one of the old trenches dug by soldiers. These had survived

well, and he followed the length of the trench to its end, keeping low and glancing behind him whenever he heard the crunch of fallen trees. If not for this distraction, he might not have tripped and tumbled hard to the ground.

When he lifted himself, he spat dirt-ridden phlegm into the soil. *Blood?*

His head ringing, he identified the rock that had caused the gash. A piercing ache filled him, and he prayed for the pain to subside. He threw his back against the earthen wall and collapsed.

Then, Terrell was flying. He tried to cry out, but his breath had been shaken from him as he soared through the air. Visions filled his eyes: billowy clouds, the deepest blue sky, the inhuman flesh of the feeler and the muscle flexing as it tightened around him. Perhaps thinking him already dead, the appendage didn't crush him. Despite feeling like he might vomit due to the offensive smell emanating from the limb he kept still. Then he saw the dome. The weathered lips parted and the teeth chattered as if hungry. His heart raced, feeling as though the organ would soon fail him. But it kept plucking out a stubborn beat so strong it made his eyes swell.

Saliva rained from the horrid mouth onto him. Feeling the cool slimy sensation of the drool, he couldn't help but strain against the tentacle. The limb constricted on him, driving out his breath all at once. Seconds later he fainted.

So, this is Heaven?

The eerie green clouds looked unfamiliar save for their wispy nature. His head bobbed to one side, and he found himself staring into Ari's glazed orbs.

He gasped, nearly screamed even. Somehow he managed to hold it in. Forcing his eyes away, he came face to face with another corpse. Rachel's body lay curled in a ball, one arm thrown at an improbable angle over her shoulder. Trapped between his two friends, he could barely contain himself.

A quick survey of his surroundings revealed a circular counter that ran the circumference of the inside of the dome. Unfamiliar electronic devices sat on the countertop—far more sophisticated than anything he'd seen. They were fastened to this console, above and below. He could grasp the purpose of only a select few, such as the peculiar breathing apparatus and what looked like an oversized brain held in a glass jar. Electrostatic charges shot out from the brain, creeping across the inside surface of the container.

He saw the witch in a purple luminescent dress that flared out around her exposed feet. Every inch of the fabric appeared torn and ragged. Her dried and matted gray hair lay in a tangled mess upon her head. Riddled with scars, remnants of flesh dangled from her jaw like rotting chicken skin. Dreadful aged bone shown through the blistered wounds, and he didn't think her alive until she rose. When she did, the dome came to an abrupt stop.

Terrell stifled a scream, pressing his eyes shut. He kept them closed while the witch neared his position, struggling to slow his breathing. He feared his acting wouldn't be sufficient, as he could almost feel her alien eyes probing him. Cool flesh touched his arm, and his

thoughts went wild with possibilities. He trembled, unable to control himself, and worried this would alert the witch to his deception.

Then the icy flesh was gone, and when he opened his eyes to a squint he saw Ari's white and pasty skin close beside him.

Screams burned in his esophagus, the pressure demanding immediate release. Still, he choked them back but couldn't remove his gaze from his dead friend.

Ari's body moved, his limp form supported by the witch. She bent her head to his crown, and Terrell forced his eyes shut once more. A slurping sound alerted him to the terror so close, but he dared not open his eyes. There was no way to escape the unnatural and horrific noises.

She flung Ari's corpse aside, and the weight of his friend fell on Terrell's legs. This gave him a clear view of the gaping hole in Ari's head. Terrell suppressed a gag, wanting desperately to withdraw and kick himself away. But he couldn't do anything until the witch moved away from him. When he opened his eyes, the witch stood over him, peering out through the side of the dome.

Ari bled onto Terrell's dark-skinned legs. His corpse sported a bony grin, as if proud of being right even in death.

He imagined Ari's glee. *Told you she was real.*

The witch bent and threw open the door to a large container. Inside, a green flame burned. Once more, she retrieved Ari's body and heaved it inside. Ari withered fast, becoming an instant puff of green smoke. Seconds later the witch closed the

door, and the internal lights of this dome seemed brighter.

Close to vomiting, the sensation of dropping several feet all at once overwhelmed Terrell. The witch crossed to an empty wall and paused until a full quarter of the dome slid away. She passed through the opening and the door shut. The dome sprang into the air, once more disorientating him.

Terrell scampered across the floor to the door and tried to identify the opening but could not. Outside, the witch stalked about the machine's feelers, as if inspecting them for flaws. She stroked them as one might a family pet, admiring each. Then, the witch ventured out along the landscape and disappeared over a slight swell.

He waited, observing how the dome breathed, the mouth opening to reveal those hideous pointed teeth and then closing. This might be his only means of escape. When the mouth opened again, he hurried down between the rows of daunting teeth, using them as footholds to lower himself. Upon making his way through, he dangled from a few of the teeth and prepared to jump.

Some twenty yards away, the witch appeared on the horizon. She hadn't seen him yet, but seeing her was enough to make him hesitate.

Excruciating pain jolted his body as the mouth slammed shut, crushing Terrell's hand. Agony disabled him, and he screamed. He dangled back and forth, the pain now all that mattered.

The mouth refused to surrender, mashing shut on the remains of his hand and holding tight with those dreadful teeth, regardless of how much he twisted or

flailed. This senseless motion came not as a result of his effort to escape the mouth, but because the dome kept trying to recapture Terrell's body.

Then he was free: of his hand, the blood that flowed from the wound, all the pain, the senses that should've awakened as he crashed to the ground. He curled his bloodied stump against his chest and rose to unsteady feet, where he wavered.

The witch spotted him and lunged forward. He shielded himself from her assault, staggering away upon realizing her attack had only been an illusion. Preoccupied by an armful of decaying corpses, the witch approached steadfast but without worry.

Terrell ran until the loss of blood had fully drained him, and he could no longer flee at all. Although he couldn't ascertain whether the witch had ever followed him, he couldn't have cared if he wanted to. His body went limp, and he collapsed, the pain too great. There in the middle of nowhere, he slid into darkness.

Long after they rebuilt the city and his children moved there, Terrell refused to visit. Beneath the structures of metal and stone was the swamp, a place where he and his friends once stumbled upon something terrifying. Though his story frightened others, no one ever found evidence of the witch or his two friends. Confident young minds, those who'd never witnessed such atrocities, deemed his truths were amusing stories.

A few weeks after Terrell's seventieth birthday, someone reported discovering an extraordinary dome,

half-buried in the sandy beaches of the northeast. Everything Terrell had seen, the lives lost to the witch, had forever changed him. He knew then that life on Earth's surface could never be what it once had been.

THE BAD MEN

WHEN THE BAD men arrived, Usa worried they'd been discovered. Long had the elders foretold of this precise moment. Now that it had come, panic overwhelmed her.

True. It's all true.

She reeled in her emotions. There wasn't time for panic. She needed to warn the others.

Usa prayed these men wouldn't follow. But they looked so inquisitive. If they did come, they would be difficult to stop.

When he'd left Earth, Roger Coughlin had been in his early twenties. His wife, Charlene, had accompanied him. Although they hadn't planned on children, being woken up between periods of cryostasis offered many opportunities, as it had with the other two couples on this journey.

Roger now had two children, a boy and a girl. Each of them was old enough to start their own family, perhaps right here on Arlos 5. Although with only a pool of three other children from which to select a suitable mate, there would be few options. They'd

already been cheated out of childhood, and now they might equally be robbed of adulthood. But someday they'd be considered heroes among Earth's survivors.

The Salvation 13 had been the last of twenty-five ships dispatched in four-year intervals. The latest series of wars had taken its toll on Earth, and time was running out. The primary mission had been to discover a comparable planet and when found, fire off the beacon. Once the beacon had been signaled, all survivors of Earth would rendezvous at their new home.

The beacons should only be used if the planet was first deemed inhabitable. Whatever natives were discovered, animals and vegetation, must all be amicable to mankind. Roger knew what this meant, too, likening it to the fate of Native Americans. Still, he'd use the beacon the split second he deemed this planet suitable, regardless of what came afterward.

"I don't register any life forms," he said.

"Roger that," Dickie answered, "all joking aside, of course."

Dickie was a decent guy, young and astute despite the constant jesting. Dean, on the other hand, could be reckless. But he'd been the best available pilot. Besides Dean's wife, Allison, was a renowned botanist.

"You reading this, Dean?"

"Affirmative, Roger."

They proceeded through a vast jungle of extraordinary vegetation. Much of it Allison believed posed little threat.

"Keep your gun handy just in case," Roger said. "And don't hesitate if there's trouble."

Dickie nodded.

Roger pointed off in the distance. "I want to explore that ridge over there before we get too settled in for the night."

Dickie grinned. "Roger that."

Roger scanned the trees. No signs of any flying organisms. The weather was characteristic of late summer, a season he barely remembered anymore.

He removed a rod from his belt and held it high. When a beep sounded he replaced the rod and checked the readouts on his wrist screen. Although initial signs pointed toward a similar atmosphere, it would take time to adapt to breathing the air here without the help of a respirator. Even then, their lungs might reject unknown trace molecules, preventing them from ever acclimating.

We need to be sure. Still too early to know with any certainty.

Appreciating the slender orange leaves on the trees, he watched them wave back and forth. It reminded him of a cat's tail swishing, fluid-like but with an occasional hitch.

"Nothing dangerous about those," Dickie said.

"Nope." Roger admired them a second longer. "Not at all."

There'd been no signs of danger. He'd instructed the others to leave the second anything threatened their mission. No matter what transpired, they were *not* to come for them, as the future of Earth's inhabitants took precedence over all else.

He contemplated being left behind with only Dickie to keep him company. They'd likely do okay for a week or two. After that, they might start bickering. Over little matters at first, and then more

once supplies dwindled. He doubted they'd last a month.

"Other than the vegetation, I haven't seen . . . " Dickie stopped, eyes trained on a nearby tree.

Roger crossed to him, curious. Then he saw it, too.

He'd seen plenty of broken limbs before, so he knew right away what this was. Fallen or snapped limbs left behind jagged wooden teeth. A branch like that might found dangling or even lying beneath the tree. A limb that had been removed with a saw had a smooth cut. But this one looked as though it had been hacked away with a sharp rock and then twisted free, leaving behind a long peel of bark.

He scanned the dense forest, looking for the limb. But there weren't any matching that appearance.

Can't be. What could have—

"You think that broke on its own?" Dickie said.

"I'm not sure."

"You guys find something out there?" Dean said.

"Nothing to get worked up about just yet, Dean. A broken tree branch is all."

"A limb?" Dean laughed. "That's all you have for me?"

Roger took the lead. "For now. We're going to make our way over to that ridge to the east. Stand by."

An overgrown forest gave way to a pinkish desert.

He glanced up at the two suns, one a silvery blue and the other a deep orange. "Come on, let's hurry. I want to get back to the ship before those suns set."

"Yep."

The ground beneath them crunched. Even with such a light suit, it proved no easy trek. Less than an hour later, they arrived at the ridge.

"Let's record some quick findings. I'm still hoping we can make it back in time for dinner," Roger said.

"You got it, boss."

Roger's earpiece crackled. "You guys better hurry up." He laughed hard. "The girls whipped up one heck of a food paste feast here."

Dickie chortled.

"Don't encourage him," Roger said. "Check out that way. I'll head up this direction."

Dickie nodded and proceeded down along the ridge. Roger started off, but after several yards Dickie alerted him.

"What the hell was that?" Dickie said.

Roger stared at him, head cocked and listening. "I didn't hear anything. You joking around again, Dickie? Because we don't have time for—"

"No Roger, I'm telling you. I heard something."

He crossed to Dickie's position and listened again. A light wind whistled across the desert. The seedpods in the trees rattled, producing an odd whisper-like noise.

Is that what Dickie heard?

"The wind, you mean?" he said.

Dickie hesitated. "No, it sounded like—"

He waited, but no answer came. "Like what?"

"Never mind. It isn't possible."

"Damn you, Dickie, *what*?"

Dickie's barely visible eyes widened to large circles, big as the reflection of this planet's two suns in his visor. "It sounded like English."

"There's nothing on the scanners, guys," Dean said.

Roger tried to see through a potential charade, but Dickie wasn't giving off any sort of vibe contrary to his disbelief.

Leaning against the stone, Roger took note of its consistency. "Dickie, what mineral do you think this is?"

Dickie retrieved a small pickaxe from his pack and hacked off a small chip. Even then, it didn't come away easy. He held it under his scanner. "Couldn't say for sure . . ."

"Dean, any chance it's blocking our readings somehow?"

"Maybe. Doubtful, but maybe."

"Wouldn't our initial scans of the planet have determined as much?" Dickie said.

"I would have thought so." Dean's voice sounded grave. "I think this is where we should call it a day, guys."

"That's a negative," Roger said. "We better check out whatever Dickie heard before we get all snug in our pods."

They explored the ridge for a half hour longer. Roger was about to give up for the night and would have if not for Dickie's discovery.

"Down here."

He hurried to Dickie's location and gazed at the opening to a cave. Strange symbols had been carved into the stone surrounding the mouth, reminiscent of the warnings found at the entrances to Egyptian tombs.

"Well, someone's been here," Roger said.

"What is it?" Dean said.

"There's some kind of writing over the entrance to this cave we discovered. Barely legible and nothing I recognize. Looks old, but we can get Charlene out here in the morning; see if she can translate it." He paused,

considering their options. "We're going in for a closer look."

"Roger that," Dean said.

As long as the bad men didn't breach the cave, it would provide them enough security. They'd stockpiled food, but their supplies wouldn't last long.

Even if they could wait this out, what good would that do? What would that mean for their future? These men weren't going to leave. Soon, others would come, claiming this planet for their own.

What then?

The great ones had prophesized this, stories retold over the years by the first air breathers.

One day, bad men will come. They'll want to take this all away.

They'd depicted it through murals, painted upon these cavern walls.

And now that time has come.

A crunch drew her eyes to the entrance. There she saw two strange beams of light. They scanned the walls, back and forth.

They're inside now.

A hand grasped her shoulder. She turned and saw Ates' grave expression, one eye eclipsed with a painted white star, the other blue, and red stripes across her forehead. Usa patted the air, instructing her mother and the others to remain out of sight no matter what happened.

"Dean, you read us?" the smaller one said.

He waited for a reply and when none came, he used hand signals to convey orders to the other man.

This short one is their leader.

She would take him out first. A leader would warn his people. Tell them what to do, how to retaliate. A weaker subordinate would seek safety first.

The leader pointed out her footprints. "Do you see that, Dickie? Keep your gun handy."

Dickie nodded and retrieved a strange weapon.

They reached the main cavern and now she saw their enormous singular eyes quite well. She waved her people back farther, as far into the bowels of the caves as they could withdraw.

Can I take both men by myself?

She'd need to. There was no room left to retreat.

Scanning her immediate surroundings, she remembered the large limb she'd taken from the tree. She had hoped to carve something decorative out of it. Now, she seized the limb and wielded it like a weapon.

Both men's lights beamed upon their ancestor's vessel, ignorant to all else.

"I can't believe it," the leader said.

They examined the extent of the damage to the hull. It had taken many of her people to relocate the vessel here. Over the years the hull had rusted, its appearance now marred. It bothered her to see their hands trace the worn areas where most of the writing had become illegible. What was left had been used to name many of their young. Ates had been named because of this ship, and then Usa, too.

The original settlers had been forced to live in what was left of the spaceship. After the ancestors died, the craft had been used as a medical facility for a long time. Now, its only purpose was that of a monument, a sacred one at that.

"What is it?" Dickie said.

"This, my friend, is what's left of Deliverance 1, the very first of our missions. It took to space some eighty years before us, in the summer of 2015."

"How the hell did it end up here? And why didn't they use their beacon?"

"I haven't a clue." The leader paused. "Maybe they found hostiles. I doubt that writing came from them. They must have had a log." He ventured into the doorway. "You wait here. I'll check it out."

"Roger, Roger."

Roger Roger disappeared into the vessel. Roger Roger's light moved around inside, exploring the hull. Then she heard a startling click.

"Dickie?" Roger Roger reappeared in the entrance, carrying a strange box she'd never noticed. "This is it."

She stared at the black box, unable to discern its purpose.

Roger Roger tucked the box into his pack, secured it and then hoisted the bag back over his shoulder. She felt sick when Roger Roger turned to the entrance, hesitating only when Dickie's light didn't follow.

He turned back to Dickie, and Roger Roger scanned what had caught Dickie's attention. Together, their lamps illuminated her people's illustrated history, maneuvering their beams until they recognized something.

"Is that— Is that Fred Dentson?" Roger Roger said.

Dickie didn't answer.

She tracked Roger Roger's eye as it moved from one painted scene on the wall to the next. He would've found the suits familiar and seen how her ancestors cast those uniforms aside. Over generations, the pinkish flesh had transformed into the distinct crimson that now defined her people. Then he came to scenes depicting their arrival, the picture of the beacon she'd been warned about.

Now is the time.

With both men distracted, she made her move.

"Usa, wait!" her mother called out, alerting them. Ates obviously knew something Usa didn't, but she couldn't stop now.

She raised the limb and attacked Dickie, leaping on his back and clubbing him. Roger Roger raised the strange weapon. Usa didn't know if he could hurt her from such a distance and therefore used Dickie's body as a shield. But she needed to take Dickie down soon if she meant to even the odds.

She swung hard at Dickie, connecting. A loud crack echoed throughout the cavern. Pain riddled her arm and she fell. Dickie also collapsed.

Roger Roger took aim again.

Usa had no idea her people had gathered behind her. Young and old, they stood in support.

Seeing this, Roger Roger turned to run. But he never reached the entrance.

Again came the thunder, loud and reverberating within their cavernous home. She saw the troubled look on her painted mother's face. Ates held Dickie's weapon, smoke curling up from its end.

Her mother shivered and let the weapon plummet to the ground. "I haven't seen one for many moons."

An injured Usa nodded. Then, remembering her lessons, what they must do to ensure her people's safety, she retrieved the limb.

Through his cracked visor she saw Dickie's face, so

similar to that of their ancestors. But they deserved no kindness for their likeness. She brought the limb down with her good arm. A distinct ping echoed as she struck Dickie's helmet.

Dickie cried out. "No! Wait. Please—"

Again, she slammed the branch against his helmet. It crashed through the remains of the visor. Red blood splattered her legs and arms.

Dickie gasped, breathing in the air that had taken the settlers a decade to adapt to. She struck him again and again until she was certain he'd ceased to breathe.

Afterward, she rifled through their packs. Held the beacon high for her people to see. They cheered victorious cries. She smashed the beacon with her limb until it, too, had been destroyed.

Injured or not, she dragged their bodies out of this cavern. And there, in the Majuae desert, under the ridge, she heard voices. She leaned in close to Dickie's broken visor and heard the man's voice within. Heard him call out for both men over and over with no response.

Then, a short while later, she saw their craft rise above the horizon. After a moment's hesitation, the ship left, vanishing into the darkening cloud-filled night.

PARASITE

THE INSISTENT RING of Aiden's cellphone annoyed him. Upon identifying the caller, he groaned and returned the phone to his pocket. Neil had cried wolf one too many times. Besides, what had responding to his brother's constant needs ever done for Aiden?

It got you dumped by your girlfriend, that's what.

Why did he always feel the need to check up on his little brother anyway? Sure, he was close enough now he could run right over. But sooner or later Neil would have to learn how to live on his own.

To his chagrin, he missed taking care of his brother. Still, he pushed the urge aside and instead reflected on the reasons he should've seen this coming.

The red flags should have popped up when his brother, who lived in their mother's old house by himself, started calling Jasmine. Blinded by love, Aiden suspected nothing. He'd thought it more of an annoyance to Jasmine than anything, but she didn't seem to mind. Plus, it was kind of nice to have someone share the burden. He never thought she'd sleep with him.

Why, Jasmine? If only we could be together again.

Outside his new apartment, he walked toward his

brother's house. Although he often longed for those better days to return, everything had become so fractured that the notion seemed flimsy at best. Yet after all that had happened and the hurt feelings, Neil still had the nerve to call.

No doubt over some trivial concern.

The cellphone buzzed against his thigh. Aiden retrieved the phone and glowered at the screen expecting a text. None came, but his brother did leave a message.

What if he's in trouble?

If something happened to Neil, he'd never forgive himself. Their father had left when they were both still young. Aiden had shouldered the obligation of helping his mother raise Neil. When their mother passed, Aiden took sole responsibility for the task. Neil's decision to sleep with Aiden's fiancée should have severed that duty for good.

He deleted the message unheard.

Halfway to his brother's house, he wondered why he'd even come this direction at all. The temptation was strong, but Neil deserved a lesson. One that was long overdue.

It never occurred to Aiden that not knowing would be the most disquieting consequence of ignoring Neil. Worry overwhelmed him. Beads of sweat formed on his forehead as he struggled to contain his curiosity.

The familiar ring disrupted his anxiety and this time he did answer. "Neil?"

"Ai-den . . . " His voice sounded strained. "Ai-den . . . "

He quickened his pace. "Neil, what's wrong?"

"Hurts, Ai-den . . . "

"What hurts?" Now he jogged. "What is it?"

There was no reply, only heavy breathing.

"Neil? Talk to me!"

With his phone pressed tight against his ear, he ran to the end of the street. The sight of the house made his heart leap. He felt like one big sucker, knowing he'd rented an apartment close by for this precise reason.

Why should I care?

Neil had hurt him bad. As such, he deserved that hurt repaid. His brother's voice did sound like he'd been in pain, though. He disregarded the details of their strained relationship upon reaching the front door and tried the knob. The door opened with ease.

Why does he still refuse to lock the door?

His expectation had been to find Neil waiting for him, an expression of terror struck on his face. He recalled having seen this exact look many times before. But upon throwing the door open there was no sign of Neil. Boxes of Aiden's possessions sat stacked in every corner, making the place seem rather empty.

"Neil?"

No answer. In the living room, Aiden stared out through the front bay window as the familiar car pulled into the driveway.

Damn. Why'd she have to come?

It became evident that Aiden moving out hadn't affected her relationship with his brother. Now it occurred to him that she might not have moved in with Neil yet to spare Aiden some grief. The idea she would do such a thing made his skin crawl. Still, his heart fluttered when she rushed inside. He quietly cursed himself for not having shut the door.

"Is he okay?" she said.

She'd become as obsessed with his brother's care

as he'd been. Neil had a way of sucking people into his terrifying world. Once there, it became near impossible to escape.

Well, hello to you, too.

Her ignorance irritated him. Disgust overwhelmed him, returning his ability to speak to a lesser degree. "He's fine."

Although he didn't know this for a fact, it had been the case often enough that he surmised this truth. Their mother had been the one who played to his brother's paranoia. Too often she'd done more to heighten Neil's fears rather than alleviate them. Each and every time Neil had been fine. His schizophrenia often ended up being the sole culprit. It only took some patience and understanding to calm him. But Aiden no longer cared to help him now that she'd arrived.

"How do you know? Have you seen him?" she said.

The fact she worried so much about his brother frustrated him even more. The base of his neck burned and the sensation crept upward as the heat infected him. He wanted to scream, to hash everything out all over again. Instead, he refused to expose his emotions. He wouldn't give her the satisfaction.

"He always is," he said.

She wrinkled her nose as if she smelled something. "He said he found something in the basement."

Aiden used to love the way she crumpled her nose. Seeing it now made his heart skip a beat. This eased when he spotted the ring he'd given her still on her finger. It represented a false proclamation if there ever had been one. Part of him wanted her to keep it there as a reminder of what they'd had together. At the same

time, another part despised her for it and wished she'd give it back in light of her infidelity.

"He said he heard scratching." She raised her brows. "Like something was trying to get inside."

"Scratching?" He considered this, pushing his jealousy aside. "Like a cat, you mean?"

He had doubts any such creature would bother this house, let alone the basement. There were windows in the basement, but they were old and beyond filthy and had long since weathered shut.

"I don't know," she said.

Neil had become more of a concern to her than Aiden had ever been. This infuriated him. When her hopeful eyes met his, his anger eased.

Her struggle to hold back the tears showed on her face. "It sounded like the noise was driving him mad. Then he said he had to go. So he could call you."

How ironic she'd chosen these words. Didn't she realize his brother was crazy? He'd reminded her of this fact many times. Maybe she found something appealing about Neil's madness.

Drifting in these thoughts, his eyes stole glimpses of the ring. She noticed this and hid her hand from his view. Whether guilt-ridden or unwilling to relinquish the past, he found hope in such an action. A belief she might someday grow tired of Neil's antics and return to him.

But would I take her back?

"Maybe he's still in the basement," she said.

His brother still hadn't answered. He'd spoken loud enough for Neil to hear even from downstairs. Of course, it wouldn't be the first time Neil ignored Aiden. Still, he thought he'd better check to make sure Neil hadn't passed out or something.

He sauntered into the kitchen and threw open the basement door. "Neil? You down there?"

No answer, but a peculiar glow pulsated off the downstairs wall. He turned to Jasmine. "Wait here."

The light didn't work, but there was plenty of illumination below. The wooden stairway creaked as he descended to the half-finished basement. Although dark, the strange orange glow lit the way. He left the safety of the staircase for the open basement and tried to discern the source of the light.

From this angle, hc could only see Neil's back, who knelt before whatever object produced the orange light. The damp white tank top he wore was covered with dirt. His sweaty hair hung like black icicles.

"Neil? What's going on here?"

He approached with care, disregarding any contempt he'd held for his brother. The closer he got the more the odd light revealed. Now he could see Neil wasn't only sweating. Perspiration dripped from him in steady droplets. Aiden wanted to run to him and make sure he hadn't hurt himself. Yet this unsettling scene encouraged him to proceed with caution.

Bits of rubble, dirt, blood, and other unrecognizable debris lay scattered around Neil. His chest heaved as he inhaled deep gasps of air. Each exhale came slow and even.

Aiden identified a large egg-shaped metal casing from which the glow emanated. Although the bulk of the object remained half-buried in the exposed earth amidst the wreckage of the wall, it looked as though it had been torn open.

Is it a time capsule? If so, how long might it have

been buried here? The noise that emitted from the object was maddening, a scratching type of sound.

Neil's fingers dangled at his sides, resting on the basement floor. Blood oozed from each worn digit, the bone of his fingertips exposed and sharpened to brutal points. This likely had come as result of him clawing at the wall, desperate to uncover the noise that played upon his paranoia.

Heart thumping in his chest, Aiden beheld his brother's fate. "You look pretty banged up, bro." His concern grew when Neil didn't falter. "Come on, let's get you to a hospital."

He'd hoped his presence would've been enough. That Neil would leave the strange pod and come with him. But Neil ignored the invitation.

Jasmine's shadow wavered in the light being cast down the stairs. "Is he okay?"

Her voice surprised Aiden. Shook him out of the trance he'd drifted into upon seeing his brother so traumatized. His answer didn't reflect the truth. "He's fine." He paused and then added, "Don't come down."

"Why? What's wrong?"

"Jasmine." He loathed her distress. "Just stay there, please."

She sighed, her shadow rocking back and forth, her impatience evident. After a moment she retreated. Then he returned his attention to his brother.

Neil's panting had become rhythmic. However, this wasn't what concerned him most. A noise throbbed inside Aiden's head. It pierced his ears and penetrated deep into his skull like an MRI. This buzz disrupted his thoughts as if something were scanning his brain.

Neil grunted and an awful sound followed like

something wet being pushed through an obstruction. The muscles of Neil's back strained, flexing. He dry heaved.

The possibility this could be some physical sickness had never occurred to Aiden. Perhaps something inside of this unusual pod had infected Neil.

He knelt behind Neil and placed a sympathetic hand on his shoulder. "That's it, bro. Get it all out."

Aiden leaned to one side to better observe the metallic object, cautious but wanting to understand what he was seeing.

"We'll get you all fixed once we call the paramedics and they come."

Could whatever infliction Neil contracted be communicable? With some reluctance, he steadied his hand on his brother's shoulder. He'd show his support despite his fears.

Neil's retching halted along with the panting and the buzzing noise. The strange orange glow diminished. It faded to a dull shimmer, giving way to the shadows of the basement.

For a brief moment, the situation improved. Then Neil turned to face Aiden, who saw firsthand what his brother had endured.

The cavity of his brother's nose had been destroyed. The strained look in Neil's eyes made it seem as though something had taken up residence inside. Whatever it was now stared out through his brother's illuminated orbs. Much of the flesh surrounding Neil's nose had melted away, leaving bone and the exposed passages of his sinuses.

Then he saw the thing that had crawled up inside of that hollow. This creature had secured itself to Neil's bone with tiny hook-like fingers.

PARASITE

A scream found Aiden's lips. He leaped away from his brother, tripped and fell. There, he scampered back on his rear.

Jasmine's quick descent concerned him. He wanted to caution her, but his voice had swollen shut. Each breath escaped him in a wheeze. With his eyes glued to his brother, he continued to crawl back to the stairs. Jasmine's meddlesome legs halted him.

When she saw Neil, she burst into a fit of screaming. Her piercing shrieks jolted Aiden out of his stupor. He stood and ushered her back to the stairs, refusing to look away.

The torn flesh on Neil's face flayed back from his teeth. The loose flaps rippled as tentacles writhed about inside of his mouth. They clawed at his teeth, prying his jaws apart and tearing the flesh there. His bony grin unnerved Aiden.

Aiden gulped. His brother looked like more of a monster than a human. Neil crept at them like a four-legged animal stalking its prey.

Aiden shoved Jasmine hard, who still shrieked as he forced her up the rest of the stairs. She went, but with reluctance.

Neil leaped, spun mid-air and dug his fingers into the wooden floor joists. From there Neil sped at them like some horrible spider. If not for the keen fingertips, he might not have been able to support his own weight. Aiden's legs faltered, worsened only by Neil's inhuman hissing.

A straining noise grew in Neil's throat. He heaved, preparing to vomit. Aiden lingered near the top of the stairs, wanting to retreat but unable to rediscover his legs. Neil hacked up something awful, which he

launched at Aiden. It looked like a giant wad of chewing tobacco.

The dark blob missed Aiden by mere inches. He located where it had struck, intrigued how the ooze now reached out for him. It looked desperate and shrieked as it tried again and again. Confident if the secretion did reach him, he'd suffer a fate similar to his brother, he kept his distance. Shrieks of agony escaped the ooze, and seconds later it fell lifeless from the wall to the stair.

Another fit of coughing and hacking shook Aiden from his daze. This time he threw himself up the remaining stairs. Neil pursued, managing the basement ceiling as if it were a jungle gym. When Aiden reached the top, Neil plunged to the base of the stairs, crashing through the wood.

Aiden toppled to the kitchen linoleum and scooted to a position where he could kick the door shut. Once it was closed, he used his weight to brace it. Neil banged, shaking the egress on its hinges. The knob turned in Aiden's hands, twisting and wriggling with Neil nearly succeeding several times. But with Jasmine's added weight Aiden managed the lock.

Safe, but for how long?

Scanning the room for a weapon, he thought to raid the kitchen knives but realized they'd been packed away in boxes. He tried to remember which box he'd put them in. Then turned his focus to Jasmine's purse. She kept a gun there for protection.

He rushed to the bag, leaving her to brace the door by herself. She cried, tears streaking her face with mascara. He rifled through the contents. Grabbing the gun he was overcome with instant empowerment.

PARASITE

A confused Jasmine stepped away from the door, seeming concerned and anxious. He was glad she moved. The beating continued, each blow splintering the wood and weakening the door. Soon it would give way to the alien force behind it.

The door busted open revealing darkness. Aiden hurried to usher Jasmine to a safe place behind him. But as he whirled back around something shot past his ear. Another black ooze had missed him by less than an inch. The wind of its path still cooled his earlobe. He had this sick feeling that its claws had taken a brief hold of his ear.

Neil spun out of the darkness and sank his bony fingers into the plaster, clawing up to the ceiling.

Aiden leveled the gun on his brother, ready to fire. Before he could get off a shot, Neil dove for him. The force of their collision sent the gun sliding across the floor.

"Jasmine, I need the gun."

She didn't respond.

"Jasmine!"

Neil wrestled him to the ground. The filed bone of his fingers dug deep into Aiden's shoulders. Neil hissed, his body retching. The bloody mass of the nasal passage offered a glimpse of his brother's unique passenger. A single-tentacled eye descended from the cavity and gazed back at Aiden.

Unable to withhold his dread, Aiden kicked and punched. He knew what Neil would soon unleash. The torn flesh around Neil's mouth quivered as the bony grin opened wide enough to expose the place where once had been a tongue. The ooze occupied that space now, loaded and ready to propel itself outward.

Aiden arched his back, recalling his days of high school wrestling. He threw his brother to the side.

Neil grabbed and clawed for him, but Aiden found his feet and scurried for the gun. Neil took hold of his shoe, throwing him off balance, so he lost the sneaker. Aiden seized the gun and rolled onto his back, surprised as another ooze shot past.

His brother flung himself into the air and Aiden braced for the impact. He brought the gun up and got the shot off.

The gun recoiled, a trail of thin smoke rising from its end. A hole the size of a grapefruit had ruined all recognizable features of Neil's face. Blood and black goo dripped from the wound, but still, Neil's body lurched.

Aiden fired again, this time finding his brother's forehead. Neil's body collapsed on Aiden, who without hesitation shrugged off the weight and rolled away. He didn't want the black stuff touching him, even if he believed it dead.

He scooted away, eyes still on his dead brother. The sorrow of what had transpired was all too real for him now. When he did look away he discovered Jasmine's fate. It stung his heart deep.

The creature had burrowed its way inside of her, already excavating Jasmine's nasal passage. The bone and flesh sizzled, which reminded Aiden of when his mother used to cook bacon for breakfast. The black ooze maneuvered itself into position. She sat cross-legged, breathing heavy. Already her eyes had changed color as her passenger observed its new view of the world.

Breaking into tears, he fell to his knees. He loved

her still. Saddened by this fate, he took aim and fired. A horrid *click* followed. Panic set in and he fired again. Once more the gun produced an empty click.

He spun open the chamber to reveal the vacant spaces. Aggravated, he threw the gun aside and whirled around to the stack of boxes marked "kitchen." As he tore through their contents, her breathing eased.

His pulse quickened as he tossed various non-threatening utensils aside in search of something fierce. Her shoes clacked against the wooden floor of the living room. Tossing a crab cracker aside, he dug deeper. He recognized the sound of flesh ripping.

Then he found what he'd been looking for and turned with the knife raised. But she'd vanished, the front door still open and the setting sun now in the distance.

A light breeze swept in and never more had the compulsion to shut that door been so strong. She could be someone else's problem for all he cared. Such a selfish thought but he'd already lost enough.

Inching forward, he clutched the knife to his chest, as if warding off evil. He almost couldn't look at his brother's corpse as he passed, the dark pool beneath the body having already spread across much of the floor. To avoid it, he took a wide berth to the door and when he reached it, he cautiously stepped out and seized the knob. His fingers found the cool of metal, but an awful sensation washed over him in that brief second of time.

Above him, clinging to the side of the house, he saw Jasmine. She spat the black ooze, and it splattered in his face.

He twisted, an effort to steady himself on the door

as the ooze excavated. He collapsed to his knees, the molten sensation intolerable. The pressure of the creature squeezing every last bit of itself into his sinuses tormented him. He'd become aware of his heavy breathing, the panting, and profuse sweating.

Horrid pain incapacitated him as the tentacles pried open his jaws to reveal his teeth. The skin tore back accompanied by shockwaves of pain, as this parasite invaded his skull. And the agony made him delirious.

He saw what his passenger saw. Felt all the torture, the anger, the hopelessness. His memories remained with him, tearing him up inside that he'd now spend an eternity by her side after all.

They'd spread, maybe even reproduce. He spotted the engagement ring on her finger, forever binding them.

STRIP POKER, CRABS, AND BLUE WOMEN

ONLY JESSE COULD end up being abducted and bare-ass naked save for the lone sock he wore over his pecker. This must be the famous Emerson Curse striking yet again. This wasn't the first time he'd woken up wearing little more than his birthday suit, though. It was however, without doubt, the strangest.

He wished he were back at the picnic table. He'd hoped to finish his hand despite never being much of a poker player. But if there ever were a game where losing wasn't all that bad, strip poker was it. Besides, strutting his stuff in front of Mallory McCoy had been his primary goal. He'd been dying to see those beautiful hoo-has from the first day he'd spotted her crossing to a table at Mickey D's. Though he hadn't looked at his cards yet, he believed he had the hand to ensure that end.

Realizing he still held those cards, he glanced down at them. *A lot of good they'll do me now*. He fanned them out to reveal his hand. "Crap, not even a goddamned pair."

He tossed the cards aside and searched for

something to cover himself. A weapon would also be nice. A quick scan of this room offered little more than the cool metal. He ran his hand along one wall admiring its craftsmanship. He surmised even the strongest of men wouldn't be able to break through these barriers.

The door would be his only way out. He'd been avoiding it up to now because he wasn't sure what the object flanking its side could be. The square device looked complex, yet familiar. But he hadn't been able to place it yet.

How did I even get here?

Then he remembered. Adam had been the first. A strange sound preceded his unexpected departure.

Janet hadn't been far behind. She rose right up into the air like a magician's assistant. She'd vanished seconds later.

He recalled the strange mist-like beam surrounding Mallory. How it illuminated her beauty.

Damn, she's gorgeous.

Despite her obvious terror at that moment, he wanted her right then and there. With her abduction, the mood had been ruined. At least he'd been afforded a free peek at her Hello Kitty panties when the light lifted her into the air.

God only knew why they'd decided to play outside. No aliens would've bothered them if they'd stuck to the kitchen. But Adam always had to have things *his* way. Look where that had gotten them.

Dumb ass.

As he thought of his friends, he wondered where they might be right now. What if both girls were with Adam? Jesse flushed with jealousy.

Nah, he wouldn't—

But truth be told, he would. *You bet your ass he'd do anything to bag both of them.*

They'd been the best of friends for a long time. But friendship only went so far in the boonies of Jersey. An old tickle to the pickle beat a firm handshake any goddamn day of the week.

Would Mallory betray Jesse? He'd been trying to convince himself he'd always remain faithful to her, mostly because he didn't want to lose her to Adam. Strip poker had been Jesse's idea because he'd known Adam's secret. When God created Adam he must have run out of clay when it came to the old Wang Chung. Once Mallory had been made aware of that detail there would be no way she could ever be interested in Adam. These extraterrestrials had thwarted his plan. Now he'd have to come up with a new one.

Find a weapon, track down Mallory, and fend off whatever aliens are holding her prisoner.

Once they got back home he'd take her out to Chili's for one of those bright green margaritas. He had no doubt after such an adventure she'd want to reward his bravery.

He cocked a brow. "That's a damn good plan."

Near the door, the smooth sensation of the floor changed. Now it irritated his feet. They throbbed as bitter cold flowed across his toes. He noticed the metal grate and how the air circulated out of the room through this vent as fast as it was being supplied.

He regarded the strange black square to the right of the metal door and traced its perfect edges. Then he ran a finger across the glossy surface. The display lighted beneath his touch.

It's a frigging tablet?

Considering some of the gestures he'd learned for his cellphone, he swiped two fingers up. Startled, he leaped back when the door slid away.

That was easy.

He peeked around the corner. What he saw both amazed and disheartened him. They scrambled down the hall unaware of his escape. He couldn't stop watching the strange alien creatures and how they crawled in such a familiar way.

Crabs!

He'd caught many crabs in Jersey's back canals, tying off and dangling pieces of raw chicken in the water. The trick had been to draw in the string slow, but he'd never had the patience for it. Still, a good part of his life had been spent catching and eating crabs, and an odd thought occurred to him. He'd once caught crabs when he was seventeen, too. On that occasion, they'd been the sorts that clung to one's balls. Just the thought of these creatures still made his junk itch.

He mindlessly scratched. Because of his itching, the sock loosened and fell away. The metal grate beneath his feet slurped the sock in. Now he really was naked.

Hell if that don't suck.

Tiptoeing down the hallway, he kept his hands cupped over his crotch. At least the floor wasn't so cold out here. He glanced in both directions, opting for the one that led away from where he'd seen the half-dozen or so crab-like critters heading.

Bulbous half-moon lights ran the length of the passage on both sides. They stood out on walls that looked like heavy slabs of dark granite. There wasn't a single window, but he saw plenty of metallic doors.

He stopped to check several egresses. He swiped each tablet in the same way. Thus far, all had proved inactive or required some other motion to gain access.

Around a slight bend in the hall, he finally discovered one door that *did* open. An overhead light flashed on. He entered, and the door slid shut behind him. An observation table rested in the middle of the room. Draped over it was a length of material that reminded him of denim.

Two stirrups were fastened at the end of the table, like those used for childbirth. These looked like they'd been installed upside-down. Several leather restraints hung loose. A few devices sat on the table next to the denim. One appeared to be a large container of what looked like clear gel.

I'll bet that's lube.

Some of the other objects reminded him of things he'd seen before, especially that black snake-like camera. Thanks to an over-concerned doctor, he'd endured his first colonoscopy many years too soon. Evaluating the rest of the tools, he decided only two were large enough to do any damage. He grabbed both.

He recognized the first of these objects. Its metal stick was about a meter in length. A large trigger at one end controlled two menacing metal pincers at the other. Pulling back on the trigger, he observed how the pincers closed. He opened and released the pincers several times as childhood enthusiasm temporarily amused him.

The other object concerned Jesse. He lifted it, noting how it sagged to one side. Shook it, and it bounced and wiggled just like a—

Like a dildo.

If this was a dildo, it was the largest he'd ever seen. It had been constructed of some durable plastic.

I bet if I swing that dong hard enough it would dislodge one of those crab's legs.

He didn't want to think about whether these objects had been used or not. Still cold, he tied the length of denim material around his waist to create a makeshift skirt. He didn't like how it felt, but if he needed to fight he'd want to cover up his tackle as best he could.

Gathering up his weapons, he placed the pincers in his left hand and the oversized dildo in his right. With that, he set out in search of his friends.

The next three doors wouldn't open. Hope of finding his friends began to falter as he came to the last door. This he thought the tail end of the ship. When he swiped the tablet the door slid away. Inside were his friends, their expressions alive with alarm.

"Jesse?" Adam's eyes thinned on him. "Is that a—" He started again. "What the hell are you swinging around there, buddy?" He smirked, his smile bright and charming as ever. "Is that a miniskirt you're wearing?"

"Never mind," Jesse said. He entered and the door closed behind him.

Mallory rushed forward and hugged him. Her fingers crept up the back of his neck, arousing as ever. "We thought you were—"

Jesse grinned. "Nope. Still kickin' like a Kung Fu chicken."

Bitterness showed on Janet's face. Pink splotches on her cheeks were evidence of dried tears. Maybe he should be more mindful of his cock-blocking friend after all.

"Listen, we're on a spaceship," Jesse said.

"We know that," Janet said. "We saw those crab-people take you away. We were worried." Her eyes centered on the giant dong. "Did they . . . did they try to . . ."

"What, this?" Jesse shook the large rubber penis. "Nah, it didn't get anywhere near my backside. However . . . " He rushed forward and extended the dildo to Adam. He wiggled it suggestively. "It might have seen some action elsewhere."

Adam swung his arm and knocked the schlong aside. A nervous laugh followed. "Get that thing out of my face."

Now that he'd wiggled the dong a couple times, he found it difficult to stop. "These creatures abducted us, and Mr. Winkie here doesn't make me feel very welcome. We've got to take these things down."

"Okay," Mallory said. She sounded anxious. "What's your plan?"

Janet and Adam closed in. Adam had been the starting quarterback through high school. He'd always been the one to come up with plans.

"Well," he conceded after a moment, "I don't exactly have one." At least not one he wanted to share.

Mallory sighed.

Seeing her let down, he said, "What if we attack the cockpit?"

Adam shook his head. "We don't even know where it is."

"I think I might," Jesse said. "I saw those bastards heading toward the ass end of the ship. So it only stands to reason . . . "

"You don't know that, Jesse." Adam scratched his

head, and Jesse couldn't decide whether his good buddy wanted to steal his thunder or do right by his friends. "I mean, we don't even know how to fly this thing, right?"

"No," Janet agreed. "We don't."

"What do you suggest then, Mr. Basketfullofjoy?" Jesse said.

"Well," Adam whispered. "I think we should wait this one out. Maybe hide here and see where these things take us."

"What? Are you crazy?" Jesse's face flushed. "I ought to stick my foot so far up your ass that you pee shoelaces for a week. That's what I think."

"No, Jesse. Adam's right." Janet patted her man on the shoulder. "We could be far away from Earth by now for all we know. If we do anything rash we might not ever get back."

Adam nodded.

Mallory's eyes were on Jesse. He liked that.

"Well," Jesse said, "it's certainly an idea." He looked around. "Where do we hide?"

Adam shrugged. "Here?"

Jesse's lips formed a doubtful smirk. "Seriously? You do know that they've already graced us with their presence, don't you? That they came and took me away? Remember any of that, Sherlock? And you want to wait it out in the open?"

Janet wore a stern expression. "First off, you're still alive. For all we know they might not mean us any harm."

Jesse thrust the dildo at Janet. "They weren't planning to fix my dental work with this thing." He wobbled it. "Guess where this goes, Janet?"

"Easy, Jesse. Come on." Adam looked around. "As long as we stay together we'll be okay."

Jesse sighed. *Oh you'd like that, wouldn't you?* But his actual response sounded more genuine. "Listen, no offense, but I'd rather find that cockpit."

The veins in Adam's throat bulged. "Fine, go ahead. Good luck then."

"I'm going with him," Mallory said.

"That's great. You two lovebirds go and find *your* cockpit. We'll be right here. Let's just see which of us makes it out of this alive."

Jesse nodded.

Janet no longer looked so agreeable. Yet she snuggled up to Adam anyway. "You should leave us one of those weapons."

Jesse regarded the dong and then the pincers. He opted to stick with the pincers.

Adam seized the dong with eager hands and shook it at Jesse. It came off as an attempt at intimidation. "You better not screw us."

"I won't."

The door shut behind them, and they hurried down the hall. He snapped the claws several times. "I think I can fend them off with this. Maybe tear a limb or two away if I'm lucky."

She offered an unsure smile.

He led her down the corridor. It surprised him they hadn't encountered a single crab-creature. That ended up being the case all the way back to the room where he'd been held captive. Beyond that, they proceeded with caution.

Jesse kept the claw out in front of him. With his other arm, he shielded Mallory. A few times his hand

brushed up against her breasts by accident. Each time he tried to play it off, but even now when their chances seemed slim he had trouble ignoring the sensation. And she didn't seem to mind.

They disregarded all other side rooms, searching only for one they believed would be marked. When no such door had been found, they settled on the very last room in this direction. It ended up being the cockpit, and not a single crab waited for them inside. The door closed, and Jesse went right to work at the tablet.

"What are you doing?"

He glanced at her and then to the tablet. "I'm trying to lock the door."

"How?"

"I don't know, but these things are similar to the tablets we have back on Earth."

He spied a raised area along one edge and moved in for closer inspection, having not noticed the thin button prior to now. Holding it in for a few seconds produced no result.

Mallory was at his back, pulling at him. He ignored her and depressed the button again. When that did nothing, he tried to recall some other common gestures.

He spread his fingers outward and heard a click. When he tested the door it remained unlocked. He did the same thing, this time sliding his fingers right and then left. Each gesture produced no result. He tried other combinations while depressing the button with no luck.

Finally, he held the button in and drew his fingers together. A red slider displayed on the screen accompanied by some indecipherable alien warning.

He slid his finger across, and an audible clack indicated success.

"There."

Her hands rubbed his back, his arms. She kissed his neck.

He'd wanted this for so long. Sadly it would have to wait. There was still work to do.

He hurried to the front of the cockpit and sat on the odd shaped stool. A large window offered a view of an unfamiliar planet. For a moment he thought they were on a collision course.

"What the—" The engine grinded, and the ship glided left to correct its course. "Damn thing must be on autopilot."

"Jesse?"

"Yes?"

"I'm glad I went with you," she said.

"Me, too." He stared out through the portal. "We need to figure out how to control this ship. Once this baby touches down I think it would be bad for us to stay there long."

As the surface grew closer, the ship began to level off. It lowered toward their impending destination.

The larger tablet appeared similar to the others. The digital controls also reminded him of a flight simulator game he'd played a handful of times. A green icon blinked off and on in the upper left-hand corner of the screen. This he believed an indicator that the autopilot had been engaged.

He identified a digital joystick and throttle control. Thought he might even know how to turn off the autopilot. Now he could almost taste that lime green margarita, as well as Mallory's lips.

The ship maneuvered across the alien landscape, through unusual pink tree formations and top-heavy mountains. It wasn't altogether so different from Earth, either. Dissimilar enough to make it feel a bit like a dream, but his mind made the obvious connections that kept him bound to reality.

All the while Mallory stood behind him, *oohing* and *awing* as they passed each of these wonders.

When they reached their destination, the ship descended. It came to a complete rest on a large slab of rock, surrounded on all sides by a vast mist-covered sea. To his surprise, the autopilot turned off on its own. Several noises followed, many doors sliding open all at once.

It shocked them both when they saw Adam and Janet. Hand in hand they hurried across the rocky surface. But there was nowhere to run.

That bastard left us without even a word.

"How the hell did he know they would be able to breathe out there?" Mallory said.

At this Jesse smiled. "I doubt he even thought of it." He heard Adam say something. "Hey, I can hear them. You think they can hear us?"

She leaned forward and rapped against the window. "We're up here, guys!"

Despite Adam's duplicity, Jesse also called out for their friends. "Yo, you listening?"

Both Adam and Janet looked up at the cockpit. Adam nodded, seeming nervous. "You hear something?" he said. "You think that's Jesse?"

She clung to Adam's thin frame and shook her head, appearing uncertain.

"Adam, we're up here," Mallory said.

It became obvious neither Adam nor Janet could hear them.

"Give it up," Jesse said. "They can't hear us."

He considered joining them on the surface until he spotted a few claws scrambling along the edge of the surface. Then there were more of them, many legs speeding around, none of the creatures seen as of yet.

Janet screamed when the first of them crawled up over the edge. It paused as if waiting for the others. And several of the crabs now made themselves visible. The crab creatures gathered and surrounded Adam and Janet, their mandibles bubbling. And when they attacked, Adam and Janet ran where they could to avoid the strange aliens. To Jesse's surprise, the crab creatures spoke a single word over and over that made him both laugh and tremble.

"Chicken."

Adam slid behind Janet. She turned and spun around behind him. He hoisted the dildo and shook it with fervor. Their situation had become grim and yet seeing the dildo like this still made Jesse chuckle.

Mallory slapped his back. "Really?"

"Sorry, it's just that—"

He couldn't finish for fear of laughing again.

Another alien spoke that awful word. "Chicken."

The crab-people closed in on Adam and Janet. Adam did his best to fight them off with the dong, swinging it wild. Other crab-like creatures emerged from the ocean. They crawled up to the surface and gazed at them with their beady eyes. They surrounded Adam and Janet. Now the dildo, no matter how much it wobbled, was no longer the slightest bit funny.

Some chanted together. From others, the word

popped out with passion. Always it was that same terrible judgment. "Chicken."

It wasn't until one of them added two other common words that any of it made much sense. The crab that spoke these words wore attire that made it look far superior to the others. "Chicken. Tastes like."

Terror filled Jesse. "We have to leave."

Mallory agreed. She let Jesse work at the tablet.

He tapped and slid his fingers across the screen. He did everything he suspected was right. The ship jerked to life. It rushed forward and spun in the air. The ship ran over several of the crab creatures, and their alien shells pinged against the ship's hull.

Then he maneuvered the ship so they could see the platform. It was too late. The crabs had now swarmed Janet and Adam. Clacking noises reverberated in through the ship's speakers as they fed upon their friends. It sounded much like the steady beat of an old typewriter being tapped upon but far more terrifying.

He steered the ship into the dark unknown with Mallory at his side, feeling hungry for Chili's baby back ribs. And that lime margarita, of course.

THE BENEFIT OF BEING WEIGHTY

I SHOULD'VE RECOGNIZED it earlier. Maybe I wouldn't have made the connection at all if it hadn't been for the throbbing sensation beneath my wedding band each time something bad happened. But I chose to ignore it. That was my error.

The wedding band in question was my third. The first I lost on our honeymoon, somewhere while wading in the ocean surf. When the second ring grew too tight, I'd removed it for relief. I still can't remember where I put it. If I had, Kelsey wouldn't have been inclined to purchase a third.

This last ring came from a pawnshop located in the boonies of what her mother called "lower-slower" Delaware. She'd relayed this joke to me upon returning from visiting her mother. She hadn't bothered to remind me of the reasons she'd needed to buy a third ring. She tended to avoid conflicts. And I loved her for these subtle kindnesses. Yet, we both knew my weight had gotten beyond my control.

A few weeks later I went fishing with my brother-in-law David. Passing the time before dinner, I'd felt the prickling sensation under my ring for the first time.

I wasn't that shaken up by his unfortunate death. He'd always been a bit of an asshole. The type of guy who needed your help all the time but never showed up when the time came to reciprocate.

We were slugging down a few beers while fishing. The lake being only a couple blocks from his house, we didn't need to worry about driving. Knowing this, I drank like a fish, already on my seventh. He, on the other hand, had been nursing the same beer from the moment we wet our hooks.

Never mind the fact we'd soon be out of beer. Nothing was biting. And I couldn't blame the fish, either. I'd never used corn kernels before and believed only a bluegill would fancy such a meal.

Then something did bite. Nipped at my bladder with the urgency of a baby bass attacking a juicy worm. Before I had the chance to relieve myself, David had some concerns he wanted to convey to me. These were no doubt the words my sister-in-law Ellen had instructed him to say, perhaps even at Kelsey's request. David couldn't give two shits about me. But that was okay, too. Like I said, I never cared much for the guy. If not for the girls, we would have never braved each other's company for even one second.

"You should slow down," David said.

"Slow down? Hell, I'm only getting started."

I wasn't lacking in confidence despite my size. I tried to make light of his comment, but in truth I knew what would come next.

"Mike, if you keep drinking—" He paused, a wrinkle forming across his brow. He struggled on his words. "Your weight is getting out of control, man."

THE BENEFIT OF BEING WEIGHTY

I'll admit his words stung. I managed to force out a boisterous laugh. This had been a natural defense, and my full bladder afforded me an opportunity to avoid the conversation altogether.

I hurried along the dock to a nearby shed. How appropriate it would be to douse his neighbor's property. But I stopped myself, deciding to reply to his comment after all, if for no other reason than to get him off my back.

Turning to do just that, my words were lost upon seeing the dark cloud on the horizon. "What do you suppose that is?"

He regarded the ominous cloud and sighed. "Nothing. We get them all the time."

I wasn't so sure. The cloud spread fast. It was at the edge of the lake before I could get out another word. "I think it's getting closer."

Again, he glanced up at the cloud, then back to his bobber and shrugged. "It's nothing."

His lack of concern perturbed me. That's why I decided to assault his neighbor's shed despite my initial reluctance.

Tucking my half-empty beer under my armpit, I let my stream flow. I expected a groan of disapproval upon him seeing me write his name in urine, but the complaint never came. And a throbbing pain deepened under my wedding band.

Seconds later, David sped past without so much as a sideways glance. He'd even abandoned his fishing pole, which I couldn't believe as he'd been the biggest tight-ass I'd ever met.

Mid-stream I saw a funnel cloud heading right for me and was overcome with urgency. I jumped up and

down, pleading for my stream to end. But you can't hurry a good piss, especially after so many beers.

I abandoned the shed, still peeing. I should've run, but I considered my fishing pole and the few unopened beers. I don't know what possessed me, but I hurried back to gather what I could. Securing my rod first, I went for the beers. I'd forgotten about my half-empty beer and when a gust escaped the tornado, I couldn't discern whether the spray in my face came from my still emptying bladder or the beer.

Ignoring all of it, I tucked bottles under my arms until I could carry no more. The tornado gained ground, and I ran as fast as my weight would allow. Lacking David's swiftness and with my manhood exposed, I needed to take a moment to wrestle with my zipper.

Several beer bottles crashed against the pavement. Intense gusts tugged at my fishing rod, bending it back over my shoulder, hindering my escape. My plight came to an abrupt end when my zipper met flesh and moved through the skin. In that moment nothing else mattered. Not the tornado, not my fishing pole, or even the remaining beers. Only my fleshy rod mattered now, and it had been mangled in the metal teeth of my zipper.

All bottles fell away at once. My fishing pole slid down my chest and then flew off into the belly of the tornado. The hook stuck with me, catching on my cheek and tugging hard as the tornado threw the rod into a wide spiral.

Finding my legs again, I ran as hard as I could but no longer improved my position. A quick glance to my feet confirmed my greatest fear. My worn sneakers had started sliding backward.

THE BENEFIT OF BEING WEIGHTY

Ahead of my position, I saw David take a hard right away from his house. Then I saw my wife and her sister standing on the front porch. They wore terrified expressions, no doubt expecting the worst.

If the tornado hadn't broken off in pursuit of David, it would've consumed me. Instead, I was thrown face forward, teeth clanging against the hot asphalt. David didn't get off so easy.

Authorities found David's body a day later, several miles away. There'd been no reason to question the ring that day. For all I knew the sting had only been in my head. I should've seen it coming and tossed the ring into the lake.

A few weeks later Ellen approached me after having one too many herself. She'd wanted to know why my fat ass hadn't tried to help David. Her words hurt, but I refused to respond. Never mind the fact I'd almost met my own demise that day, and David had left me behind without so much as a warning.

Somehow I managed to take the high road, thinking sooner or later the alcohol would wear off and she'd have to live with the guilt of her hurtful interrogation. Plus I knew firsthand that people could say and do the cruelest things when they'd been drinking.

As I lay in bed that night, listening to rain pelting my house, I struggled to discern the reason why my wedding band burned my skin.

The following morning, while my wife cried in my arms, she shared how the rain had made the road so

slick. Ellen had died in a car accident, and I regretted having not volunteered to drive her home. If not for her words I may have.

Still, I didn't put it all together until the demise of my wife's mother. Kelsey always told stories of how her mom used to cook enough to feed a small army. That is, except for when I came to town. For some reason, the loss of her daughter made her ever more conscious of my shortcomings this visit.

The meal was lighter than usual, a single steak cut into thin strips to feed all three of us. If not for Kelsey being pregnant, I wouldn't have protested. In retrospection, I should've kept my mouth shut.

Her mother's response hadn't been one I expected.

"How are you ever going to raise a child in your condition?"

She gestured to my stomach. The woman had long been ignorant to the fact I'd held down a decent job for over ten years and would continue to do so while her daughter stayed home with the baby. But things had gotten personal this time, and she didn't stop there.

"All you do is laze about and eat," she said. "It's a wonder you aren't fatter."

There it was, out in the open. That gem of an insult found us leaving before we'd even finished our meal. Which didn't matter really, as it hadn't been much of a dinner. Even if the cold-hearted bitch had been kind enough to serve up dessert, I would have chose to starve.

On our way home, I convinced Kelsey to stop at Taco Bell. The burning sensation returned before we could reach the drive-thru. I tried to remove the ring, but it wouldn't budge. I didn't tell my wife, but it felt

as though the ring had grown roots deep into the bone of my finger.

When the storm rolled in, my first thought was to skip the fast food and head straight home. We'd all be safe. But something inside of me needed to return to my mother-in-law's house, to check in on her.

From the road, everything looked normal enough. The idea the ring had anything to do with my sister-in-law or her husband had just then popped into my head. The throbbing intensified as the storm reached the old woman's home. A single bolt of lightning struck the house dead center.

What were the odds? My wife loses three family members in a few short weeks, and all of them had made some degrading comment about my weight. At least these natural events had spared my life. I suppose that alone is the benefit of being weighty. But I didn't for one moment think it would be so kind with my wife's life or our unborn child.

I loved my wife and although I was certain she loved me back, eventually, if only by accident, she might remark about my weight. Or how about our innocent child, who might someday ask why daddy was so fat? I needed to do something fast before either of them got hurt.

Normally I'm a bit of a wimp when it comes to pain. I've seen my fair share, including the incident at the lake. I'd needed several stitches in my manhood after that one. And the hole in my cheek took two full weeks to heal.

Desperate, I took up a cleaver and a bottle of Jack Daniels. Jack and I had shared plenty of good times in the past. Many of those days ended in pain, so it

seemed fitting to have such a loyal companion along to help me.

It wasn't until the bottle was half empty that I worked up the nerve. If I hadn't been so drunk, I might have only taken my ring finger. As it was, I took three of the fingers on my left hand. I'd taken precautions, kept a bucket of ice ready so the digits could be reattached. But I'd never anticipated the sheer shock of cutting off one's own fingers.

A deep darkness fell over me. I remembered nothing until waking in this hospital.

I feel good now, but far too weak and drugged to move or speak. I've contemplated everything, how best to convey all of what had happened to my wife. I've rehearsed my words over and over in my head.

"You're awake?" she says.

I nod, but she doesn't see it because my actions are so slight.

She lifts my wounded hand and shows me the bandage. "You've been out all day. Why would you ever do such a thing?"

I choose my words carefully and try to explain. All that finds my lips is an incomprehensible mumble and some drool.

Disappointment spreads across her face. "You almost ruined your ring."

Inside, I smiled at this detail. My eyes scan the bandaged hand and verify the ring is no longer there. *Thank God.*

She places a hand on her belly. "I wish you wouldn't have done this to yourself."

I understand. She's been through so much lately. Soon she'll know why once I've had a chance to explain.

THE BENEFIT OF BEING WEIGHTY

She replaces my injured hand on the bed and works her way around to the other side. "Well, you're lucky, mister."

With minimal strength, I let my head roll to her.

She grins as she takes my other hand in hers, my good hand. I'm certain this time she notices my grin.

She speaks in a most affectionate tone, which I appreciate because of how hard this must be for her. "Did you do this because of what my mom said?" Her eyes appear serious and glisten with tears. "Because of your weight, Michael? We can get it under control, you know? Before it's too late. I can help you."

I frown, worried. Then I remember the ring is gone and force my smile to return. Drool trails down my face.

"We have a baby on the way, and you really should try to lose the weight and be healthy. Can you do this for me?"

I barely manage a nod, but it seems this is enough for her. She leans in close, turns my hand and kisses my palm. There, I see something horrible.

Dear God, they've transferred the ring to my right hand.

In the distance, I hear a roar of wind. Helpless to do anything, I start to cry, but Kelsey doesn't notice.

AFTERWORD

When I started this journey some six years ago, I had high expectations. I think a lot of authors enter this business thinking they'll make it big, and then, reality hits like the iceberg in Titanic. It's a point in a writer's career where they can accept their fate and choose to go down with the ship, or they can fight. Personally, as I've mentioned before, I'd thrown in the towel. Feeling a bit like Rocky Balboa after that first championship match, I'd thrown what stories I had together in a collection and washed my hands of this writing business.

If not for the kindness of Gene O'Neill, who took a moment out of his busy schedule to drop me a note, I might not have struggled on. And if not for Mort Castle's reflection on my work, I may not have believed I actually had some skin in this game. So, I have those two (among many other professionals) to thank for taking a brief moment to offer encouragement in one form or another. They gave me the confidence to push myself, the desire to write better fiction, a quest I know now has no end. But I love the journey, and I live to write because of it. I would be remiss if I did not take a moment to thank Joe Mynhardt for giving at least two of my collections a good home. I'd also like to thank his staff for helping see this project through.

As I have in previous collections, I always take a moment to mention a few words regarding each story, what might have inspired the tale or what I was thinking at the time. Most of these came of several thoughts or images that seemed to fit together, so in keeping with tradition I'll attempt to reveal a little truth about each story to keep up with the tradition, starting with the first story and working through to the end.

"The Chamber" deals with the concept of guilt, and how far one might go to alleviate their conscience. For this story, I'd been focusing on the opening to the movie Saving Private Ryan, which is a powerful scene. I couldn't shake that image and after several weeks that image started expanding in my mind, turning into something quite different. So I'm looking at things from another angle here, trying to examine that guilt over a lifetime. For this particular story, I visited the holocaust museum in Washington DC for further inspiration, as I wanted to do the victims of these heinous crimes the justice they deserve.

Back when I lived in Chicago, we had a large window in the front room that offered a view of the entire yard and beyond. I remember staring out that window for hours on end, imagining a world no one but I could see. So, while "Valerie's Window" isn't about that imaginary world, it definitely focuses on some details regarding that window. Valerie represents that malleable part of a human being that sometimes falls victim to the cruelty of others, in this case specifically a crime of verbal abuse and extraordinary fetish. Her story is one of retribution and overcoming one's own fears.

AFTERWORD

"A Window to Dream By" is a Lovecraftian story where I'd originally meant to portray a haunted hotel. However, the day I wrote this story it was stormy, and weather can often inspire a very different path. When the idea struck me, and the story began to venture into other realms, I embraced it. And while this isn't the haunted hotel tale I'd originally thought it would be, it does serve as an example of the possessed hotel room.

Several years back they thought I had sleep apnea, so I went through a series of sleep studies meant to identify the problem. While it turns out I didn't, these studies gave me plenty of time to reflect on circumstances. I jotted down details of a secluded room with no windows, where a camera up in the corner of the ceiling saw everything I did. "Each New Day Unknown" explores that room and the secrets within, loosely based on the details of those studies and how I felt after going several months without good sleep.

As a parent, you sometimes find yourself confronted with fears you hadn't expected. One for me was that of losing my children wherever we went. One time, in fact, my son did run off in a crowd at Disney World, which was quite terrifying. I remember the hitch in my chest, the worry and concern as I ran after him, trying to find him among the horde of people. "Gone" dissects that fear, in a way making an attempt to sort through the anxiety I experienced that day.

"Under the Drift of Snow is Another World" is a bit of love story actually, despite the deception and infidelity. This one had a bit of a Poe feel for me from the moment I began putting the words on the page, though I had no end at the time. As such, I found myself exploring the possibility whether we might maintain relationships as we pass through to the great beyond. The concept for the snowdrifts comes from my childhood in Chicago, when my friends and I would dig tunnels under the large frozen drifts of snow.

"Blackbird's Breath" is based on a true story to a degree. My wife and I really did have a blackbird get stuck behind our fireplace, and thus the research regarding the construction of the fireplace, as I struggled to find a way to free the bird. And yes, I did try to feed, tried to help it escape, and in the end attempted to put the poor thing out of its misery once I learned it could not be freed. All told, the event lasted a trying four days, where I got little sleep. As you can see, it haunts me still.

I'm a fan of all tropes, no matter how old or tired. Throughout my fiction you'll come across attempts at breathing new life into these ideas. "Desolate" focuses on a story of rage, one similar to the zombie infection brought on by a mutated rabies contagion. But I wanted to use something as simple as a berry to create patient zero.

I used to take solo hikes quite a bit, mostly working through the loss of my niece who died far too young from no fault of her own. I'd found this hill by the local lake I liked to visit, a track through the woods that led to huge boulder at the edge of the lake. I spent a lot of time reflecting on life at that rock and what I'd lost. Many details in my stories go back to that rock. Also, pieces of my niece tend to show up throughout my fiction. "Lost in the Woods" is a story of lost hope, as we always wish we could bring back those who've died, but how that isn't possible no matter how hard we desire.

AFTERWORD

"Final Breaths" is a sort of tribute to my brother's niece, who also died young. Death has always troubled me, so it tends to be a focal point in many of my stories, as I feel some need to explain mortality. Anyway, I forget whom, but someone suggested I write a story about her. I ended up mixing in details from my dad's passing, as toward the end of his life he swore he saw people standing at his hospital room door. I like to think he saw the people he'd lost in life and that they were really there.

Some boys struggle to connect with their father throughout their lives. I'm no different, as my father and I had many differences. But we were also a lot alike in so many ways. "Closer" focuses on one such struggle, though unlike most, this one involves differences of a greater magnitude.

Sometimes you hear details about a friend's life you can't quite forget. When they're so powerful, they can end up haunting you. There's a certain hurt that goes with them I cannot quite explain, but these images haunted me for weeks. "Flocking Birds" finds its roots in those stories of a mother who had a sickness, one that left me aghast. And while this story doesn't focus on any facts from that woman's life, it does have details taken from those stories.

Growing up my one sister had this plain looking jewelry box and when opened, a tiny ballerina spun around inside. Doing so activated a small metal cylinder that spun in its guts. Tiny metal prongs picked at the cylinder creating a whimsical tune. I'd always thought that box such an innocent pleasure, so with "Pirouette" I wanted to explore that innocence within a maddening environment where one world exists within another to provide an escape.

I've always rooted for the little guy, and who better than Boris. If you haven't picked up on the Easter Egg to "To Save One Life" you might not be looking in the right place. Research the lesser known songs by The Who, and you'll find what inspired this story.

At times, I've considered how little we know about our own planet. What if there were gateways between worlds, paths that could unite the monsters of old with the modern world? "Of Both Worlds" is a story of discrimination and seclusion that leads to a gatekeeper of sorts by mere happenstance. This is a kind creature seeing one of those worlds in color for the first time like a child, and slowly shifting to the other side. Much of these stories involving caves have roots in a childhood experience in a historic cavern.

I once visited the above caves later in life and they played Beethoven's "Fifth Symphony" while colorful lighting alternated upon the various formations. It was quite beautiful, but my focus was on the people in the background who'd begun their descent into the depths of those caves. I've always been a little terrified of such an adventure, as I worried about getting lost in those caves. "Breathing Cave" is that precise experience.

I had this dream once of a ghost chasing some old guy, where it finally caught the man and said, "Tag, you're it." So, "Soul Tapped" began there, and then sat in a folder with only that bit for a long, long time. This was one I almost didn't write, but eventually other details about that elderly man came to me, and slowly things began to fall into place.

The idea for "The Water People" also came to me

in a dream one night, but this time with almost the entire story written in my head. I guess this could be referred as a bit of an epic dream, with so much detail. Anyway, it had a Lovecraftian feel, so I played up that classic horror take.

"Water Snake" plays upon a very real pond, one where my friends and I used to fish long ago. We never caught anything in that pond, which gave us much time to reflect on what might be hiding in the depths of those waters. One day we showed up and hundreds of water snakes had infested the pond, so we never returned. But I never forgot what that looked like when all those snakes swam for us.

"Evolved" is a story of transformation, which I guess could speak legions of how I feel at times. Again, I hit upon discrimination, playing upon the differences in people. It's a topic that bothers me to a large degree, as I loathe everything that separates one person from every other. But this story is also about evolution and how it too could be perceived in a discriminatory way, as if change somehow makes one awful. Here we explore the closest of these beings, one so engrained in the lives of others, but the differences are too much for his people to bear. Therefore, separation leads to contempt, and brother fights brother.

Having grown up in the suburbs of Chicago I remember this amusement park called Old Chicago. A horrible wreck happened there when I was young, so it's always remained in my thoughts. While "Buried Beneath the Old Chicago Swamps" offers a glimpse into those days, this story is really my homage to a tale that inspired my desire to write, that of the story of Baba Yaga.

I've always been consumed with space from the first day I looked upon the stars and wondered what exists beyond. But, seeing what we've done to this world, how we've mistreated this planet, I struggle with how much we take what we have for granted. So I couldn't keep this anguish out of "The Bad Men," which explores the future of mankind on a very small scope. This isn't the end of humanity, but a refusal to let the old ways persevere.

When you have migraines as bad I did before I found the right medications, it reached a point where I'd do almost anything to relieve the pain. But more so, it almost felt like something was growing inside my head. So, "Parasite" started there, with me hating my sinus cavity and imagining what could be festering there.

"Strip Poker, Crabs, and Blue Women" is my way of teasing New Jersey a bit. If you've even made that long road trip back from the shore on a Sunday, you'll understand. Seriously, it's meant in good fun, and hopefully everyone gets a good chuckle out of it.

"The Benefit of Being Weighty" focuses much on little scenes from my own life. Mind you, my wife has always been quite supportive about my struggle to get my weight back under control. I don't like to make excuses about my weight, but like many others I have been fat shamed, and it's no fun. This was my Hitchcockian attempt at thwarting that sort of insensitivity.

So, I've given you a little behind the scenes look about where these stories originated, much like I have in the last two collections, *These Old Tales* and *Fresh Cut Tales*. As always, my goal remains the same, to

AFTERWORD

write the better story. In this, I hope you find me successful. With luck, I'll have many more stories to share with you for years to come. And so, dear readers, I hope you will continue to stick along for the ride.

Pleasant nightmares,

Kenneth W. Cain

THE END?

Not quite . . .

Dive into more Tales from the Darkest Depths:

The Final Reconciliation by Todd Keisling—Thirty years ago, a progressive rock band called The Yellow Kings began recording what would become their first and final album. Titled "The Final Reconciliation," the album was expected to usher in a new renaissance of heavy metal, but it was shelved following a tragic concert that left all but one dead. It's the survivor shares the shocking truth.

Where the Dead Go to Die by Mark Allan Gunnells and Aaron Dries—Post-infection Chicago. Christmas. There are monsters in this world. And they used to be us. Now it's time to euthanize to survive in a hospice where Emily, a woman haunted by her past, only wants to do her job and be the best mother possible. But it won't be long before that snow-speckled ground will be salted by blood.

Visions of the Mutant Rain Forest—the solo and collaborative stories and poems of Robert Frazier and Bruce Boston's exploration of the Mutant Rain Forest.

Tales from The Lake Vol.3—Dive into the deep end of the lake with 19 tales of terror, selected by Monique Snyman. Including short stories by Mark Allan Gunnells, Kate Jonez, Kenneth W. Cain, and many more.

Sarah Killian: Serial Killer (For Hire!) by Mark Sheldon—Follow foul-mouthed and mean-spirited Sarah Killian on an assignment from T.H.E.M. (Trusted Hierarchy of Everyday Murderers), a secret organization using serial killers to do the dirty work for their clients. Sarah's twisted sense of humor alone makes this Crime Fiction / Horror / Thriller a worthy read.

Gutted: Beautiful Horror Stories—an anthology of dark fiction that explores the beauty at the very heart of darkness. Featuring horror's most celebrated voices: Clive Barker, Neil Gaiman, Ramsey Campbell, Paul Tremblay, John F.D. Taff, Lisa Mannetti, Damien Angelica Walters, Josh Malerman, Christopher Coake, Mercedes M. Yardley, Brian Kirk, Stephanie M. Wytovich, Amanda Gowin, Richard Thomas, Maria Alexander, and Kevin Lucia.

Run to Ground by Jasper Bark—Jim Mcleod is running from his responsibilities as a father, hiding out from his pregnant girlfriend and working as a groundskeeper in a rural graveyard. Throw in some ancient monsters and folklore, and you'll have Jim running for live through this folk horror graveyard.

The Final Cut by Jasper Bark—Follow the misfortunes of two indie filmmakers in their quest to fund their breakthrough movie by borrowing money from one dangerous underground figure in order to buy a large quantity of cocaine from a different but equally dangerous underground figure. They will learn that while some stories capture the imagination, others will be the death of you.

Blackwater Val by William Gorman—a Supernatural Suspense Thriller / Horror / Coming of age novel: A widower, traveling with his dead wife's ashes and his six-year-old psychic daughter Katie in tow, returns to his haunted birthplace to execute his dead wife's final wish. But something isn't quite right in the Val.

Tribulations by Richard Thomas—In the third short story collection by Richard Thomas, *Tribulations*, these stories cover a wide range of dark fiction—from fantasy, science fiction and horror, to magical realism, neo-noir, and transgressive fiction. The common thread that weaves these tragic tales together is suffering and sorrow, and the ways we emerge from such heartbreak stronger, more appreciative of what we have left—a spark of hope enough to guide us though the valley of death.

Devourer of Souls by Kevin Lucia—In Kevin Lucia's latest installment of his growing Clifton Heights mythos, Sheriff Chris Baker and Father Ward meet for a Saturday morning breakfast at The Skylark Dinner to once again commiserate over the weird and terrifying secrets surrounding their town.

Pretty Little Dead Girls: A Novel of Murder and Whimsy by Mercedes M. Yardley—Bryony Adams is destined to be murdered, but fortunately Fate has terrible marksmanship. In order to survive, she must run as far and as fast as she can. After arriving in Seattle, Bryony befriends a tortured musician, a market fish-thrower, and a starry-eyed hero who is secretly a serial killer bent on fulfilling Bryony's dark destiny.

Wind Chill by Patrick Rutigliano—What if you were held captive by your own family? Emma Rawlins has spent the last year a prisoner. The months following her mother's death dragged her father into a paranoid spiral of conspiracy theories and doomsday premonitions. But there is a force far colder than the freezing drifts. Ancient, ravenous, it knows no mercy. And it's already had a taste . . .

Eidolon Avenue: The First Feast by Jonathan Winn—where the secretly guilty go to die. All thrown into their own private hell as every cruel choice, every deadly mistake, every drop of spilled blood is remembered, resurrected and relived to feed the ancient evil that lives on Eidolon Avenue.

Flowers in a Dumpster by Mark Allan Gunnells—The world is full of beauty and mystery. In these 17 tales, Gunnells will take you on a journey through landscapes of light and darkness, rapture and agony, hope and fear. Let Gunnells guide you through these landscapes where magnificence and decay co-exist side by side. Come pick a bouquet from these Flowers in a Dumpster.

The Dark at the End of the Tunnel by Taylor Grant— Offered for the first time in a collected format, this selection features ten gripping and darkly imaginative stories by Taylor Grant, a Bram Stoker Award® nominated author and rising star in the suspense and horror genres. Grant exposes the terrors that hide beneath the surface of our ordinary world, behind people's masks of normalcy, and lurking in the shadows at the farthest reaches of the universe.

Things Slip Through by Kevin Lucia—When a child mysteriously disappears from a small town and even his mother seems indifferent, it's time for the new sheriff to step in.

Where You Live by Gary McMahon—Horror is everywhere, in the shadows and in the light. It takes on every shape, comes in every conceivable size. But most of all it's right where you live. With the WHERE YOU LIVE short story collection, Gary McMahon delves into the depths of dark and brooding horror in every day events, objects, and the ghost of human nature.

Tricks, Mischief and Mayhem by Daniel I. Russell— Tricks, Mischief and Mayhem. These are not just some of the themes lurking in this tome of horror, but the names of three mischievous carnival clowns. Along with them you'll meet some of Australia's most popular monsters and legends, along with a popular cast of ghosts, demons, and zombies. Hell, there are more than a few stories portraying nature fighting back.

Samurai and Other Stories by William Meikle—No one can handle Scottish folklore with elements of the darkest horror, science fiction and fantasy, suspense and adventure like William Meikle.

Stuck On You and Other Prime Cuts by Jasper Bark—A word of caution gentle reader, these tales will take you places you've never been before and may never dare revisit. They'll whisper truths so twisted you can only face them in the darkest hours of the night. They'll unlock desires so decadent you'll never wash their taint from your flesh.

If you ever thought of becoming an author, I'd also like to recommend these non-fiction titles:

Horror 101: The Way Forward—a comprehensive overview of the Horror fiction genre and career opportunities available to established and aspiring authors, including Jack Ketchum, Graham Masterton, Edward Lee, Lisa Morton, Ellen Datlow, Ramsey Campbell, and many more.

Horror 201: The Silver Scream Vol.1 and *Vol.2*—A must read for anyone interested in the horror film industry. Includes interviews and essays by Wes Craven, John Carpenter, George A. Romero, Mick Garris, and dozens more. Now available in a special paperback edition.

Modern Mythmakers: 35 interviews with Horror and Science Fiction Writers and Filmmakers by Michael McCarty—Ever wanted to hang out with legends like Ray Bradbury, Richard Matheson, and Dean Koontz? *Modern Mythmakers* is your chance to hear fun anecdotes and career advice from authors and filmmakers like Forrest J. Ackerman, Ray Bradbury, Ramsey Campbell, John Carpenter, Dan Curtis, Elvira, Neil Gaiman, Mick Garris, Laurell K. Hamilton, Jack Ketchum, Dean Koontz, Graham Masterton, Richard Matheson, John Russo, William F. Nolan, John Saul, Peter Straub, and many more.

Writers On Writing: An Author's Guide—Your

favorite authors share their secrets in the ultimate guide to becoming and being and author. *Writers On Writing* is an eBook series with original 'On Writing' essays by writing professionals.

Or check out other Crystal Lake Publishing books for more Tales from the Darkest Depths.

ABOUT THE AUTHOR

Kenneth W. Cain first got the itch for storytelling during his formative years in the suburbs of Chicago, where he got to listen to his grandfather spin tales by the glow of a barrel fire. But it was a reading of Baba Yaga that grew his desire for dark fiction. Shows like *The Twilight Zone*, *The Outer Limits*, *Alfred Hitchcock Presents*, and *One Step Beyond* furthered that sense of wonder for the unknown, and he's been writing ever since.

Cain is the author of The Saga of I trilogy, *United States of the Dead*, the short story collections *These Old Tales* and *Fresh Cut Tales*, and the forthcoming *Embers: A Collection of Dark Fiction*. Writing, reading, fine art, graphic design, and Cardinals baseball are but a few of his passions. Cain now resides in Chester County, Pennsylvania with his wife and two children.

Website:
kennethwcain.com

Newsletter:
http://eepurl.com/caUofP

Twitter:
https://twitter.com/KennethWCain

Facebook author page:
https://www.facebook.com/AuthorKennethWCain/

Facebook:
https://www.facebook.com/kennethwcain

Pinterest:
https://www.pinterest.com/ozmosis7/

Instagram:
https://www.instagram.com/kennethwcain

AUTHOR'S PLEA

Greetings, Reader. You've reached the end of my book, and I hope that means you enjoyed it. Whether or not you did, I would like to thank you for giving me your valuable time to attempt to entertain you. I am truly blessed to have such a fulfilling job, but I only have that job because of people like you; those kind enough to give my books a chance and spend their hard-earned money buying them. For that I am eternally grateful, my friend.

If you would like to find out more about my other books then please visit my website for full details. You can find it at: kennethwcain.com. There you'll find a link to sign up for my newsletter. Or you can email me. You'll also find my social media links, which you can use to follow or contact me. I would love to hear from you.

If you enjoyed this book and would like to help, then please consider leaving a review for the book on Amazon, Goodreads, a blog, or anywhere else readers visit. The most important part of how well a book sells is how many positive reviews it has, so if you leave me one then you are directly helping me to continue on this journey as a full-time writer. Thank you in advance to anyone who does.

Hi, readers. It makes our day to know you reached the end of our book. Thank you so much. This is why we do what we do every single day.

Whether you found the book good or great, we'd love to hear what you thought. Please take a moment to leave a review on Amazon, Goodreads, or anywhere else readers visit. Reviews go a long way to helping a book sell, and will help us to continue publishing quality books.

Thank you again for taking the time to journey with Crystal Lake Publishing.

We are also on . . .

Website
http://www.crystallakepub.com/

Books
http://www.crystallakepub.com/book-table/

Blog
http://www.crystallakepub.com/blog-2/

Newsletter
http://eepurl.com/xfuKP

Instagram
https://www.instagram.com/crystal_lake_publishing/

Patreon
https://www.patreon.com/CLP

YouTube
https://www.youtube.com/c/CrystalLakePublishing

Twitter
https://twitter.com/crystallakepub

Facebook page
https://www.facebook.com/Crystallakepublishing/

Tales from The Lake Anthologies Facebook page
https://www.facebook.com/Talesfromthelake/

Writers on Writing Facebook page
https://www.facebook.com/WritersOnWritingSeries/

Beneath the Lake Videocast Facebook page
https://www.facebook.com/BeneathTheLake/

Google+
https://plus.google.com/u/1/107478350897139952572

Pinterest
https://za.pinterest.com/crystallakepub/

Tumblr
https://www.tumblr.com/blog/crystal-lake-publishing

We'd love to hear from you.

With unmatched success since 2012, Crystal Lake Publishing has quickly become one of the world's leading indie publishers of Mystery, Thriller, and Suspense books with a Dark Fiction edge.

Crystal Lake Publishing puts integrity, honor and respect at the forefront of our operations.

We strive for each book and outreach program that's launched to not only entertain and touch or comment on issues that affect our readers, but also to strengthen and support the Dark Fiction field and its authors.

Not only do we publish authors who are legends in the field and as hardworking as us, but we look for men and women who care about their readers and fellow human beings. We only publish the very best Dark Fiction, and look forward to launching many new careers.

We strive to know each and every one of our readers, while building personal relationships with our authors, reviewers, bloggers, pod-casters, bookstores and libraries.

Crystal Lake Publishing is and will always be a beacon of what passion and dedication, combined with overwhelming teamwork and respect, can accomplish: Unique fiction you can't find anywhere else.

We do not just publish books, we present you worlds within your world, doors within your mind, from talented authors who sacrifice so much for a moment of your time.

This is what we believe in. What we stand for. This will be our legacy.

Welcome to Crystal Lake Publishing—Tales from the Darkest Depths

We hope you enjoyed this title. If so, we'd be grateful if you could leave a review on your blog or any of the other websites and outlets open to book reviews. Reviews are like gold to writers and publishers, since word-of-mouth is and will always be the best way to market a great book. And remember to keep an eye out for more of our books.

THANK YOU FOR PURCHASING THIS BOOK